NIALL WILLIAMS

Boy and Man

HARPER

Harper
HarperCollins*Publishers*
77–85 Fulham Palace Road,
Hammersmith, London W6 8JB

www.harpercollins.co.uk

Published by HarperCollins*Publishers* 2008
1

A catalogue record for this book
is available from the British Library

ISBN: 978-0-00-721348-1

Set in Sabon by Palimpsest Book Production Limited,
Grangemouth, Stirlingshire

Printed and bound in Great Britain by
Clays Ltd, St Ives plc

Mixed Sources
Product group from well-managed
forests and other controlled sources
www.fsc.org Cert no. SW-COC-1806
© 1996 Forest Stewardship Council
FSC

FSC is a non-profit international organisation established to promote th
responsible management of the world's forests. Products carrying the FS
label are independently certified to assure consumers that they come
from forests that are managed to meet the social, economic and
ecological needs of present and future generations.

Find out more about HarperCollins and the environment at
www.harpercollins.co.uk/green

For the two Deirdres

Everything that rises must converge.
        Flannery O'Connor

ONE

I am no longer a boy.
I am a man. Almost.
And I am here.

The sun shone. The Master went to the top of the hill and flew the kite. There was brisk wind and it took only a few sharp tugs and the twin cords tightened and the yellow and red sail took flight. At first it danced drunkenly. It swooped, as though the earth and not the air was its element, and the Master waved both hands above his head like the conductor of an invisible orchestra and the kite rose sharply into the blue. He unspooled the lines and kept his gaze focused on the thing that moved further and further from him but was yet connected. The wind pulled the cords tight but the line that was drawn from kite to man was curved into the distance, and a movement of the Master's hands took moments to travel to the sail in the sky. Soon it was small and almost freed. So far up, it achieved a serene grace, its colours dissolved, its line invisible to any that might have looked up and noticed it from the winding roads below the hill.

It was April, the countryside thereabouts already in bloom.

1

Over stone walls, yellow gorse blossom was draped. Bare branches of the thorn trees were spiked with white flower. The day itself was blue and mild. Spring had come softly to the west of Ireland and it was warmer even than the springs in the memory of old people. The first grass of the year was crisp and had made a dry whispering as the Master had climbed up through it.

Now he flew the kite. A short man over sixty with a tuft of white hair, he had only just come back into the world. Much of it he had forgotten. He knew because he had been told that he had been in a car crash. He knew because he had been told that he had been thought dead and then took breath and lived inside the quiet of a coma more than a year. So too he was told he had once been a Master at a primary school at the edge of the village. He had a wife and one-time a daughter who were both dead now. He had lived with a boy, his grandson, but the boy had run off. To such telling the Master had listened without comment, as though it told of another. He blinked and sat quiet, his blue eyes seeking in the fire any semblance of himself in the tale. But the life just spoken of did not seem his own. Some details – a red cup in his kitchen, a bottle of Power's whisky half empty, some books, *David Copperfield,* a dog-eared copy of *The Confessions of Saint Augustine,* a pair of shoes with the laces tied and the heels broken down, the worn tweed of a jacket – such things seemed to speak of him and his earlier life, but even these seemed obscure. He had the feeling that he did not belong in the world, that perhaps he was meant to have died, and had somehow missed his exit. Now he was left in this After-place. The couple who cared for him, Ben Dack and his wife Josie, were the only ones to whom he felt any connection, but even that seemed tenuous. Who were these people and why were they caring for him? He didn't remember them. They were not his relations. Why should they have brought him into their own house? For the Master the world was a jumble of things without meaning. Was that red cup *important* in some way, that boy's jumper, that old book? These objects from the past, how did they matter if he couldn't remember them? And if he had come back to life, as they said, what kind of life was it? The country too seemed barely recognizable to him. There were familiarities, brand-names, place-names, but Ireland itself as it passed across the screen of the evening news seemed another country, and he a foreigner in it. To neither the past nor the present was he connected.

The kite lay against the sky. It sat in the wind unmoving, and on the grassy hill below it the man was intent on the lines that rose upward. Time was nothing to him. His morning and afternoon would be divided by the arrival of hunger, when he would tie the lines to his leg and sit to tea-flask and sandwiches. He had no purpose or plan other than to remain there flying the kite. And while he did, a silent figure on the hill beneath a perfect blue sky, he was forgotten by the world he had forgotten. While the hours passed, the kite moved only little. Once it arrived in the high it held still and the Master did not indulge in any tricks, no stunts of flying. He simply watched the twin cords, looked up along the angle, tested the tautness of the lines, and waited; as if for answers he fished the heavens.

The sun shone on Jerzy Maski, lifting blocks and laying them to make rise the wall to the second floor of a new house on the outskirts of the town of Ennis. He had come from Poland a month earlier. Within two days he had a job, and was one of a crew of twenty-three that came like a dawn army in dusty cars and vans to build an estate of seventy-six houses. He was twenty-one years of age. He was fair-haired and strong, and liked to sing when he was drunk in the evenings when the eight other men in the house he shared spoke of Poland. They knew they were in the country only temporarily. They knew that after this estate there would be another, and more after that, but one day they would be told there was nothing more to build in that country. And the knowledge of that made easier the absence of Poland for Jerzy Maski. His English was poor and these people were different. This month had been his first away from Jaslo in southern Podkarpackie not far from the Carpathian Mountains. He did not mind the work, and while he was lifting the blocks and tapping them into place, while the walls were rising about him, he could forget the thing he felt most strongly. He could hide in work the feeling to which he would never confess: that if he paused long enough there would rise in his heart an unbearable longing to have his mother's hands hold his face.

From the upper level of scaffolding, he saw a lorry bounce over the deeply potholed entrance to the estate and his uncle Laslo called up to him to come unload. He descended the ladder swiftly and his uncle smiled at his nimbleness and strength, nodded consent to an inner argument and led the way out through the doorless hall.

Laslo was in his late fifties and compensated for his baldness with an outrageous moustache. He smoked sixty cigarettes a day, wheezed all of his breath and joked that hell would be no difficulty because so much of him was smoke already. 'Smoke and these boots,' he would say, 'these will do me in hell.'

They crossed the packed dirt of Eden Crescent, the semi-circle of walled but unroofed houses, the way randomly stacked with deliveries, pipes, rolls of insulation, white aeroboards, plastic sheeting torn open and flapping in the breeze.

The lorry driver had already climbed down. 'What a day. What a day what a day what a day. Cripes yes. Warmer than July, eh?' he said, and clapped and rubbed his hands together. A short man with a ball of belly, he was red-faced and beaming. 'Island in the sun men, am I right?'

They looked at him.

'What is he saying?' Jerzy asked under his breath.

'I have no idea. Smile at him and nod.'

'And point is. Point exactly is, the world, the sun, and the layer between. That's the point. "Are we getting nearer?" says Mickey Cotter. Nearer what says I? "Nearer to heaven or to hell," says Mickey. That's a point. By jingo yes. Heaven, says Ben Dack. Choose heaven. But what a day what a day. Twenty-three degrees. Two three. Dear Lord thank you very much. *Go raibh mile maith agat* if you're tuned in in the Irish, eh?'

The two Poles nodded away, and Ben Dack took this for encouragement. He clapped his hands again and said, 'You're doing some job with this country, men. Some job, indeed. When this country's finished boy oh boy says he.'

Laslo nodded, Ben nodded back. When in turn Ben looked at him, Jerzy nodded too, and then the three of them considered for a time the half-circle of house shells. Somehow a cigarette had appeared on Laslo's lip and, hands behind his back like a general, he surveyed the field and through the thicket of his moustache softly leaked the smoke.

'I'll make a start,' Jerzy said, but his uncle touched his arm, 'Wait. Wait a minute. No need to rush. Take a moment. Nod again.' Laslo extended a hand as though they were speaking about the development. 'Good ya,' he said and nodded.

'Oh ya,' said Ben Dack. 'Certainly ya, most definitely ya. As the man says, you're the men can turn fields into factories. No bother to you. And no argument from Ben Dack because stands to reason, doesn't it, there's more of everything now, more of us more of you more cars more money more. That's the word, more. Eden Crescent, Eden Dale, Eden Meadows. Must be fifteen Edens in Ennis alone. By cripes. Did Ben Dack ever think he'd see it? In Ireland. Because this isn't Poland as Josie says. And – you'll like this – I says, isn't it? For devilment because Josie's a saint and you'd want to sometimes, you know, well but also my point, my point obtusely as the fella says, is aren't all places the same and the longer the world goes ahead spinning isn't one place spinning into becoming another and isn't that maybe the way because that's what Time makes of it. And so what? So Poland Ireland wherever. Irepol. You get me?'

Laslo withdrew the cigarette and nodded.

'What did he say?' Jerzy asked. 'He said Poland.'

'He said that young man from Poland is a bull, must have women everywhere. Like his fine bull uncle.'

'"Because what's a country?" says I. And my saint Josie comes at me with that little furrow in her brow like she wants to say Ben Dack you've lost the last marble now. And "what's a country?" she says and I says right exactly because look there's no lines drawn from above. You get me? Not a single one. My point. Clear as daylight. Countries are made up. Am I right? Countries are all joined together and only pretend to be separate. Am I right?'

'He is insane,' Jerzy whispered.

'Don't whisper. Nod.'

They nodded profusely, and for some moments made a strange triangle of mute acquiescence, and then all three looked back at the house shells and in Polish Laslo said, 'Are they not the ugliest houses you ever saw?'

Jerzy burst out a laugh, and Ben was pleased because the simplicity of his nature was such that he felt sympathy for all strangers and wanted them to be at ease.

'With this fellow we could nod all day,' Laslo giggled. 'I think he would not mind.'

'But our necks would ache.' Jerzy said, and then couldn't stop the laughter coming now. Suddenly it bubbled airily up inside him, quick bursting gasps of it, first one then another; each he tried to stop but couldn't. Now the laughter grew upon itself and he opened wide his mouth and made a soft near noiseless wheezing as though he had a series of 'h's caught in his throat. He sounded not 'ha' but only an aspirate 'h' and his eyes watered with the effort. He squeezed them shut and bent forward and put his hands on his thighs and laughed down to the ground. Laslo and Ben were laughing too now, heartily, a bizarre human comedy none could explain, but as each looked at the other and had their laughter renewed they were helplessly bound. Each in their way – with shut eyes and wrinkled up nose, with mouth open and head back or tight-lipped, the chuckles snorting out – lost themselves to the laughter. Ben Dack clapped his hands. A giddy joy ran around in them, and for some time neither could they speak nor stop, but in that sunlit Eden Crescent were three men laughing in the mystery of what happens.

TWO

The population of Ethiopia is approaching seventy-two million people.

In the evening after his supper, the Master sat in an armchair by the corner of the fire. While Josie was still working in the kitchen, Ben Dack was engaged in the one activity that could count as his pastime. On a large wooden board set upon the dining table, he worked at a jigsaw. Some years before he had been given one as a present and afterward out of politeness more than interest he had made it. His next birthday Josie had given him another one. She had seen the contentment he got when he tapped a piece into place and the image became clearer. So the jigsaws had continued. Ben Dack never bought one for himself and always showed surprise when it was given and always soon afterward opened the box and began. When the puzzles were finished he used wood glue and then varnish and a simple frame. So now these were the pictures that hung on the walls of the Dack house. It had never occurred to Ben to break up the jigsaws and put them back in their boxes.

That evening the puzzle he worked was 'The World's Hardest Jigsaw', it said on the box, a large image of blue sky and clouds. There were no obvious landmarks, nothing that might indicate where a piece belonged, only sky. By this evening Ben had joined the flat-edged outer pieces, which framed a jagged emptiness.

'Don't mind me now,' he called over to the Master, 'you have the television up if you want it. Won't bother me.'

'No thank you Ben,' the older man said. He watched the fire. The turf glowed softly.

In front of him the muted television showed the country that was his but that was still unfamiliar. When he glanced up the news was of murders and road killings, of crises in hospitals. The most frequent word on world news was terror, and if he tried to consider this he grew frightened. For him the past was not only another country; worse, it seemed an implausible invention, one in which he was once the Master of a village school and had his grandson with him and they flew kites and read books and never felt afraid. The past was innocent and unbelievable.

'All done,' said Josie, dropping the weariness of herself onto the couch. 'You all right Joe?' she asked.

'Yes, thank you Josie,' the Master said.

Without looking up from the piecemeal sky, Ben asked, 'Your programme nearly on, love?'

'Yes, love.'

Ben left the puzzle then and sat beside her and rested his hand in her lap. Sometimes she held it and sometimes gently turned it with a kind of mild curiosity, the hand of another.

She turned up the volume. In the last item of the news a reporter walked out on a dusty landscape in Africa, explaining how fourteen Chinese businessmen had come to Ethiopia to negotiate oil rights. They had been kidnapped by rebel forces, who did not want the government selling the country's natural resources. Now, in a dry hollow of sand, the fourteen bodies had been found. The handheld camera showed them.

10

'Sweet mother of God,' Josie said.

The Master's chin rose and trembled and then he wept. It was something to which Ben and Josie had become accustomed. Since his return to the world he had been given now to these sudden moments of strong emotion. They arrived prompted and unprompted, could be brought on by anything, or nothing that was apparent. The Master simply wept. And these incidences, at first alarming, had in time been accepted by Ben and Josie as part of the after-coma; the bits of wreckage that must sometimes float down into the Master's spirit out of the past. Always, he apologized, but was helpless to stop, though always too his chin battled against trembling and his brows lowered in a vain effort to hold at bay what came through him.

He wept.

Ben and Josie let him be. They offered neither tissues nor consolation, and in time the weeping eased and the Master grew serene again. While Josie watched a country singer on the television, Ben watched the Master and wondered what he was thinking. Was he thinking at all? Did he just sit without any memory of anything other than flying the kite earlier that day? Was that it? Was he blank? Josie had said he was probably happy. 'It's a kind of happiness isn't it? To be alive and not to have any worries at all, isn't that wonderful sure?' She had said it because after the first months when Ben had tried often to get the Master to remember, she had been hurt for both of them when nothing had happened. It was not that Ben had wanted acknowledgement or any connection between himself and the man who had reminded him of his dead father. It was that he wanted some meaning out of it. What was the point of what the papers called the miracle, the Lazarus man, who had been dead and come back, and for what? To sit all day, or go and fly a kite? When Ben Dack's heart bruised on this, his wife had tried to convince him it was for the best. 'If

11

he remembers he will have pain,' she told him. 'Without it, he has a chance of happiness. Leave him be now.'

And because he didn't want to disagree with her, Ben said no more.

The country-and-western singer finished, and sang another.

'There's a break coming,' Ben said.

She turned his hand in her lap. 'You want tea so.'

'Did I say anything about tea?'

'Tea and biscuits I suppose.'

'And biscuits! You're a saint you know that? Absolute, one hundred and one per cent saint. Not another like you on the planet, says he.'

She stood and saw the simplicity of him she loved.

In the break Ben tapped his hands on his knees, glanced over at the Master, then back at the screen. Then he got up quickly and went across to the one bookshelf where they kept the telephone books and the farmer's almanac and under some of these he found the Master's copy of *David Copperfield* and brought it over to him. He opened it on the newspaper clipping that had been stuck inside and handed it like that to the old teacher.

'There now, take a new look at that,' Ben said quietly. 'Go ahead. Give her a shot.'

'Yes Ben,' the Master said, with the strange politeness with which he had returned to the world. And he looked down, first at his book, and then at the piece of newspaper. He lifted it up and held it directly in front of him.

It was a picture of a boy.

The prisoner did not know what country he was in. He thought it was Germany or maybe Poland, but he could not be sure because when he was taken he was blindfolded and made unconscious. He saw only the small cell he lived in and the other he was brought to when they wanted to ask him questions. He was happy at least to see the cell. For the longest time he had lived with his eyes tied with a cloth that smelled of ammonia.

He did not have any record of the days. He knew it was a long time since he was taken, but he did not know it was three years.

How is it so hot? Ireland they said would be rainy and cold. Rainy and cold. But it is hot. Hot as Jaslo in summertime. And as soon as the image crossed Jerzy's mind, he felt something reach into his stomach and twist out homesickness. Jaslo in summertime. He had been a boy with a boy's freedom, fair-haired and strong and running along the roads in the hum of bees and the sweet sharp scent of pine from the foothills of the mountains. Jaslo. He had not thought of a future then. He had thought only of home, and of his mother, and never dreamed he would build walls in Ireland. It seemed not his life that he was living now but another's that ran parallel and this sickened him and he fought the sickness with hard work.

He hurried for another block and laid it on the wall. About him the others worked without pause. *Like machines, machines that make walls. Cement in our skin, thinned out each night with Polish beer. Each wants to go home. I know. Each one. Not just me. But Laslo says this is a man. A man is work. A man is not crying for his mother. For his home. This is today's home. Tomorrow's somewhere else. Jerzy Maski is not a boy. It is stupid to miss Jaslo, a small place. There is nothing there. No money. Who can live in Jaslo now? Only old people.*

He laid the block and trimmed it and went for another. He thought of his elder brother who had gone away to become a priest and then not become a priest and then for shame not returned. He wondered where he was in the world and if he

13

ever thought of his younger brother and if he knew that one day a letter had come from their Uncle Laslo saying there was work for good money in Ireland.

'You go,' his mother had said. 'Yes you go.' She wore black fifteen years after burying her husband.

'I will stay with you.'

'I don't want you under my feet,' she had said, and turned the lowered wings of her eyebrows to the fire.

And he had not said he would prefer university and to study architecture, for he did not want to hurt her having to say they had not the money. 'I will go but come back when the big mountain of money is here beside you,' he had said.

But now that he was in Ireland, and the money was good and the work was plentiful, he thought Poland grew further not nearer each day. Some mornings he woke well before the six o'clock start and thought of himself rising into another life back in Jaslo. He allowed himself the imagining of it the way you might a chocolate in a box, deliberate and pleasurable and too soon passed. He had himself rise from the bed and come down and light the fire and go outside in the little yard at the back and take the axe to the logs. He let himself feel the cool air coming from the mountains and to see his breath plume away on the morning. He lay in the bed and imagined he was this other and already could smell the first thick wood smoke coming down from the chimney with the press of cold air. He could see himself in the woollen jumper and thick trousers and even feel the easy swift motion of the axe and hear the crack as the log split sharply. He was there, paused in the after-stroke, and able to look out into the trees on a cool morning and hear the birdsong and be perfectly still in the opposite life to the one he lived now. He could see himself carry the logs inside and see each corner of the house in which he had grown up, know each chair and how it felt to sit in, and know the sounds of the latches on the presses, the song of the kettle. And these, in this other life, were all perfectly clear to him as he lay in the bed waiting for the alarm. They were as near as dreams, and he clung there on the edge of them, not yet realizing the life he had made up was his father's.

So, with the alarm, each day he left that other life and went to lay the blocks.

In the evening Laslo complimented his work and passed him another bottle of beer.

'You were working fast today,' he said. 'You are a very good worker, Jerzy, but no more laughing,' Laslo teased. They both smiled. 'What was he saying? I have not one idea.'

Jerzy finished the beer, took another.

'Soon you will be singing,' Laslo said.

But Jerzy did not sing that night, nor escape the melancholy, and at last rose and went out the front door of the little house and walked down the road beneath the April stars, swaying slightly with the beer and the sense of loss. In some ways the country was no different to Poland. At night you could pretend it was Poland. There was no one speaking. There was only the mild dark and the moon. He walked, saturated with loneliness. It leaked from him. He went out from the tight street of houses where televisions flickered blue and gold against the curtains and gates were closed on their cars. He said out loud 'Jerzy Maski' to none listening and then bowed and waved his hand in a wide sweep, as if to a partner in a dance. He staggered backward two steps, widened his eyes with surprise, then stumbled down off the kerb onto the road. He laughed to find himself so. 'Oh,' he said. 'Oh-oh.' And laughed some more, then he walked on down the centre of the road. His forehead was cool and yet beaded with sweat. The streetlights were wild blooms against the blue. In sudden moments he filled with loathing and ridicule. *I am an idiot. What is Jaslo to me? I am a man now. Stop stop acting like a baby, a* niemowle.

In the centre of the Ennis to Kilrush Road, Jerzy Maski

sang the first verse of the Polish national anthem. He sang it in a loud and manly voice and stood to attention, and for moments afterward, he was all right. But too soon, hope or resolve buckled in him and he flung his head forward and vomited. He was bent over like that when the first car came toward him. He lifted his head into the lights and arced his arm to block them. He cursed and saw the Latvian plate as the car flew past, its horn blaring. There was another car travelling fast behind it. In it were five men. The back passenger window was open and leaning out was a man with shaved head who yelled in a language Jerzy did not understand. He was extending his arm in an aim. Was it a gun he held? As the car whooshed past, the man's hand jerked upward twice as though he released two shots. Then he withdrew back inside the car as it turned sharply towards the road to Limerick.

The moment returned Jerzy to something like clarity. He patted his chest and looked at his fingers for blood. Then he closed his eyes and shook his head hard, as if to shake from the framework of thought a thick, cloying grief. He blinked at the moon and then – as if in the throes of revelation – he walked purposefully down the broken line of the road. His arms he crossed, holding onto himself, his eyes he turned downward. If a car came and hit him so he would die. It was chance. Life was chance.

He walked past one o'clock and two. Single cars flew past. Beyond the town the countryside was stilled, as if it dreamt itself into a fairytale. But Jerzy Maski, moon shouldered, blue eyed, a blaze of fair hair, carried an invisible bowl of sorrow out of the town to Eden Crescent. When he realized he had not been knocked down, he went in among the half-built houses of the new estate and, in one of them, unroofed and unfloored, he passed like a ghost, and sat on two upright blocks at the dark opening where soon would be built a hearth.

16

THREE

The remains of the oldest-known modern humans were found in Ethiopia. They are estimated to be approximately 200,000 years old. They were excavated at a place near Kibish. Here, at the bottom of dry rocky layers of sediment of a lake that had once been washed by the waters of the Mediterranean, a team of archaeologists which included Richard Leakey made the discovery that changed all previous estimations of how long humans had been walking on the earth.

The Master stared at the picture of the boy. He was a boy twelve years of age, with dark straight hair and sallow skin. His expression was serious, as if he had decided against smiling for the photograph or was otherwise occupied by some troubling thought. He looked out from the picture at the Master the way faces do on the memorial cards for the dead. He was gone. He was lost in the world somewhere. Perhaps he too was dead. The Master had been told what had happened. On the morning of his Confirmation the boy had turned away from the altar rails. That night he had run away. It was presumed out of shame. He had left a note saying he was going to look for his father. But his father was unknown, the boy's mother had never told. There were only two traces of the boy afterward. The first was that Ben Dack had identified him as the one to whom he gave a lift in his lorry as far as Dublin; the second, that he was one of the victims of the BBC bombing who had been brought to hospital but later left without being discharged.

And this was three years ago. For a year or so Ben and Josie had constantly kept in touch with the police to keep alive the search. They had posters printed. They had spoken on the radio. Ben had gone to London and seen the hospital ward and spoken to the nurse. He was told there was a file with Interpol, he was told that the search would never end, but in the time since the boy was put on file another two hundred and seventy-six names had already been added.

The boy was gone. He was in the world of the missing.

The Master held the newspaper clipping before him, and was still holding it when Josie returned with the tea. She saw him and passed Ben Dack her mild disapproval in her grey eyes.

'It does no harm,' he said.

'Tea now,' she said a little loudly to the Master, handing him the mug.

'Oh thank you very much, Josie.'

'Put that away now and enjoy your tea.'

He put the clipping back inside the copy of *David Copperfield* and balanced the book on his knee.

'I'll put that away for you.'

'No. No thank you, Josie. It's fine,' the Master said.

'You remember I read it to you?' Ben asked.

'Ben!' Josie knitted her brows at him. She was such a woman as combined strength and gentleness. Though she was slight, though her frame was small, and when her face settled it settled most frequently into a look of kindness, she could be forceful too. The moment she realized she had raised her voice slightly too loud and the men turned to her, she looked away across the room, as though something alarming had run there, and twice she patted in place the back of her hair.

But Ben paused only a beat, then to the Master continued, 'No no, do you remember I read it out loud? First book I read like that since I don't know when. I'm only saying, yes indeed, Aunt Betsey Trotsy and Mr Dick and Steerforth and Uriah Heep. By jingo yes. They're in my head I'll tell you that. They're right there.' He tapped his forehead with the flat of his hand. 'My point is . . .'

'Ben, your tea!' Josie's face flushed; she sat a little more erect. She found her hands needed pressing together.

'Sorry Josie, sorry. My Josie's a saint, aren't you pet? Yes, pet.'

The Master took his mug and balanced it on the book.

'My point is, real as real they are,' Ben said. 'That's my point.'

'Shsh now, my programme's back,' Josie said somewhat abruptly, and regretted her abruptness, and without turning from the screen reached over and put her hand near her husband's.

And so they all remained that evening before the television and the fire, sipping strong tea, the husband and wife in the dance of relation, and growing tired in the ordinariness of time. Across from them the older man, like a visitor from another domain, sat with quiet politeness and the vague look of someone hearing everything explained in a foreign language.

The country singer introduced a guest, Michael Tubridy, the traditional flute player. A tall man with glasses and a brown suit, he appeared bashful in the studio, as if out of his element. He said the piece he would play was an old air with many names but he knew it as '*Bruach na Carraige*

Baine', Bank of the White Stones. He lifted the flute to his lips and played, and when he did he himself seemed to vanish; instead there were western fields at evening, soft rain falling, cattle standing. There was light turning slowly grey and stone walls glistening and the long deep quiet of the land. Grass damp and heavy darkened. Small winds moved, but nothing else. The slow air, both beautiful and mournful, on its melody brought to every room that ghost-scape. The music was ancient and spell-like and while it lasted nothing else was. Josie put her head against Ben's shoulder. He shut his eyes. Then, a final long note and the air was ended.

The Master suddenly stood up, as though he had been told something of great importance.

'You all right, Joe?' Ben asked.

The Master was standing before the television, and again his chin trembled and he struggled, making a small moan. He balled his fists against his sides and tilted his head upward, as if to keep whatever rose in him from falling out. He turned and left the room.

The bedroom that was his was small and spare. The ceiling sloped along one side of it where a skylight opened to the night. There was a narrow table and a three-drawer chest. There was a picture of the beach at Inch in Kerry, a long pale tongue of sand and foaming sea. On the table was a black-and-white photograph of him and his wife, Mary, taken on their wedding day. He came into the room and put the book on the bed. Then stood into the skylight and looked out at the rectangle of stars. He did this to compose himself. He was aware of his trembling and tried to breathe through it. He was strange to himself now. He had had to accept so much that was unacceptable. Here he was in this room in a house not his own in a life that didn't seem his own either. 'You are here to get better,' was what Ben Dack kept saying to him whenever he showed upset. 'You are here to get better.'

But he was not getting better. He was the same, one day after the next. He had whole parts of himself that were blank. He looked at the picture of Mary and sometimes he could remember her. He could remember a dress, pale green and yellow buttons, and the backs of her legs as she turned to walk ahead of him into some room. But then he couldn't remember her face. Or he had her face in front of him as he woke up, her face as it was in sleep when she was lying beside him, but he could not get his memory to open her eyes. What was the sound of her voice? He tried to hear it, tried to make up phrases she must have said to him, tender or not, tried to put back together a morning, a breakfast, or when he came home after school at four o'clock and what did she say to him? What was her phrase?

The vacancy in him was a torment. It meant there was nowhere for feeling to harbour. It was one thing to suffer loss, but even grief nurtures the heart. He was a man standing at the skylight waiting for something, anything, to return. Even when he wept, he did not know clearly why. So often he had asked himself, *What if I don't get better? What if this is what there is? I should have died. I was meant to die, and by chance didn't. So?*

Now the moon and her stars sat in the mild night. He studied their stillness. His breathing steadied. Through the skylight he could look across the night valley, the dark rumple of field and hedgerow. He could make out the far horizon by the few lights of the farmhouses. He tried to remember the names of those people. He had most likely taught their children. But if the knowledge was there, he couldn't summon it; instead there suddenly came to him some of the names of stars and constellations. Out loud he said, 'Vega in Lyra. Hercules. Cygnus and Aquila. Auriga, Arcturus in Bootes, Ursa Major. Pegasus.' And these may have been words in any language, he may have spoken to an invisible other, but that they suddenly came to him gave him comfort.

Below, a murmur rising through the floorboards, the rosary began. It was still a nightly ritual in that house. It had been since Ben Dack and Josie were married, and was broken only briefly one year when they had discovered they couldn't have children. There had been six months. Then without announcement one night Josie had begun the 'Hail Mary' and Ben had slipped to his knees before the fire and it was back in their life. They prayed it with soft voices and heads half in sleep. They prayed it as if it was not second nature but nature itself, and though they knew that elsewhere in the country it had all but passed into folklore, they ringed the prayers one after the other and let them climb where they might.

So it was, if you had passed that house that night on the narrow road that ran past three small farms, the sheds and hay barns and yards with tractors, the slatted houses of restless cattle anxious for the grass of April, you came to a long farmhouse with a light on downstairs and the heads of a man and woman praying the midnight rosary, while above them a skylight was open and a man was peering outward into the dark.

The dark he stared at was himself, and now into it some glimmer that had come from the music. *He used to play that air.* 'Bruach na Carraige Baine'. *He used to play that on the flute.* And this moved him profoundly, and he tried to rescue from the dark an actual scene when the boy might have played, tried to remake it for himself. *What room? In the school? Or in the house? Upstairs in his bedroom was it?* And he crossed to the bed and picked up the copy of *David Copperfield* and took out the clipping with the picture again and stared at it hard and he tried to combine the flute and the picture and see the boy playing. It was just there. It was just in that place beyond where he could picture it. *He played that. I know he played it.* And the return of that sliver of knowledge was like a shard jabbed into his forehead and he wanted to pull it out and press it further at the same time. He shut his eyes and tried to hum the melody. He put his two hands into the wiry white of his hair. Near-remembering was unbearable. He got a foothold on a mossy step and then slipped back into nothingness. For an hour, longer, he tried to find something solid in the half-memory of the music, something in which he could find solace. *He played it more than once. When did he play it? When? Remember you fool. Remember. Come on. Don't forget him. Don't.*

The images all fell as he grasped for them. The ache was unendurable and he went from the room and down the stairs where the lights were already out and Josie and Ben gone to bed. He went to the dresser where there was a small metal stand for keys and from these he took the one marked 'Joe's Car' and he let himself out through the back door.

The night was velvet, a soft mild dark. He crossed the yard where Ben had parked the lorry facing outward for the morning and in the hay barn he saw the yellow car that he had been told was his but that he could not remember. It had been repaired since the crash but only occasionally driven by Ben, to keep the engine alive he said. The Master opened the door and sat in the driver's seat. He sat awaiting epiphany, but none came. The cold damp of the interior, the cracked places in the plastic of the dashboard, the missing cigarette lighter, the twine-tied winder of the passenger window; he looked at the clues of each but they led him nowhere. *Did I smoke once? Did I tie that twine?*

He held the steering wheel to see if he could find his own hands there, but there was nothing. Then he turned the key. He put the car into gear and released the handbrake. *There was something in that, in the feel of the release. Wasn't there? Wasn't there something familiar about that?*

He couldn't be sure, and he couldn't bear any longer the nearness of his own mind and so he drove out of the yard into the night.

I remember how to drive.

I remember this, shifting the gears, first, second, the narrow slot to third. He drove down the country road, lighting it briefly and leaving it back into darkness behind him. A cat crossed into the ditch. He peered forward, gaining speed now. *Hum the air, hum it now, come on. How does it go? Remember. He played it. He played it one what one Christmas concert was it in the school was it picture him remember you old fool remember*

The road dipped and came around a sharp bend and then out by McInerney's where a light was on in the calving cabin. A dog barked as he passed, but he had shut it out under the humming of the air and he had it now clearly in his head. He had the first passage and he knew the boy had played it and he knew that something was coming back to him at last. On the edge of revelation he drove more quickly. Black fields flew past. A horse startled and flew off down along the wall, briefly winged with light, a flash of mane and then tail and then gone into the darkness. Hedgerows thickening with April shouldered the road. The Master found his heart was racing and with it the car moving faster. *Come on come on.* He hummed the air louder still. He sped the car onward, roaring forward when what he wanted was to get back to the past. At the narrow bends not far from the village he came upon four of Daly's young cattle broken out and grazing the road grass of the ditch. He was upon them before he could think. One hind-kicked at the light and then jumped the straggle of barbed wire, breasting the tangle of it into the field, bellowing, chased by the others. The urgent night noise of the countryside was short-lived. The animals found they were in sweet grass and forgot pain. A car came against him and

24

did not dip its lights and he cursed it on approach but did not slow down and wanted to close his eyes from the dazzlement, and then did.

A silent moment before the crash. A perfect instant of nothing. His own mind trying to make contact with himself. With eyes shut and muscles tensed the instant was forever.

The cars slid past like two knives, a pulse between them.

The Master sped on through the village and past the church and out where Tommy O'Shea was standing at the crossroads, nine pints full and deciding which was the road home. He drove with his foot pressed to the floor now, as though the pursuit was at its hottest and the truth nearer each second. His breath Steamed the windscreen and he sleeved it with his tweed jacket and made a worse smear and sleeved it again *come on come on you can remember, remember, everything is in your head, it's in your head all the time* And then, when the revelation should have come, when he felt it was just a fraction from him there on the edge of his mind, it went.

He was blank.

He knew he could not remember and he took his foot from the accelerator and let the car slow until it came to a stop not fifty feet from the wall where he had crashed three years before. He had come there because he thought he was remembering and that was different to being told. He had thought he would belong to himself again, but now, stopped on the road in the night, he was lost once more. He was a white Lazarus, a meaningless resurrection.

Then, because he thought it was in his head, because he thought the entirety of his past was just behind that less-than-inch of his skull, he unsnapped his seatbelt and then he put the car into gear and drove straight at the wall.

FOUR

The grandson of Noah was called Ethiopis. His son was Aksumawi. It was he who established the Kingdom of Aksum in the country now called Ethiopia.

For four hundred years a snake took power and ruled Aksum. The snake had to be fed milk and virgins until a warrior came and slew the snake and became ruler of Aksum. His name was Angabo. Soon he married the Queen of Sheba and she ruled there with him. When he died the Queen of Sheba took almost eight hundred camels and went to visit the great Solomon in Jerusalem.

The child of that love was called Menelik. He was born in Aksum where Sheba had returned. When he was twelve years of age he wanted to see the face of his father. He journeyed back to Jerusalem and was received there.

He stayed for three years.

When it came time for Menelik to go back to Aksum, Solomon gave him the Ark of the Covenant to protect him, and so that the blessing of God be brought from the people of Israel to those of Ethiopia.

This, the boy called Jay read. He read it from a book he devoured in the corner of a room he shared with twenty-two patients that he cared for in the House of Angels in the city of Addis Ababa in Ethiopia.

He looked up from the yellowed page. His face was deeply tanned. There were three sun-wrinkles at the outer edges of his brown eyes. His dark hair was cropped short. He wore a white T-shirt that had been washed with coloured ones and turned pale blue and donated to Africa in some European city, and khaki trousers he had cut to shorts. His feet were bare and brown.

I am no longer a boy. I am a man, almost.

Then, as though to think it made it real to himself: *I am here in Ethiopia.*

Often it did not seem possible to him. Often he thought what he was living was an Afterlife. He should have died in a bombing in London, or in another in Paris in that first plagued season when terror had crossed Europe. But he had not. There was no one alive in this world to whom he felt connected. His grandfather, the Master, was dead; so too the person he had left home to find, the shadow that may have been his father whose name may have been Ahmed Sharif. His life had come to such dead-ends, to may-have-beens. Bridget had rescued him by bringing him with her here, to this place where she was welcomed as a nun and he as an orphan, one of the lost in that country of orphans. The children he cared for were more lost than he was, and in such a way do the lost find themselves. They were ones who had seen their mothers curl up in corners of tin shacks to die, who had seen their fathers shot, their sisters raped, their brothers become boy-soldiers and vanish or die. They came, many of them, carrying the malign inheritance of AIDS, a disease whose name in English was cruel and bitter, the boy thought, and for which there was only the lower-lettered aid they gave there. These children, some of them nearly his own age, had given the boy a purpose in his Afterlife.

What do you do when the world in which you find your-self is beyond any you have imagined? What do you do when you no longer have an idea called home, when you are outside of knowledge, of understanding, where you know nothing, and all that there is are sick children in a hot place, fever and pain and the staring dark eyes of the innocent?

What the boy did was to erase himself. To become the one who carried water. The one who emptied bedpans. Washed tin plates. Scrubbed bed sheets in the large tin sink, hung them in the sun and brought them in stiff as boards and smelling faintly of *bokra,* the large lemon-like fruit of that country. He was for sweeping floors, for stamping on insects whose names did not exist in English. For washing floors, living in the smell of disinfectant until the acrid odour was his own skin. He was for beating away flies from the faces of the sleeping, for holding plastic beakers of water to the cracked lips of unconsoled children who looked out on the lined-up beds as though waiting in an antechamber of Heaven.

This was the Afterlife of the boy, Jay, and within it he had seen close up many things, and most especially death. Death was always near. In the three years he had spent in the House of Angels he had witnessed all manner of spirit-passing, as Sister Bridget called it. He had held the thin fingers of some even as life left them. This witnessing had caused him to think of death not as an ending but as something other: a falling away, as though a chrysalis phase was over and another, an invisible phase, had began. *Where do we go?* he asked himself often. *Where is this place that must be packed with spirits? Even if a soul takes up only a little space, think of all that have been since Time and how many there must be.* Once, in what he thought of now as long ago, he had walked away from Confirmation and set out to find his father, telling God to prove that He existed by helping him to find him.

29

But the father had not been found and the boy stopped thinking that God ever listened and the long ago was a fairy-tale. They had been childish imaginings. He did not think of God in that way any more. If God existed He was elsewhere. He did not pass through Africa. No longer did the boy address the sky or seek answers in the silence. Yet, frequently, ghosts were about him.

Frequently, he had a sense he would describe as nearness. He did not know if this was a remnant of having been an imaginative child, or from so much aloneness, but he was pleased to be sometimes visited by such a strong sense of company. Sometimes these were figures from his first year travelling across Europe, the blind boy Nuno he had met and brought back to his home in Portugal, the tattooed Maori Whatarangi, the Bob Dylan priest Gus. Most often it was his grandfather, the Master.

So now, as he lifted his head from the coverless book on the strange noble and mythic history of Ethiopia and told himself, this is where I am, I am here in Ethiopia, he had a feeling he was telling it not only to himself. He was telling all those, living and dead, who knew him.

And, he had a feeling that *he was heard*.

He has a life here. At least he has a life.

That's why I brought him here. Because where else was he going to go? And it wasn't selfish. Really it wasn't.

I mean, I knew I was coming. I knew I couldn't go back to Birmingham and the convent. How could I?

And this is what I am supposed to be doing. I know it is. And I am grateful every day for being here.

How strange that must sound, to be grateful to be in such a place of suffering. But also there is joy. There is.

And anyway, if I am wrong You will guide me.

Won't You?

If I am wrong and neither of us should be here. If this wasn't what You intended, You will let me know, won't You?

Dear Lord You will. A sign. Any sign would help. Please guide even such a mad one as me.

Sister Bridget's prayers were not prayers. They were one-sided dialogues where the other spoke mostly in silence but sometimes in signs. These might be various, a change in the light, the ringing of a distant bell, a knocking at the door, sudden showers of rain during the '*belg*' in April, the flight of a white bird. She supposed the world was not merely a surface, that the physical contained within it something else, *as do we*, she would tell herself. *It makes perfect sense.*

She prayed seated on the narrow bed. There was a short pause while the patients ate and she could take a moment to herself. Three years in Africa had made her pink face golden. Her hair was cut short, her arms thickly freckled. She had the look of a European touched by that continent, the simplicity of her clothes, sandals, the compassion of her eyes.

The boy moved back and forth with bowls and cloths and refills of water. Over the years she had seen him grow and was proud of him, until she chastised herself for pride and kept instead to a kind of quiet gladness. Their life was as strange as a thing imagined. But sometimes she was able to accept that it could be so. One thing can lead to another, was a thing her mother used to say, as if that explained anything.

One thing can lead to another.

Her days at the hospital were full, her evenings too. She had come to love these people. She loved the faces she saw in Addis, the old men with their sticks and their ancient expression, in equal parts knowledge, bemusement and resignation, the proud watchful faces of the young, the dignity in the women. It was a noble city. Like almost everything else in her life it was not as she had imagined. She had not imagined the clear air that was almost alpine, the junipers, the eucalyptus and the fig trees. She had not imagined the beauty of the Entoto hills, but neither the grim shanties of the Kechene district. She had smiled when she learned the city's name meant 'New Flower'. She had not expected the perfect manners of the Ethiopian people, how they bore themselves with grace, how fiercely some held their Christian faith. She had not expected their humour. The city itself was a surprise. Addis was neither dirty nor lawless. There were tower blocks that gleamed, chrome and glass cafés, hair salons, marble-fronted banks with uniformed guards, streets filled with white cars. There were all the outward evidences of a global city, but so too there were beggars and lepers. There were animals herded through the same streets as Mercedes. There was a ragged nomadic population of the diseased. Men, women and children came from the mountains, came from villages that were no more, who had the shirts on their backs only and drank from the city's fountains and sat on the pavements in a kind of desolation Bridget hadn't seen before. In Addis she had had to learn a difficult lesson, that here there were always more than she could help. And there always would be. Here she had had to admit to the smallness of what she could do, and then do it anyway. This was among the first lessons of Africa, but it was a beginning.

'You need my help?' she asked Jay.

'No. No thanks. Everything's good.'

She thought he was remarkable. When he had a task he took to it with the kind of seriousness especially endearing in boys. Whether he was in charge of tidying a press, sweeping floors, cleaning toilets, he did it with earnestness. Sometimes Bridget thought this was because when he was working he was not thinking; he could put aside his sadness. That was why he liked to be busy. *Was that it?*

He moved among the children in the beds quickly. He was tall now and long armed and full of energy. For each of his tasks he had a method and this never varied. So if he gave the bowls out from left to right and collected them right to left, this he did every day the same. *It's the way he is. He likes the order because so little in his life has been that way. And there's nothing wrong with that. This is our life now. I may never leave. He may never leave, and isn't that all right? Isn't it? If it isn't you need to tell me. You need to send a sign.*

Suddenly she heard commotion at the entrance.

There was a loud shouting and a stick beating on the door. She went down the stone corridor calling '*Usshi usshi*' which meant 'okay' and she said it louder and over again as she came but it made no difference. The banging continued until she opened the heavy door and blinked against the dazzle of sunlight, extending a flat palm above her eyes to see an old man, skeletal, bald, with baleful watery eyes. He wore a brown cloth over one shoulder, part dress part sack, and a ragged pair of red tracksuit pants that ended well before his bare feet. The moment Bridget opened the door the man fell forward to his knees and grabbed onto her dress. He bowed his head and spoke quickly and Bridget could understand only that there was urgency. He kept his head lowered and when she tried to reach down to lift him up he shook and reached out an arm to point behind him on the street.

There a girl was lying, unconscious.

When the old man began knocking on the door, or perhaps before that, when he had borne the lifeless body down the street on his back, calling out, carrying the girl and his story,

33

people paused, and some had blessed themselves but others hurried to clutch tokens of luck – bones, hair-knots, brooches, anything – and locked their doors against ill-fortune. But some others had followed. Now there was a small assembly of elder women who were drawn to witness sorrow, and leaning boys who hung back across the street but watched hawk-like for what was next to be revealed. There was wailing in the air. There were bowed heads and hands raised, appeals and cries. The old man was talking, telling something Bridget did not understand but she went at once to the girl, and crouched down and moved back the covering from her face.

She was perhaps seventeen. Her eyes were closed but she bore no mark or outward evidence of disease. Did she breathe? Bridget couldn't tell. There was too much noise. She raised her head, called out for quiet and all fell silent. She put her ear against the girl's lips. *There's breath. Isn't there?* She looked up for help but then the old man began again, chanting his tale and prompting a response of wailing from the women across the way.

'What is he saying? What are you saying?' Bridget called out.

One of the boys stepped down from the doorstep and to show his courage and intelligence came across to tell her: 'She is from the east, Miss, a village. He says soldiers came because of Chinese oilfield, because Chinese were killed. The soldiers shot her father, then they took her away. Two days, the men.' He looked down at the ground and did not tell further.

The old man spoke, the bones of his face working, his long-fingered hands clasped together.

'Then what? What?' Bridget asked.

'He says she is dead in life.'

'Dead in life? What does that mean? That doesn't mean anything.'

34

'She was found on the road beyond the village, like this.' The boy shrugged, pointed, but explained no further. 'He brought her here to the city for . . .' The boy searched for the word. He raised his right hand from his waist into the air above his head to demonstrate.

'How long has she been travelling?'

'Many days.'

The old man had finished speaking and was turned now to look directly at Bridget. The women had suddenly stopped making noise and Jay had come outside to the doorway.

The boy suddenly had the word. 'Rise. Rise up! He brought her here, Miss, so that she could rise up, rise up again. You can make her rise up.'

FIVE

The Master remained perfectly still. His head had hit the windscreen and popped back and hit the headrest and he was looking now puzzled at the weblike crack in the glass in front of him. He stayed still a long time. The headlights were still on and showed the concrete pier tilted and the seven-bar gate knocked out of its top support and hanging at a crazy angle. The empty field was lit before him, a quadrant in which each tuft of grass was held in illumined focus, and there, standing, turned towards him, a hare. In the moments after the crash the Master was not sure that he was there. The clarity of his vision was startling. He watched the hare watching him and did not know if it was a hare in this life or the next. Then, with the illogic of those just crashed, he considered he himself was the hare looking back at the dead man in the car. He was looking at the motionless white-headed figure in the tweed jacket and grey shirt and seeing, as in all crashes, the pointless end of life, the still and twisted angle of the body behind the wheel, the lifetime of hopes rising like steam from the engine and evaporating into the night. He was seeing the frailty of the old man and how easily he had been broken, and that, after all, what had his life been? He was only that body stilled in the yellow car, that labouring heart in a framework of poor health that should have stopped before.

As the hare, he studied the scene dispassionately. He turned his head to one side and saw the collected dreams of the old man just then fading away. He saw the days of his boyhood when he ran barefoot and lived in scolding in a household of sisters. He saw his afternoons in a field with a football and his solo runs out-swerving his shadow, his thrilled eyes wide with the marvel of himself. Here was the short solid figure of him as a young man considered stubborn and within a hair's-breadth of arrogance, the arrogance slipping away like sand the evening he stood in front of Mary Conway. Here, the college nights in Dublin he took her dancing, the peak of his dreaming when suddenly he saw life was a feast laid out before him. His marriage, the cold sweat on his forehead the night his daughter Marie was born, his abashed eyes, the tuft of his hair he couldn't pat down, as if some part of him was permanently upward, optimistic; there they were. The days of Marie's girlhood when he was already a schoolteacher, and what he didn't have time to acknowledge was human happiness was his, the birthdays, the timber flute she played, the hand of Mary taking his; these each like clouds formed and passed upward. So too the terrible days of his life, the cancer that began, the times he fled into a bottle, the horror day of Mary's funeral and his hand a numb lump of flesh shaken. Here he was in that aftermath, a drunken master and poor father; here he was arguing away the priest who came to sack him; so too there was the birth of his grandson, this brown bundle brought from England in his daughter's arms, the father she wouldn't name. The time when he had imagined wretchedness and grief were accounted, and that in that family there had been suffering enough, and then was proven wrong as his daughter died; this a foul black twist like smoke rose too from the scene.

All this, the hare saw. The lifetime dreams of the old man climbed into the air above the crashed car.

Then there was the boy, the boy he was left with who became his life.

There he was.

The moment he appeared, the hare, while still standing, made a sudden darting turn of his head, as though he sensed the approach of something yet invisible into the scene. Again he turned his head sharply and raised slightly the exquisite sensitivity of his nose. His ears twitched. The polished blackness of his eyes considered the night and what might arrive in that rough field now. And whether he saw further into the present or the near future, whether what he sensed was real or unreal, he leapt. His speed was astonishing. An instant, and his tail flew out of the headlights and the Master was returned to himself and sat watching the hare vanish. It went into dark, but what was left was the returned memory of the boy.

He could remember.

He touched his forehead; there was no blood. He turned off the lights and got out of the seat into the night. He was stiff but unbroken. He palmed his forehead and flattened the top of his hair and shut the car door and walked out onto the road.

Then he walked back into the village. He went along the centre of the road and no car came or went, and only once did he encounter someone. Out of opposite dark came a man similarly walking, the way some say you meet your soul. He was dark on darkness first, a smudge in the near distance, silent as an idea, a figment. The Master considered that each saw the other, but neither helloed nor coughed nor otherwise saluted. They approached along the night-road as though each had been *sent,* for each were likewise in an absolute aloneness and perhaps they were to be for each other in some way significant. So it might have seemed. The two men came steadily closer. The Master could see the other was younger than he and fair-haired and perhaps the slight looseness of his gait spoke of drinking or strong feeling. At ten yards both were looking at each other as they approached: one from the east, the other from the west. The Master moved slightly to one side of the middle of the road, the stranger the other. And they passed by, strange and quiet, the Master nodding and, shoulders high at first with apprehension, hands buried in his jacket pockets, the man nodded back and strode on.

He was not from there, the Master thought. He was probably Polish or Latvian and very young, he thought, and then thought no more about Jerzy Maski. He walked back in through the village. Tommy O'Shea was no longer standing at the crossroads. The village slept, its one-hundred-and-twenty-four dreams hanging above Church Street. With steady purpose now, he walked back out the end of the few streetlights and passed back by the places where Daly's cattle had broken out and then along the winding bends once more.

When he arrived at Dack's he tried to let himself in quietly, but the metal latch slipped on the catch and fell. 'Shshshsh,' he said to it immediately after, and then came in the back door and down the two steps into the sitting room. The fire was well gone but he crossed and sat before it and was looking down into the white turf ashes as Ben Dack came down the stairs wrestling a dressing gown.

'What's up, Joe? Everything all right? I mean you're all right. Only I heard the door, you weren't out were you? Josie thought she heard a car a while back and I says it's me who's usually driving in dreams.'

'I was on a straight road,' the Master said.

'What road? When was this?' Ben gave his head a vigorous rubbing with both hands, then fisted his eyes.

'I was on a straight road, Ben, and there was a tractor and a trailer and I thought I could pass it. That was the crash,' the Master said. His voice was clear and calm, then his chin trembled and he worked to control it, drawing in air through his nostrils and tilting back his head a little. He would not collapse. 'We called him Jay,' he said. 'We called him Jay because in school he was teased about his name and when he was eight years old he said he wanted to change it. And I wasn't sure what his mother would want and I said we'd better think about it and that same afternoon we went up the hill and took the kites because he liked flying kites. And while they were in the sky he turned over to me and had to shout a little because it was windy. "What about just Jay?" he said. And I said that was perfect. And he was very happy then. We flew the kites a long time. He liked loops. He liked when the kite came swooping down as though it would hit the earth and then at the last minute flew back up again. He called it a 'j' because he was clever like that and could connect things so quickly.'

He paused. In the middle of the night in that small front room of the Dack house he was illumined by the past. It was as if in the crash someone had come slowly down the mossy steps bearing a torch into the cavernous dark of him. Whole parcels of time, wrapped and shelved and forgotten, were then discovered inside him. He had not access to everything, but he knew now that they were there. The marvellous was his own mind; in it was the torn tapestry of days. The torch was held up and a portion gleamed.

'We called him Jay,' the Master said again. 'He loves the novel *David Copperfield*.'

'There now,' Ben Dack said.

'He plays the flute because I told him his mother did,

though he never heard her. There is a tune called "Napoleon's Retreat". He likes "The Who" because I had the old LPs and because he liked the name "Who" without any question mark. He likes cocoa, Josie,' the Master told her as she appeared at the foot of the stairs.

'Oh Joe,' she said, gently.

She sat beside him on the arm of the chair and she took his hand in hers and looked into the ashes. Ben Dack put his hand on his mouth and then rubbed his head again and then took a step off in the direction of the kitchen, stopped, turned, punched his right fist into the palm of his left, nodded.

'You're remembering,' he said, 'you're remembering! You're remembering Jay.'

'Yes,' said the Master, 'his name is Jay now.' And then his face creased and his chin rose and he said, 'And Ben, he's not dead.'

He said it calmly; he said it as though telling himself also. 'He's not dead. He's somewhere.'

SIX

Bridget and the boy brought the girl inside. She made a moan when Jay bent down to pick her up but did not open her eyes. She weighed nothing. When she lay on the bed her limbs were lifeless, like sticks. The dust of her travels was on her features and Bridget told Jay to bring a bowl of water and a fresh cloth. When he came back, two small boys followed him. They stood at the doorway and stared.

'She is breathing but . . .' Bridget held the girl's wrist. 'Her pulse is so slow it's . . . I am going to get Doctor Pellier.' She rose from the bedside. 'He will be down at the clinic now. I won't be long. Just stay with her, Jay.'

When Bridget went out, the two boys came forward. Their names were Dembe and Bekele. They thought Jay was a magician because he knew all things, and had taught them the magic of letters to make English words.

'What is she?' Bekele asked.

'She is sick bad,' Dembe said.

'Sick bad-bad,' Bekele told him.

'Shsh!'

The boys dropped their faces for ten seconds, then pressed forward again. Jay watched the girl. He looked at her perhaps as he had never looked at a girl before, the profound mysteriousness of her. He took the cloth and dipped it in the water and wrung it tightly and then, with absolute delicacy of touch, as though she were a figure from a dream that would vanish under his fingers, he brought the cloth to her forehead and cleaned off a curve of the dust of the road. She did not move. He dipped the cloth and wrung it and again brought it to her face. He washed her brow, then her temples, then rinsed the cloth again, then he told the boys to take the bowl and empty and refill it freshly.

'What is she, sick-bad?' Bekele asked again.

'Yes, sick-bad,' he said. 'Go quickly now and bring back fresh water.'

The two boys stood looking.

'Bekele go now. Quickly.'

'You will make her all-good?'

'Water, now, go!'

They ran together, spilling the water, down the hallway.

Jay looked at the girl. Where he had dabbed on her forehead glistened now. He had not dried away the water. Or was it that she was hot? Was it a fever? He laid his hand upon her brow. To touch her was strange. More strange in this moment than anything he had known. There was no fever, and she bore no outward sign of disease. But when his fingers touched her brow he felt something beyond his experience. He felt how *real* she was, how *solid*, how she was *another*. He could not formulate it in words yet. He could not explain the full dimension of his surprise, or even why he should be surprised. But he knew it as he touched her. It was startling, just that moment when he laid his hand on her forehead. He left his hand a moment on the shining skin.

'Water fresh-good,' Bekele said.

Jay withdrew his hand. 'Good boys thank you.'

'Good boys yes,' Dembe said. 'You make her all-good?'

44

'Shsh now.'

Jay took the bowl and prepared the cloth again, and he brought it to her face, this time gently washing first one cheek and then another, then the line of her nose which even in repose seemed raised in pride. There were some blisters on her skin, but they were not sores, he thought. They were the marks of the road where she must have fallen or been knocked and pressed down. He tried to dab the dirt out of them but it was not easily done. Tiny traces of blood shone. He rinsed again and cleaned her chin. Her lips were dry and cracked and seemed pressed in a firm line, as though the last thing she spoke was refusal. He looked at them and was filled with misshapen feelings of awkwardness. They blundered into his heart and were like weird visitors discovered when you did not know the door was open. He turned around to the boys as if to see if they had noticed.

'Shsh,' he said, though they had not spoken.

They showed him back the puzzlement in himself.

'Go see if Doctor Pellier is coming. Quickly.'

Bekele ran out. He was the runner. He had grown up in a mountain village. He would run for everyone, he would run to the end of the world, run for his country until he held gold. Dembe did not move.

'Jay Jay is sad,' he said. He pronounced the name as though it were *chaychay*.

'Shsh.'

Dembe picked at his fingers, pinching tiny pieces of upset. Jay turned back to the girl. Suddenly he felt he shouldn't look at her. He looked across the room at the far wall. It was roughly plastered, a once-white that – like everything else in that country – faded to brown. Even white was not white there. At the corner the walls were off-plumb and, where after some settlement of the ground, stones in the building protruded and the plaster had fallen off. There was a second bed, dressed tightly in sheets and a grey blanket, so taut you could not think of a person entering it. Then, just beneath it, Jay saw a black hard-bodied beetle and he pointed to it and Dembe went quickly and picked it up between thumb and forefinger, wriggling pincers, and threw it out the window.

'Good boy,' he said, and Dembe smiled whitely to be back in favour, but this time did not risk saying anything.

Where's the doctor? The girl's arm lay where Bridget had left it. She had not moved even slightly. He looked at her hand, fallen open over the edge of the bed. He looked at the creases across each finger, the paler pink in the dark skin, the broken roads on her palm. *Where's the doctor?* He brought his own hands together palm to palm and patted the prayer-like pose of them against his lips. Then he quickly released them, took the cloth and dipped and wrung it partially, then squeezed it gently so water dripped on her lips. The drops sat proud an instant then trickled sideways to the pillow. They had done no good. He wet the cloth again and now leant forward and was within the thin slow breathing of her and the awkward company of his feelings shifted about in his heart as if no seat would suit.

He touched the cloth to her lips. He touched it as gently as he could imagine possible and yet her lips moved under the pressure and her nostrils opened slightly and he looked to her shut eyes thinking she would waken. But she did not. Single drops of water – two, three, four – he let fall now along the parting of her lips and then, whether she knew or not, her lips pressed together and opened slightly and pressed again as if she was new to tasting or had thirsted to the point of forgetting water. It was the action of a moment, nothing more. It happened, and then there was no sign that it had. Her eyes remained closed, her breathing the same. But he had seen it. The company in his heart crowded the space so

46

he had to lean back and open his mouth for air. He looked back at Dembe who studied him as though to discover the secrets of magic.

'What is keeping them?' Jay asked the boy, who did not understand, and he backhanded his brow and was surprised to discover it clammy with sweat. He thought he should get up now and step away from the girl. But he turned to her again and looked at her as if the features of her together could explain what was happening to him. Where her lips had parted the pink flesh had torn slightly. There was a pencil-line of blood. This he was leaning forward to wipe when the quick slap sound of bare footsteps in the hallway startled him.

Bekele ran his smile right back to the bedside, neither out of breath nor seeming exerted in any way. Bridget and the doctor followed.

Doctor Michel Pellier was a mid-sized Frenchman of fifty, with thick black hair and the deep-set blue eyes of one who still found appalling the capacity of life to produce suffering. Like all who came there from elsewhere, his personal history had opened a wound to which only Africa seemed a possible salve. For the many that discovered this a misdiagnosis, there were some for whom the remedy was perfectly matched, and Michel Pellier was one such. Africa had saved his life when his wife left him.

'*Attends,* step back, please.'

He felt her brow, then lifted her thin wrist. 'She has not moved?'

'No.'

'*Rien?* Nothing?'

'No,' Jay said, then just before the doctor noticed the bowl of water on the floor, added, 'I cleaned her face.'

Doctor Pellier lay the girl's arm back on the bed. He turned to Jay. 'I see,' he said.

Bridget too looked at Jay, and he felt the unwelcome visitors shuffle about in his heart. There were not enough chairs for them; they sat on sills, stood in close knots in heavy coats, whispered.

'Did she do anything Jay?' Bridget was asking.

'No. No she didn't.' He felt guilty when he was innocent. He held his hands together. 'Well she, she maybe . . .'

'*Oui*?' Doctor Pellier narrowed his eyes, as if the point being made was far away behind the words.

'She maybe drank a little of the water. I wet her lips and she just . . .' He mimicked the action. 'Just that. She didn't open her eyes. She didn't do anything.'

The doctor looked at the puzzle of this a moment, then turned to the girl and bent over and raised first one eyelid and then the other. He addressed the nun. 'I must examine her. *Tu dois rester, pas les autres.*'

'Go back to the ward, Jay, and bring the boys and keep an eye on things for me, will you?' Bridget asked.

'Will she be all right?'

'I will come and tell you soon,' Bridget said, and could see already a difference, as though some part of him had become transparent.

He went down the hall, the boys following.

'Is she bad-bad?' Bekele asked.

But Jay did not answer. He came into the ward where several of the children had lost their bedclothes to the floor, where a chamber pot had been spilled, where a boy of five years old with a bandaged right eye was crying hard. And to these Jay gave his attention and energy, swift and focused and effective, filling the time with purpose, though the awkward company within him remained.

SEVEN

At first there were the beatings in the dark, questions in the light. The prisoner told the truth but the truth was the wrong answer and did not set him free. He told it when he knew he would be beaten for telling it. He told it though the telling brought him to unconsciousness, and pain woke him later in a cell where the dark was total. He was left there without food or water and could not say for how long. There were no days, and of all the things that he missed the worst was light. He lay in the dark hugging the brokenness of him until they brought him out again.

Tell us, Ali. Tell us where you were going to plant the bomb.

I told you. I know nothing about a bomb.

Are you an idiot, Ali?

My name is not Ali.

We know your name is not Ali.

Jay is out there somewhere.

In the days following the Master's discovery of this in the clearing fog of himself he was perturbed and more given to weeping. He would come into the kitchen to Josie, his eyes glossed with a rescued moment. 'I took him fishing,' he said. 'I have the whole day of it in front of me. I have us packing to go, the sandwiches, the tea-flask, the net-bag, the, the *happiness* of him. I have all of it, right here in front of me,' he said, and then his chin rose and he made fists to fight what came through him, though it was not an enemy.

'He is out there somewhere Josie,' he said, and it was enough to make him seem a man of water, his face dissolving before she had even time to tea-cloth her hands and come and hold back what was flowing away.

Memory returned now, a river thickening by the moment. It pushed aside stones, nudging them partway so what came first was a quickening eddy, then a swirl – the broken-heeled sneakers he wore, how he never undid laces, how his clothes amassed on the floor of his room – then a whole rushing torrent – the day when Marie brought him home for the first time, having conquered the fear of judgement, that particular warm smell of him, the perfect minute hand clutching his grandfather's finger, how he seemed to want that finger more than any other, and how they were then bound like that, wordlessly connected for hours.

They came now, such moments, flowing into him, carrying what could only be called a bitter joy. There was no consolation for the loss. Sorrow was like a transforming illness in him. Although once stocky and strong, the Master now bore the frail baffled air of having been knocked down and got up only to discover some inner parts seized. He was what people meant when they said the stuffing had been knocked out of them. Inside his old tweed jacket he might have fitted another. The skin of his face was delicate and pale and made beautiful by weeping. When he shaved himself each morning he was astonished the blade did not tear it away, so fine did it seem. His hair, once tufted with a kind of irrepressible

50

front curl, had fallen flat, as had his eyebrows, lowering onto eyes that were always wet, always bringing to their blue surface broken pieces of the past.

He told Josie some detail he remembered and she sat him down at the kitchen table and listened and fed him tissues and took the lumpish discards like a sour harvest that she hoped would be finite, of which in each of us there is only so much.

Afterward, the river slowing to a trickle, the Master would sniffle once or twice and apologize.

'Don't be silly,' she said, then, in case he had forgotten, 'We have told the police again you know.'

'Yes, Josie. I know.'

'If he is out there they will find him. They find lots of people. They can send the search all over the world now.'

'He *is* out there,' the Master said.

She nodded and pushed together the hoard of used tissues, dropping them into the bin. She ran the water for her hands and looked out of the window. She did not ask the question that was always there when she thought of the boy because she knew there was no answer: *if he is out there why does he not come back?* Was it better to believe he was dead or was out there alive but had some dreadful secret or shame or hurt that made him not want to come back? She ran the water and kept her hands within it, watching the flow sluice over her fingers some moments, as the idea suddenly came to her: *he needs to be searching. If he believes he is out there somewhere he can't just sit, he has to be searching.* And before she had taken her hands to the tea towel she had decided, *We'll get him a computer. That's how you search for things now.*

That evening, when Ben returned, the Master was sitting with the copy of *David Copperfield* by the fire. He was not reading but he held the book in his two hands and from the balls of his feet rocked himself very gently.

'Well now,' Ben said. It was neither question nor statement but his round face smiled and his thick eyebrows floated upward, as if in him hope was irrepressible. 'Got your car fixed again,' he said and winked, 'but you're best to tell me now when you want to take her out, eh?'

'Ben?'

'Yes Joe.'

'Ben, there are some other books, some books I remember. Can you bring me home to get them?'

They went after tea. They arrived at the house before dark and came up along the garden path where the daffodils had died back and their brown heads bowed at angles to the ground. The garden missed its gardener and, like all such, seemed to grow loneliness. The grass was wild, the hedges top-heavy and falling outward. Bushes had thickened and pushed one into the other, crowding up towards the house. Plants that had once been chosen for their colour and form were straggled twists and spires, the whole of each bed entangled in a miry struggle. Nettles, dandelions, buttercups were embedded everywhere. The warm spring had jungled all plantings and what had come up had fallen over and what was low to the ground was choked, the whole scene one of wilderness and ghosts. A wooden bench, weathered thin, lost its legs in weed. Behind it, two trellises for roses had been pushed over by the wind and now pinned the growth into the grass where the top curve of an old ball gleamed. There was no wind now, only the comfortless stillness that sometimes occupies graveyards and is like a hand on the shoulder pausing everything. It was not death but life that was recalled there, all the vivid, thoughtless bustle of the everyday in that garden, the comings and goings down the garden path, the Master walking out through the gate and down the road to the

52

school, the boy on a blanket in the grass in his first summer, the first buzzing of bees trafficking from lily to columbine, pulling sweetness out into the air. It was such a place that had once been lovely. But the ragged world inside the hedges now showed nothing of that life. What love remained was hidden. The pine trees in the plantation across the road had grown ten times faster than time. They towered into the evening so shadow fell where once had been sunrise and set.

From an unseen branch, the two-note song of the cuckoo. It was plaintive and sounded again over that wild garden a song strangely hollow and sad. Perhaps because they could not bear to stay there any longer, the two men came up the path, taking in and keeping out what they could of the deep melancholy around them. Ghosts of childhood and youth, of love and marriage passed them. The red paint of the front door was flaked to show the yellow one beneath it. The windows likewise were wind-and-rain-scoured to show something of the yellow place that had been when the boy was young. It was in all manners the House of Memory, and when Ben turned the old key in the door the sound of the clack itself as the lock slid back was like some cogged mechanism working in the Master's mind. They stepped into the hallway where Ben waved aside a drapery of webs. The house was damp, and the smell thick and heavy as a buried cloth drawn from the ground. Daintily, small spiders finger-walked up onto the ceiling. Although Ben had come back occasionally to collect books and clothes and tried briefly to air the house, it was quickly reclaimed by creatures and dust. An old stone house in the west of the country seemed always trying to return to the ground. It was as though the stones themselves were always heading homeward, and would win out in the end.

When Ben turned on the light switch, the room that was revealed wore in all aspects the sorry air of decline. In the chimney, black tar streaks of soot glistened; in the hearth the fallen excess of twig leaf and feather of the nest above. Dust, dust everywhere. A grey film was laid faultlessly over couch and chairs, along the table that was still set for the unheld party of the boy's Confirmation. Bottles wore an opaque coat, glasses for the fierce aunts that never came had now drunk the dust of three years and made soft places for spiders and other creatures who liked their crystalline cool.

Briefly the two men stood awkwardly alongside the evidence of a life's shell. And although Ben could imagine a family life in these armchairs, feet crossing the linoleum, hurrying to and from the kitchen, the thought was painful. He did not like to be there, and did not think it could be good now for the Master. So, once the light had thrown the sad little room into vivid display, he pointed to the books along the mantel.

'There you go now.'

The older man looked but didn't move.

'Will we just take the lot?' Ben asked.

Then the pale face with the watery eyes turned to him and said, 'Ben, why am I alive?'

'Well. Well now.' Ben let the fullness of his eyebrows head to his hair and then discovered it needed scratching, furiously.

'I should have been dead. And was dead, and then wasn't. That's what I think of, Ben. And it makes no sense to me that the last person I loved should be gone and I'm still here. So that's why, Ben.' He turned slowly then to take in the full room and its many ghosts. 'Because it doesn't make sense. That's why I know he's out there somewhere.'

Ben smoothed a hand over the up-scratched hair. 'I've thought of going looking, don't get me wrong,' he said. 'I have and I have told Josie. I said I could take the time and take the lorry even and head out, go to England, go anywhere

54

they said he might be, and just look for him. I said to her: how do you find someone in the world? You go looking and you keep looking because someone will have seen him and sooner or later you'll meet someone who has met someone who has met him and that will put you on your track. Cripes yes, I've thought that, Joe. I've thought the world is just people. That's what it is, and it just needs asking and looking. Just people. It stands to reason. You go somewhere, you ask. You ask all day every day and you go one place to the next and ask there and you don't give up but the problem is, the problem is if . . .' He hit the wall in his thinking. He didn't even see it coming. 'I mean . . . if he's out there . . . if then . . .'

The Master was already there. 'Why doesn't he come back,' he said.

The silence falling was curdled by fear and unknowing. The thought of the boy hurt made the thick lumps of dead air un-breathable. Ben squeezed his fat fingers into a clasp and the Master tilted back his head, fighting his chin.

'Yes,' he said at last. He looked over at his rescuer. 'But he will come back, Ben. That's what I understood last night. I have to wait. He's out there somewhere and he's going to come back. That's why I'm alive. That's why I have to stay alive. That's why you rescued me.' The weeping was welling again but he shook his head to deny it and swallowed. 'I wish to blazes this didn't keep happening to me,' he said. But this time Ben Dack was not uncomfortable, and waited the moments for the emotion to ease.

Then the Master said, 'It is his birthday today.'

'Is that right?'

'He is sixteen.'

'Well now,' Ben said. 'Well now.' And for a few moments they were quiet in the thought of that, each differently imagining him somewhere in the world. But the imagining was vague and without satisfaction; there was no actual *scene*, no reality to it, and it could not sustain their feeling.

The Master turned to the shelf and took down five or six volumes to bring away with him. Smells of dust and old paper were released. One thin book in particular he held out in front of him and blew a million mites to the air before peering down at the old cover, studying its title as though it were a message from the past. 'This one I will read for him. I will read it for his birthday,' he said.

EIGHT

'Jerzy!'

Laslo came into the shell of the house where the crew that included Jerzy was taking their break. They sat shirtless on blocks and unwrapped tinfoil from what they considered the best thing about Ireland, the breakfast-in-a-roll, the eggs and beans and rashers and sausages and tomatoes and mushrooms and sometimes fried potato, all packed into and spilling out of a heated tube of dough. The Poles did not go to restaurants, they ate from petrol stations. They liked the curt clean exchange with the cashier, the hot window of food you could see and point to, the practicality of filling car and body at the same stop, returning there on the way home to collect beers. They liked routine. Habit is how you keep homesickness away. It is how you make familiar the strange, Laslo had told Jerzy. You make some things you do, and you do them again each day. And that way you make a life.

Jerzy was not sitting with the others. He was still on the upper wall, tapping a block into place. Laslo came up the ladder.

'*Pomylony chlopiec!* Crazy, did you not hear it was break?' he said.

'I didn't want a break,' Jerzy told him, carrying on with the block, trimming the excess cement with a smooth cut of the trowel.

'You get paid no more for no break. Come on, breakfast-in-a-roll. Take the break. I don't want you to collapse. What will I write to your mother?'

Jerzy stopped. His bare torso was muscled and tanned and shone in the sun of morning.

'Come on, come eat with me,' Laslo wheezed, and for relief tapped his breast pocket and took out a flattened pack of cigarettes, lipping one and lighting it with a fluency of years, then squinting one-eyed through the smoke.

In what would be the downstairs box bedroom, Jerzy and his uncle sat.

'I know you are unhappy,' Laslo said. 'But the unhappiness will go away. What you need is a girl.' He one-eyed smiled, smoked. 'Big Irish girl maybe. You have seen, I know you have seen. Some not bad eh? Though not for marrying. Your mother would kill.' He laughed into a cough and then coughed until tears. 'What do you say, Jerzy, some not bad?'

'We don't speak English. We are strangers here.'

'They like that. They love that. More strange the better. Not the usual. We are . . .' He stroked his the magnificence of his moustache, raised both eyebrows heavy with suggestion. '. . . like Italians.' The eyebrows danced like extra moustaches.

'I should go home.'

'No. No no. You are just homesick a little longer. Then it will be over. You will see. You will be able to go anywhere. You will always have Jaslo here in your heart but it will not hurt so.' He flicked the dead butt and watched it fly and tapped out another from the pack. 'We will all go back. We know we will. We will all be old men in our own villages talking about the countries we built, the places that would

58

not be if we had not come. Without us this country would be what? Fields. No, you must stay. There is nothing at home for the young. Even for me and I am not that young.' He laughed and punched Jerzy on the shoulder and drew a smile, and for a while the two of them said nothing but ate the divided breakfast-in-a-roll. Then the beeping of a lorry reversing signalled the end of break, and Jerzy thanked his uncle and went outside where Ben Dack was delivering another load.

'What a day, eh?' he said, jumping down the short step from the lorry onto the dusty site. He wore a check shirt of red and green that was too warm for the beautiful day and began at once to carefully roll the sleeves. 'By jingo yes. Another scorcher says he.' He put his face briefly to the sun, as if for a kiss, then winked at Jerzy Maski. 'Fabulous country, eh?'

But Jerzy was already moving around to unload the lorry.

'They always give you this job, don't they?'

Jerzy didn't know he was being asked a question. He dragged off two large bales of fibreglass insulation.

'Hot as Poland, is it?'

Jerzy took another two.

'I'd say it is. I'd say hotter,' Ben said. 'It's not the way we're used to here, you know? Indeed and it is not. No. We don't know what to make of it. You know? We don't. It's like . . .'

Jerzy was gone again. Ben waited.

'. . . it's like we went to sleep and someone took the whole island and just sort of floated it down to the Canaries or some-where. You know? You know the Canary Islands? Ben Dack's never been and why would you go now says the fella. Why would you? Why would you if we're going to have this?'

Another two bales he took behind him. There were forty more.

'I was thinking I might like to go to Poland,' Ben told him. 'I mean to see what you people have seen. Because it stands to reason. Every day you're the lads I'm meeting. Polish.'

Jerzy paused and looked at him, nodded.

'Yes, Polish,' Ben said a little more loudly, then pointing towards the east of Ennis, added, 'Po-land, Po-land.'

And in that look, in that moment while Jerzy Maski's expression changed, Ben Dack joined the dots, he would tell Josie later.

It was a look both painful and proud and released in the younger man a sudden swift flow of language. His blue eyes shone. He spoke quickly, urgently. He brought thumb and forefinger close together as if telling of something small, and this he held out before him, insistent, then opened both arms wide to indicate a great expanse, then right-palmed his own chest three times. An instant then he shrugged both shoulders, sharply shook his fair head, widened his eyes to show what he told was marvellous, and with one hand then outreached as if in appeal. He said further phrases then, tumbling one after the other quickly, his animation growing as though he pleaded Justice or Love or any absolute of humanity.

And all of this in Polish. The sounds of the language were like crashed words to Ben Dack. They were words that kept hitting harshness, Zs and Ks and CHs, as though a chainsaw took them roughly. It seemed language fierce and masculine and proud, and in the young man's delivery was charged electric and fizzed as it came through his teeth.

'Wait a minute wait a minute wait a minute,' Ben said. He held up both hands and Jerzy might have turned away but for the smile.

'Hold on. Hold the horses now one tick.' Ben patted a

hand on the top of his head, as if he was thanking his brain. Twice more, as if it were a dog that had just pleasantly surprised him. Then he extended his hand.

'First things first. Ben. That's me. That's who you're talking to. Ben. Ben – Me.'

'Ben-me.'

'No no, no cripes wait no. BEN.'

The younger man took the hand. 'Ben.'

'Bingo.'

'Bingo.'

'No, jeepers. No. No. Just Ben.'

'Just Ben.'

'Ben. Yep. And you?'

'Jerzy.'

'Jer. Good man. Jer.' Ben couldn't stop smiling: an idea was running wildly around inside him, whooping, giggling, tearing full speed down the corridors of his brain and not caring who heard or what might be in the way.

'Jer,' he said, 'you want to learn English? English. Speaking. Learn lesson, yes?'

'English?'

'Yes.'

'English no. Polish.'

'Yes, but, teach. Lesson Jer. Good. Very good.'

Jerzy shook his head. He told Ben, *'Ja nie potrzebuje zeby uczye sie Anglielski. Ja jestem udajacy sie dem do Polska wkrotce.'*

Ben did not understand a word.

'Yes, lesson very good, perfect,' Laslo said. He had come out when the next two bales had not arrived in the house. He spoke quickly now to Jerzy and briefly the Polish flew back and forth between them like mechanical birds while Ben Dack squinted up at the impossible blue of the sky.

Laslo told Jerzy if he learned the English for three months

61

and could say sentences, then he could go home. That was their deal.

'Yes, some lesson,' Laslo said at last to Ben. 'You are teacher?'

'Oh no,' Ben said. 'By cripes no. But I know a good one.'

NINE

*At present Ethiopia has one doctor for every 72,000 people.
This is the worst ratio in the world.*

*Ethiopia contains one of the largest concentrations of poor
people on the earth. It ranks 170th of the 177 countries in
the United Nations Human Development Report. Eighty-one
per cent of the population live below the poverty line.*

Jay sat on his bed at the end of the room and tried to
concentrate on reading facts. The children were to go asleep,
and, although some had, others moved on their beds restlessly in the close heat of evening. They asked for water. He
filled a beaker for one and another raised a head to ask the
same, and then from a bed across the other side a hand was
raised. So it always was, in the hour before sleep finally came
to the ward. Jay knew it was not always the water they
wanted, but the reassurance of a presence; to some he was
mother and father both. His was the last face before dreams,
and these could be torrid and relentless. They could wake
screaming, their eyes wide but their minds shut into a horror
they had witnessed. Because of dreams, sleep was not what
they sought. So, in the last hour of evening, sporadically the
hands came up for water, the children propping on an elbow

63

and making big twisted faces of unease, eyes polished with fear.

'There, you are all right now. *Usshi usshi.* You will be all right,' he said. 'All good. All good.'

The eyes did not move from his face. Even when a child lay back on the sheet he kept his dark crystal gaze fixed on Jay.

'Close your eyes. Go on, it's all right. Close your eyes.'

But the child closed them for an instant only. None wanted to go into the darkness alone, and though he knew that they did not understand him when he spoke English, and of Amharic and the other languages spoken there he had only separate words, he had discovered that the best way to bring them into sleep was to tell them stories. The sound of his voice would accompany them.

He would read from any book in English he could find, guidebooks, fat paperback novels left behind in the bus station, and sometimes he would say inexact passages he remembered from the most-read book of his childhood, *David Copperfield*. To his audience it did not matter. The words flowed past them and soon they were borne away on that river into sleep.

So, this evening, to stop his mind from going elsewhere, he remembered a favourite passage in Chapter Fifteen of the Dickens novel. He had read it so often in the past he could say it by heart, and this made it more comforting, as if the telling was out of time, was something from his old life that had carried over, like a well-worn jumper holed and thread-bare at the elbows.

'*He never looked so serene as he did then. I used to fancy, as I sat by him of an evening, on a green slope, and saw him watch the kite, high in the quiet air, that it lifted his mind out of his confusion, and bore it (such was my boyish thought) into the skies. As he wound the string in, and it*

64

*came lower and lower down out of the beautiful light, until
it fluttered to the ground, and lay there like a dead thing,
he seemed to wake gradually out of a dream; and I remember
to have seen him take it up, and look about him in a lost
way, as if they had both come down together, so that I pitied
him with all my heart.'*

They were asleep.

Jay withdrew to his bed. His thoughts were like ashes
blown. The dead Master, the lost father, those strange unreal
days in Germany with Gus and Nuno and Whatarangi. The
bombs.

And within the ash of these now, the girl.

'Happy Birthday.'

Bridget whispered. She carried a plate of cut papaya, guava
and banana. 'I am not good at cakes,' she shrugged. And
when she saw the look in his face, she said, 'It is your birthday
isn't it? I checked your passport.'

'Yes.'

'Well happy birthday.' She smiled broadly, and when she
did the whole of her person was revealed, the optimism of
her heart, the ability she had to be glad. She looked over the
sleeping children. 'Come on,' she whispered, 'we'll celebrate
out here.'

They withdrew to an alcove in the hallway. Two of the
African nurses came by and Bridget told them, 'It is his
birthday,' and they made small silent clapping gestures so as
not to wake the children, and they hurried away.

'You can pretend it's cake,' Bridget said.

'No, I love papaya. This is . . . thanks.'

'You're welcome.'

Jay did not look at her. He was afraid she would see how
much he wanted to ask her about the girl.

'Really good, really fresh,' he said, and backhanded the juice on his chin.

'So, sixteen?'

'Yes.'

'It's hard to believe.'

'Why?' His eyes came up.

'No, not that you're not; I mean, in some ways you're the oldest young person I've ever met, and I don't even think of you as one age or another, but when I say to myself now 'Bridget, he's sixteen,' I think when I was sixteen I was just going to school and doing my homework and wondering if I'd ever be a grown-up.' She shook her head at the memory, her freckled face kissed by Africa. 'And here you are, such a world away from all that. Really.' She paused. She had something important to tell him and she wanted to approach it right. There was a runway she had to find. She took a piece of guava. 'So, what do you think?'

'Of what?'

'Of being sixteen. I mean, do you think where you would be if . . . you know, in another life? What the other sixteen-year-olds are doing?'

'Not really.'

'But you must.'

'I don't.'

'Really?'

'Really.'

The runway was nowhere. They ate awhile, each burdened with unasked questions.

Outside complete darkness had fallen. Moments of still-ness were rare in their life there. When they came, Bridget often thought of the globe and the enormity of Africa on it and the speck in the north that was Ireland, and she thought of it turning slowly and ceaselessly and how in its turning Africa never got any closer to Ireland. She thought what it would be to look down from a great height in space, to be able to zoom in on that continent and deeper zoom right to that spot where she was trying to figure out how to tell the boy what had come up. As always, she asked for help. It was the nature of her relationship with God: *You made me a bit slow, You have to guide me.*

'Why were you looking at my passport?'

'Well . . .'

Now he was looking directly at her. The runway was there before she wanted it and there was no pulling out.

'Something has happened,' Bridget said. She bit at her lower lip, released it. 'And it's really fortunate. You know sometimes we look for signs. We look for something that will tell us what to do, and well, I mean we are here, and we are doing great work and you are terrific, really you are. But . . . well . . .'

'But well what?'

The night was so hot. Suddenly she felt it pressing on her. She lifted one side of the V-neck of her cotton blouse and flapped it slightly.

'Well . . . I've had a sign.'

Jay looked at her and was afraid of what was coming.

'Just listen, okay?' she asked him. 'We haven't had a fight and I don't want to have one and you know I feel responsible for you. If it wasn't for me saying come with me to Ethiopia you wouldn't be here and I often think to myself 'how in the name of God did you come to think that would be a good idea Bridget?' But it was, as it turned out, and really like I said you've been terrific. Terrific. But well . . .'

She still hadn't landed it.

'Bridget, but well what? Tell me.'

'Well, Sister Eucharia got a letter. There's this foundation and they heard about the hospital and they want to donate money.' Her face was so flushed. The back of her neck was dripping. He wasn't saying anything. He was looking like he was about to be hit in the face.

'But they have this gala dinner thing and they want to hand the cheque over with the publicity and all that and they asked Eucharia to come. But you know she's not that well and she doesn't want to leave here and well, she asked me to go instead.'

Jay leaned back as the relief lightened him.

'That's okay, that's fine,' he said.

'No, the thing is. It's in Ireland, and I want you to come with me.'

She felt the bump. It was as clear as though the wheels had only half-engaged and the ground was wild and uneven. His eyes didn't change. For a moment they had the same serious straight-ahead look at danger coming, then the idea crashed into him and he moved the way teenagers move, with random loose gestures, his right hand rubbing his right knee, pulling his T-shirt forward on his chest, tilting back his head, turning to one side to examine the air above him to the left. He was a study of physical response while staying in the same seat. He had an itch on his forearm. He lifted one bare foot off the cool floor, angled it on its heel, lowered it again. He had a pain somewhere, he was sure. There was a pain but he couldn't find it in his body yet. But it was coming. It was coming now.

'Jay, I want you to come back to Ireland.' Bridget reached forward and put her hand on his arm. 'Will you, please?'

He didn't think he could speak. He didn't think a future could come crashing into you like this.

'Will you, Jay? You could come back with me and I'd be your guardian and we could get you into a school and get your exams done and then go to university. You know? Normal things. You're too smart not to go to university.'

Vast pieces of broken life were flying up about him now.

He knew he had crashed. He knew this was happening. But he could not get out of the seatbelt. He pushed a hand into his hairline, making the short hair stand, then he rubbed it back and forth as if to feel the electricity of himself.

'Jay?' Bridget's voice was kind.

He knew she had spoken out of love, but in the crash he had to save himself.

'No,' he said. 'No.'

Once he had said it he could stand up. 'I don't want to.'

His legs were shaking. He was back as his ten-year-old self and hated the sound of him. 'You go. I'm staying here,' he said.

Then he walked away from her, back through the night ward, his face on fire, his mind fizzing. Crackling in his head, sparking like a live wire the thought of Ireland.

He went to his bed at the end of the darkened room and lay on the blankets. It was too hot. He pulled off his shirt and threw it on the ground. Still the live cable crackled. He got up and stood by the deep sill of the open window. He looked for stars but could not see any.

He was so hot. Both hands he rubbed vigorously at his temples. He went to the table where a night jug of water was kept and he poured a beaker's worth and drank half and splashed the rest on his face. But in his wide-awake eyes now he was aware of another crackling, a second conduit, and realised that for seven hours some part of him had not stopped thinking about the girl.

TEN

The walls were off-white. Maybe they were painted white once, or maybe it was a white with a name. *Maybe Grecian White Summer Cloud White*. Time had tarnished them. There were cracks. One of the cracks came down the wall like the eastern coast of Africa.

He liked to think of this. Then he could escape for a time the knowledge that he was a prisoner.

Summer Cloud over Africa. He had been to various countries in that continent. For a whole day he tried to think of nothing but that. He sat on the floor and held onto his knees and tried to put himself back into Africa. He tried to feel the heat of Kenya, or when the wind came through the grasses. But wind was impossible to imagine. His room – he did not call it a cell, because he did not want to think of himself as a criminal, because he was innocent – was windowless and airless. He knew it was summer when the walls dripped. He knew it was winter when the cold came up through the floor.

The name of that plant in South Africa, what is it? He hugged his knees and rocked himself, his thick dark beard cushioning the bones of himself. He tried to focus on just that name, to find it in the corner of his mind. It did not matter if it took an hour, if it took ten. Shut-eyed, he rocked. He remembered travelling the Cape coast and coming inland to a place where he saw the huge flowering heads of this plant, what was it called?

The name? The name?

Protea.

When he had it, it was such a victory he almost cried out. Then he could picture the plant perfectly and see exactly the place.

With all of his spirit he tried to be in that elsewhere, and in this way escape that room that was somewhere in the world built under the ground.

The kite sat in the wind, white against the blue. Though the day seemed breezeless on the ground, once the kite could get airborne – the Master practised at small runs, wrist-jerks, overhead pulls – then its framework tautened, and with sharp flap-sounds climbed the sky. It was the pastime of a boy and in the course of flying it now the Master could only think of him. He stood on the hill in the deep warmth of the coming summer amidst the ghosts of love. Watching him while he tugged at the lines, head at a tilt to the heavens, was his wife Mary and his daughter, Marie. He felt them about him. He knew they were watching from what he called the other side of life. But he also knew that the boy was not there with them. He was not dead.

It was a thing of faith. He was going to choose to believe it. In his mind in recent days was the thought of those who from time to time passed across the television news briefly, the vanished children. They were those who had stepped from their parents' side in supermarket or street, whether by choice or by force, and were then that aching space, that photograph with a question mark on the television screen.

The Disappeared. A scattered population neither alive nor dead, but existing in memory and prayer and petition, in the invisible spaces between our lives.

He is out there somewhere. He is not dead.

Jay.

Jay. Are you all right?

Are you all right?

I am going to believe that you are. I am going to believe that you are out there doing something that you have to and that when you have it done you will come back to see me.

That's what I'm going to believe.

You can hear me, can you?

You know I'm the same old fool I always was. The only thing I did right was I didn't die. That's me, that's your old Joe.

But I miss you, you know?

I sometimes think that one day I will be flying the kite here and looking up at it and talking to you and then I'll hear you call out to me and I'll turn around and you'll be coming up the hill.

The kite remained perfectly still in the high cathedral of the blue. After a time the Master lowered himself to sit on the thick tufted grass, the lines running up from his hands. Then he lay back and moved the spools over his chest and kept them there so that to one unfamiliar with kite-flying, or to one looking up from below, it might seem that there was a man with a piece of him ascended into the sky.

Her name was Desta. For four days she didn't wake. Doctor Pellier attended her with his swift intense manner but gave no indication of her exact malady. He did not like to jump to conclusions. While he examined her he sometimes spoke to himself in French, and then gave clear instructions to the

African nurses in Amharic, but Jay, standing by the door, could not understand other than that the tone was grave. The doctor visited her three times each day. He took blood, checked her fever, her heart rate, responsiveness, the pupils of her eyes, then repacked his small bag and swept past, heading away into various other of the many clinics in Addis, pacing the blazing streets as if they were the rounds of his purgatory.

Jay had his own duties still, and, perhaps because, for the first time since he had arrived, there was somewhere else he wanted to be, he threw himself into them with greater energy. Quickly he moved from one bed to the next. He was a machine of care. He brought out the breakfast bowls; he brought the empties back. He raced the coarse broom down the floor and under the beds, then splashed the disinfectant from the bucket and slapped the mop, squeezing it hard, scrubbing all the time at invisible dirt and germs. While he was busy he could keep himself from admitting the thought of what Bridget had proposed, and to a lesser degree could keep away the thought of the girl. When he bore the bucket of dirty water down the hallway, he passed the room into which they had moved her. When he came back again he glanced in. Mostly she lay motionless, as though she had fallen into that world and was not yet sure it was the right one.

Because he already felt how strongly he wanted to, he did not allow himself to enter. His feelings were strangely contrary and unfamiliar.

Why did he care at all? There were many that were sick. There had been other girls of that age. He had cared for them, spoken with them, helped while their bandages were changed, sat with them in the big room where the butter-flies were painted on the wall. But none had brought inside him this uneasy company of feelings. When he heard her name told, something quickened in him. When he overheard the simplest phrase about her the company shifted around restlessly in his heart. He felt himself blush while he tried to accommodate it. His face surely betrayed him. And sometimes, as he overheard Bridget speak with one of the nurses about her, he hurried past like some hot creature scurrying for the shade.

But her name was Desta. This he had heard.

Desta.

If we begin in names, he had not begun right. He hated his own name and became only a portion of it. But hers landed in his brain like a book, a full rich world; in his mind, playing, the sound *Desta*, part of destiny, and of destination too.

Desta.

'Well?' Bridget was at his side. 'Have you had a chance to think any more about it? About going home.'

'No.'

'No chance or no going?' She smiled, trying to make a light approach.

'No home,' Jay said. 'There's no home there.'

Her smile went away. 'But about what I said, about university?'

'I want to stay here. This is my university.'

She pressed her lips together, knowing she was about to hurt him, then said, 'What if you were not allowed?'

It was something he had never considered. The shock widened his eyes and he stared at the idea. Bridget spoke quickly, 'If I go, I mean. If I go, well, I am your guardian sort of, and I know not really, not legally, but we came here together and I think they mightn't want . . .'

'I would stay in Addis,' he said. 'Even if I had to leave here.'

He was flushed again, and sudden, and he looked as if he

was about to walk away from her again so she put her hand on his arm.

His eyes couldn't meet hers. He stood, his head low, stopped like a child unchewing a mouthful of disliked meat.

'Jay, really? You would stay in Addis?'

He nodded, and Bridget glimpsed something of the turbulence in him and pressed his arm. 'It's all right. Let's decide nothing. We'll talk again.'

'I am not going,' he said. And this time she was the one who nodded and walked slowly away, thinking as she went, *It's like there's a hole clear through him.*

Desta.

He was there when she woke on the fourth day. Doctor Pellier was examining her with Jay standing with fresh water by the bed. It seemed random, unprovoked by medicine, she simply opened her eyes and blinked, as though some account in Cures & Healing had been rebalanced in her favour and she was returned to the column 'Living'. The doctor saw the moment. He knew it was no action of his but that he was its witness, and he held up both palms and said '*Attends, attends!*' and snapped his fingers to the astonished Jay to bring the water closer and he took a moistened cloth to her lips. In her company, strangely, a persistent black fly buzzed. It was elsewhere or unnoticed before, but now, even as she touched her lips together and blinked again, the fly came down over her. Jay smacked at it, it flew away, and around and back again and again he smacked wildly, as though the thing were Death and he the guardian against it.

'*Attends, doucement, doucement!*'

The girl looked at them, at the room, the fly in the ceiling space. She touched her lips together.

'*Ici, attends,* hold her head up a little bit,' the doctor said.

Her hair was short, the back of her neck warm and moist.

'Here, drink a little, *doucement.*' The doctor placed the beaker to her mouth and, her eyes not leaving his face, she drank.

'*Bon, c'est bon. Ça suffit.*' He put the cup to one side and took out his thermometer. His manner was the same intense focus as every day. He did not exclaim or show any joy. He smelled like smoke and ash. He wore the deep creases of his brow exactly the same and betrayed no pride or victory in the miraculous.

'Now, *ouvrez,* open the mouth, please. A little bit.' He mimed it. Jay's hand remained behind the girl's neck, holding her. She looked up at them as though they were not real, or far away in a world she hadn't yet come to. With black fury the fly passed. Jay watched her take the thermometer, and close her lips over it, all the time her dark brown eyes looking up at them. The minute passed slowly. When her eyes settled on him he made an abashed smile, but at once let it fall behind a studied earnestness such as Doctor Pellier wore.

He laid her back on the pillow.

'Does she still have a fever?'

The doctor shook out the instrument, dipped it in disinfectant, re-pocketed it in its plastic case. He took out his stethoscope, showed it to her.

'I have to listen,' he said. He put it against Jay's chest. 'Listen to the breath.' He inhaled, exhaled.

She simply stared back, showing no sign of understanding or caring.

'*Eh bien,*' he made a gesture, old as France, that was part raised eyebrows, part pouted lips, part short blown *sifflet* of air. Then he listened to her chest.

The girl moved only her eyes. She looked at Jay then away. The black fly crossed low, hunting the source of heat. Jay swatted at it one-handed.

When the doctor had finished, he cradled the stethoscope in both hands and looked at her, looking the way a foreigner looks at Africa, with that pity and sorrow and helplessness that hurts like ice in the heart. Then swiftly he bagged the instruments, and turned to go.

'Will she be all right?' Jay's question jumped from him.

Doctor Pellier paused at the doorway, a cigarette was already coming to his lips, the match flaring. '*Quelle question*. How can she ever be all right?' he asked, and then in smoke was gone.

'This is for you, Joe,' Josie said. 'This is from me to you.' She handed him the laptop and he held it delicately like a great black bird fallen into his hands. 'I've had it set up,' Josie said, 'the way you have to. I had a man I used to visit at the hospital one time, Michael, and he's the business with these computers and he's well again now and so.' She looked at him, the pity and kindness of her evident in the lineaments of her face, the soft grey of her eyes. She was small, her hair that had once been fair was mostly silvered now, and when she gave the gift she crossed her arms on herself and her face set in a sad smile. In the years since she and Ben had discovered they could not have children, Josie Dack had taken to visiting hospital patients, and there she had discovered the near infinite variety of human suffering. She was a listener, as Ben Dack said she would have to be, married to him, and was one of those people who liked to draw no attention to themselves but instead act as a quiet conduit for compassion. She had that kind of gentle loveliness that is called grace.

The Master didn't know what to say. There had been a computer in the school but it was the pupils who swarmed around it. His chin trembled with gratitude, and before he might further lose his composure, Josie said, 'Come on now, Joe, and I'll show you as much as I know.'

They brought the laptop upstairs to his room and Josie switched it on and showed him the long cable that had to run down the stairs and across the sitting room to the phone jack.

'This connects you,' she said.

'I'm very grateful to you, Josie.'

'Not at all, not at all, you'll be doing me a favour, you see. Because Ben wants to be looking for him, and this way, that's what you'll be doing, and he'll be more easy in himself, you see? So, it's me should be thanking you. Now sit down there, and you can begin.'

They watched the screen the way computer beginners do, like a window on marvels.

'That's the Windows page,' Josie said. 'Then you click here.' The browser opened. 'Now type in "Missing Children",' she told him, and watched as he leaned forward and with the first finger of his right hand and an intense deliberateness hit each key to spell out the words.

'Now, Enter.'

In a moment the screen changed. There were thirty-six million seven hundred pages linked to the words 'Missing Children'.

The Master turned to Josie, and it was as if together they were travellers come over a ridge and found before them a vista vast and shocking and in its dimension unimagined before.

'This is where you start from,' Josie said.

ELEVEN

Time was nothing. There were meals passed through a grille in the door, but whether these came at regular intervals, whether in that place there was anyone who thought *it is five hours since they were fed*, or the meals happened randomly, the prisoner couldn't say. He was hungry for a long time and then perhaps his body forgot hunger. The thinness of him was remarkable to himself. He watched the narrowness of his own wrists inside the metal cuffs. He had no mirror nor any surface to see himself. He could not be sure he could picture his own face any longer. He brought his cuffed hands up to feel his bearded cheeks, his nose. He tried to think of himself before. He tried to put himself back, like a toy figure onto a street, to see himself in the world. He tried to recapture a particular place, say, a street on the outskirts of Paris where there was a mosque and poplar trees. He had been there. What was he wearing? What were his clothes then? Could he remember the shoes of three years ago? There were khaki trousers; they had pockets halfway down the legs. A . . . what? What kind of shirt? Colour? He couldn't remember the colour and he didn't want to invent one. He wanted the exactness, and it seemed to him of absolute importance then. He must be able to remember. *Come on, try. Try. What was I wearing? What? What was the weather? I had written the article and went there. Come on. The details. What?*

He couldn't remember. And he grew greatly upset at just this. For he had the sense that he was being erased little by little, that there in that windowless room where they left him without questioning now, where he met and saw no one and the lights were turned on and off without warning, he was even being forgotten by himself.

Bridget, you asked for a sign, Bridget thought.

And you got one.

But only you were told to go.

The rest you added on yourself. Bridget's own Masterplan.

Can you get a sign and then turn it just slightly the way you want?

All right, maybe he is supposed to stay here now. But are any of us supposed to do anything? And how do you know unless it's really really clear, and even then if you're dim like me you need not only a sign but the glasses to read it.

Am I supposed to go without him?

Am I? I'm sorry but could You just tell me.

I got the sign but just before You go on to someone else could You just pop back and tell me? Go without him or not? Just a quick sign.

Anything.

Not even a lightning bolt or anything like that. Can just be small. Right now. Have to go with him: a knock on the door right now. Can leave him here: no knock. Is that fair? If I mean right now is it just this very second, or do I need to arrange a time? Does it take a few seconds to reach You?

Because You could be busy.

82

Of course You're busy, I'm sorry. You've got the whole world. But just, let's say, in ten minutes at half past. A knock on the door and I have to what? I can't remember which it was, is a knock he has to come or I don't go or . . .

Bridget, Bridget, stop that.

I'm sorry.

All right. Just.

I know You're with me. I'm sorry for asking.

In the name of the Father and the Son and the Holy Spirit Amen.

She finished her prayer and came to where Jay was washing dishes in the metal sink.

'Well?' she asked, 'how does it feel to be sixteen?'

'No different to fifteen.'

'No, I suppose.' Bridget took a cup and held it out and he filled it with water.

'Do you remember how sick we got at first when we drank the water?'

'Yes.'

'We've learned a lot, haven't we?'

'I want to learn more. I want to learn Amharic. I know some things, but if you are in Africa you shouldn't only speak English,' he said, studying the plate he scrubbed.

She sighed. There was no way around it.

'I don't want you to stay here, Jay,' she said. 'I want you to come back with me. Then later on, later, if you want you can return.'

'I told you. I'm not going.'

'Why?'

'Why?'

'Yes. You want to stay here. Because you are afraid.'

His eyes flashed to her. 'I am not afraid,' he said.

But she pressed on, 'In a strange way this is a safe place for you. But I think you are hiding here. You are not living your life. You are hiding from it.' She bit her lower lip, her cheeks were burning.

'I'm not leaving,' he said again. 'I don't care what you think.'

'Jay?'

'No, I don't care.'

'Can I ask you something?'

'What?'

'You know when you left home, you said you went to find your father, and you told me you made a kind of dare. You dared God to show himself. If God existed he would prove it by bringing you to your father?'

'It was stupid. I was a child, it was childish. My father's dead.'

'How do you know?'

'If my father was Ahmed Sharif he died in a bombing in Germany. If he wasn't then I don't know who he was and I will never find out so he's the same as dead. Why are you saying this? I am doing good here.'

'I know you are.'

'I am helpful. I work hard.'

'I know. I know, Jay, but . . . is this it? Is this the end? You're going to be a nurse in Africa?'

'My mother was a nurse.' He said it, quick and sharp and defiant, and turned fully towards her, his voice glassy with emotion.

'I didn't know that,' Bridget said softly. *How stupid I am. How stupid.*

'I'm staying here.' He put the dishcloth back, as if it were the argument, folding it, carefully hanging it on the edge of the metal sink.

'Can I ask God to look after you while I'm gone?' Bridget asked.

'Not just me,' he told her, and she felt humbled and moved

to discover that just now she could see into the deeps of him, into the place where he was most wounded, where he did not believe he was loved.

The Master wanted to put the boy into the site at once. Josie stayed with him some moments to be sure he knew what to do, but he was still the schoolteacher and showed his impatience at taking instruction.

'Yes, I understand Josie. Yes. I know.'

'Just tap it, you see?'

With the four fingers of his right hand he hit the touch-pad firmly, as though it were a door he knocked.

'You can just . . .'

'Yes, Josie. I know.'

'Each time it will give you options.'

'Yes yes, yes.'

She stood back, folding her arms, wrapping the sides of her pale blue cardigan over. He looked back at her. 'I am very grateful, Josie.'

'I know you are, Joe,' she said, and she put her hand on his shoulder and then left the room.

He leaned in over the keyboard and slowly fingered letters. Across the top of the screen in bright orange was written *Alert! Have you seen these children?* Below this the photographs of three teenagers and the dates they had last been seen in Ireland. A sidebar showed Useful Links to the Global Search Network, as well as *Help Now: Report a Sighting or Distribute a Poster*. There were Website Friends, Resources for Parents, Police. There was a prompting to watch 'Evening Prayer' last thing at night on the television because photographs of missing children were shown. The Master clicked each link and each one opened the possibilities of another, as the chain of the disappeared grew longer. He felt his heart grow heavy the deeper he went. He clicked the icon for Global Network and saw listed those countries who were partners in the search engine: America, Argentina, Australia, Belgium, Brazil, Canada, England, Greece, Ireland, Italy, Mexico, Netherlands, South Africa, Spain. *Is he in one of these? Could he be even in Mexico?* Quickly he realized the vastness of the unknown would crush his spirit, the outrageousness of the odds against finding another in the world would weigh him down until he would topple over into hopelessness. Believing Jay was alive was easier than believing he could be found. *He could be anywhere.* And even beginning to search for him was like reopening a wound and risking that this time the infection would not be contained. *I have to have the courage to believe in this. I have to believe the unlikeliest thing.* To relieve some of the weight on his heart he tapped the touchpad to bring him back to the page headed 'Enter A Child'. Before he could type anything he rubbed his face hard with both hands and scratched at the silver-grey stubble. He ran his palms back and over his thighs. He looked away from the screen above him at the cream ceiling, his eyes palest blue of water under sunlight. The silver wisps of his eyebrows were unkempt and moved with tiny tremors as though engaged in a struggle to rise. His lips he pressed tightly together and now began to give the details of his grandson. He filled the boxes *Name, Age, Height, Eye Colour, Home Address*, and the one most painful, *Missing Since*. He brought down a sub-menu under *Case Type* where the options were *Concern for Welfare, Missing from Home,* and *All*, and this he clicked. He didn't know how to add a photograph and chose the option *Add Later* and then he clicked Enter. A torch icon shining in circles appeared.

In the instants while the search engine turned, the Master could not breathe. He felt he went through a grey cavernous place, himself with a dim torch, and there on all sides were the tired and ragged bodies of the missing. His imagination showed them to him, a wretched silent population of the sought after, the prayed for, the ones from every country who had slipped from the ordinariness of life on an ordinary day, by choice or not, and by the next dawn were already an unhealable wound in those left behind. The torch passed over them; he had a vivid sense of it, a clearer image than anything he had pictured since he began to remember. They were here, those whose faces were frozen in family photographs and appeared on posters for a time, briefly gazing back from the place into which they had already vanished. In the vast cave where the Master went now he saw them, each instant there were more. While the torch turned on the screen they multiplied, an entire population of lost children, those who had fled and those who were taken. As a schoolteacher he had come across all kinds of the young; he had known their hurt and upset, every dimension of inconsolable crying, of irreconcilable disappointment, passionate stubbornness, blind outright refusal, absolute fury and righteousness and denial. But usually there were resolutions, usually by the end of the day the hurt was lessened, and when from the window he had watched the children running out of the front gate yelling with delight, he always marvelled at how quickly time healed the young. But this was the very opposite. Here an air of grievous hurt continued without end. Here in the murk of the deepest cavern was nothing but suffering; here Octavio Luis missing from Madrid since the fifteenth of October two thousand, here Gerd Hammand missing from Dortmund since August twenty-sixth two thousand and two. Sylvia King, Jennifer Walsh, June Carey, Thomas known as Tommy Bowler, Kenneth Woodfall, Fabien Rigot, Diego Bolano: here they were like souls stalled between worlds. The histories of their fractured childhood were in their eyes, the Master saw them in vision and was transfixed. Pity and anger made tight his chest; it was as though he came upon a great, darkened school-house in the forgotten world and opened its gate now and came inside. But what could he do? Alongside the details of each lost child were the names of the searchers, parents, a brother, an aunt who had not given up hope. The dimension of the suffering crushed him; his chin rose and freely tears came to his eyes. He wanted to be able to say *it will be all right,* he wanted to be able to offer something of hope when he himself had only the most slender now. But he could not.

The searching torch stopped. *No match found,* it said. Beneath it, *enter your contact details. Website updated daily.*

In the Contact box he gave himself the username 'Joe' but this was taken and he tried then 'Master' but must have mistyped and in moments was told his username was now 'Mater'.

He could do no more. He pressed the heels of his palms into his eyes. He felt what it must be when you come to the place where you once lost a limb, where the phantom hurts with terrible nearness and what might have been pierces into what is.

He closed down the computer lid. He sat there, unstarred night filling the skylight over his head.

At last he rose and came downstairs. Josie did not ask him how he had managed or what he had discovered, for he wore the weariness and disappointment plainly. He sat by the fire and let the time pass. *I am an old man. I am just an old man.*

When Ben Dack came home and saw him he asked if the Master would read aloud.

'I don't think so, Ben.'

'Right. No problem. Just a thought. Only asking, as the man says, because sometimes it gives me a bit of a lift you know. It does. Just when you're reading, I don't know, Ben Dack's the last man to be able to answer Ben Dack's questions as Josie will tell you, but my point is there's something. Stands to reason really. Being read *to*, if you get me, it's hardly there any more, is it? And it's a shame, honest to goodness, because well . . .' Ben Dack puffed his cheeks.

'All right,' the Master said before Ben could continue, and he took down the novel and began.

He read about the old man who fished alone in a skiff in the Gulf Stream. The man had gone eighty-four days without taking a fish, and was now considered *salao*, the worst form of unlucky. The Master read about a boy who had felt sad to see the old man come in each day with his skiff empty and about the strange relationship that began between them.

He read aloud while Ben Dack worked at the puzzle of the sky. Muted in the corner of the room, the television showed scenes from the world. It showed deserts and dry riverbeds. It showed ice dripping itself away like a translucent clock of doom. But the Master concentrated on his reading, pausing only when a heavy black fly kept crossing near the book and he would wave it away until some moments later it returned.

'More flies this year than ever, you notice that?' Ben said, looking down at the sky with the hole in its centre. 'The weather of course. Number one. Number two the weather as well. Whole story. Ireland is going to become Africa, hot wet Africa. Absolute. But sorry for interrupting Joe, carry on, "salao, *which is the worst form of unlucky.*" Ouch, as the fella says. Carry on.'

The Master read on. It stilled him to read. He could go into the story and for a time while his own voice was saying the words he could feel connected to something. The story had a shape, and it had meaning, and while he was reading it he was comforted in a way. He had said he would read it for the boy, not only because it was a story of an old man and a boy and fishing, but also because it was a story of outrageous misfortune that yet contained hope. Sometimes in the reading he paused and raised his head just above the book and looked at a place across the room. *I am reading to you. I am reading this for you out there somewhere.*

His thought was nothing more than that. He tried to picture just where Jay might be then, what he might look like now. But although he could imagine a figure, there was always vagueness and the imagining was unsatisfying. Now too there were the frozen faces he had seen on the website, and these kept coming between him and his grandson.

The Master read on, his reading no different to the praying of another, a reaching into the invisible.

He was in mid-sentence when a knocking came on the door. Ben brought in the short stout figure of Laslo, who stroked his moustache once for confidence before extending his hand. Behind him was the crouched blond question mark of Jerzy.

'Ah,' Laslo said, 'the Master teacher yes?'

Vigorously he shook the old man's hand, who held the book to one side and looked startled at the genial face before him.

'Joe,' Ben said, bellying between the couch and the jigsaw table, and tapping Laslo on the shoulder to step back to show the younger man behind him, 'This fellow here is Jerzy. He's hoping you might teach him a bit of English.'

Bridget left in the night. There was a car to take her to the airport where she was going to fly first to Nairobi and from there to Cairo and then to London and on to Dublin. The route had been planned by economy, the cheapest flights on the lesser-known airlines.

'I am still afraid of flying, you know,' she had told Jay, 'in case you are moved to come with me to mind me.'

But she knew he would not come, and she had stopped trying. It was hard to leave him. She would be gone for three weeks only, but she was fearful of change, and wished now she hadn't accepted Sister Eucharia's offer. She couldn't even think yet of Ireland, of crossing back into that world that seemed to have no connection to this one. But she was the kind of person who believed obstacles are only seen from distance and got smaller if you approached directly. It will be all right, was Bridget's most common counsel to herself and others. So this is what she was telling herself as she stood before Jay in the downstairs hall of the House of Angels while the waiting car sounded outside in the night.

They stood beside each other like a history in two volumes, each so familiar with the other's part, each seemingly incomplete. Bridget wore a khaki skirt and shirt and her brown hair pushed back off her forehead showing the intensity of freckles her skin had thrown out against the astonishment of the African sun. A small leather case of her things was beside her.

'Well.'

'Well.'

'This is it,' she said.

'Yes.'

She gestured with her free hand, took a half step back. 'So, how do you like the outfit?'

She was like a small girl with enormous feelings.

'It's great, very African-traveller,' Jay said, and then studied the black-and-white tiling of the floor.

'Not sure the suitcase will hold up to all the flights.'

'It will. Don't worry.'

'Oh no, I won't. Have enough to worry about.' She smiled a smile that threatened to make something break in her and she caught her lip in an action so familiar that her teeth line was there.

The car engine was running high, the fumes of the exhaust travelling in from the warm dark.

'I'll bring you back something,' she said.

'A map of the world.'

'Really? All right,' she said, a little bemused, unaware that he wanted it to show the girl Ireland.

'You're to take good care of yourself,' she said.

'You too.'

She looked at him and then couldn't look. There were double buttons on the sleeves of the khaki blouse and she saw that she had only fastened one. Her shoes were polished, the laces double-knotted.

The weight of the unsaid stunned her breath.

The driver tapped twice on the car horn.

'Well,' she said, 'this is it then.'

'Yes.'

'Better get going. Always-late-Bridget.'

But she did not move. She stood with the old suitcase in her hand. She simply stood. Was it a long time, she did not know but Jay too stood opposite her on the checkerboard of the floor. Then there was the slap sound of the suitcase dropping and she was holding him against her. She held him and he let himself be held but he did not cling to her lest he would not let go. The embrace threatened tears and she tilted her head to deny them and then suddenly pushed him back from her, still holding him by both shoulders. She looked at him a moment longer, this boy becoming man who had made her imagine she could be his angel. Then she swiftly kissed his forehead and let go.

'Goodbye now,' she said. 'Goodbye Jay. I'll see you soon.'

She went through the door and got into the car, apologizing to the driver. Jay stood in the porchway. As the car drove off she looked back at him. She looked until the car reached the end of the street and turned into the dark.

She could not shake off the feeling that she would not see him again.

TWELVE

Jay wept.

He wept the hot confused tears of his age. He wept for ordinariness, for the everyday, for a home in the world. He wept for a father and a mother, and pressed his face hard into the thin pillow so that those sleeping in the beds about him would not hear.

When it was emptied out of him he rolled over and put the wet pillow aside and lay flat in the dark.

Where are you? Where are you all in the dead world? Where are you gone?

Often in the past he had felt what he considered the *nearness* of his grandfather, a sense that the old Master was right there, that Jay could almost feel him in the same room and sometimes he could take comfort. He could believe in the logic of a ghost world. He would tell himself many great minds had been certain of it. A whole mythology of Ireland was based on it. We are spirit as well as body. *My mother is there. She is as near to me as my hand in the dark here now. Her spirit is right there.* And he had thought then that if he closed his eyes, if he closed off all parts of himself, if he could just make himself spirit too, then it followed he would be able to *feel* her. He longed for it in a kind of agony. Not just to know she was there but to feel her, and have the deep consolation of that.

Yet, in the dark of himself he could not find her.

He tried then to think of the Master. He tried to remember a day they had together, thinking that if he could, then he might remake it in a way. If he could imagine it perfectly, if he could recall each thing said, what they were both wearing, what the room was like, what the air smelled like, what each thing felt like – the plastic tablecloth with the knife nicks in it – then he could be back there for as long as he was remembering, and that would be comfort of a kind.

He thought of this. Then he leaned over and from beneath his bed took out the old journal from his bag. He had stopped writing in it a long time ago. He had stopped when he reread passages in which a juvenile, innocent boy was asking God where he was. Now he propped the book on his knees and lay a torch on his lap.

'In the cottage there is one main room with a large fire-place and above this is a shelf with hardcover books. On both sides of the fireplace are other bookcases, each crammed with books in no particular order.

He wrote himself home. He did not write 'I' but 'he' for the boy who lived there, and he did not give him a name.

In the small hours of morning he heard a noise in the hallway, staggered footsteps, and he came with his torch to find Doctor Pellier with a bottle, paused for support on a windowsill. A half-inch of cigarette burned at his mouth.

'Doctor?'

'*Hein?*'

He shone the torch on himself. 'It's me. Are you all right?'

The doctor squinted as though far away. He sucked at the cigarette, shrugged at the question, 'Who is all right?' he asked, and then flicked the butt to the floor, tilted the bottle to his mouth.

Jay stepped out the butt. 'Do you want me to help you?'

'For what? Though you are the helper you cannot help me, I am helpless, unhelp*able*.' He smiled a sad smile at the noose of language.

'Down here by the kitchen there are the seats.'

'Yes yes yes, seats are good.'

He let Jay lead him.

'Will I make you some coffee?'

'*Bon café* in Ethiope, very good; better than even Paris, and so cheap. Same coffee costs six hundred and twenty per cent more. *C'est vrai.*'

'I'll make us some.'

'You make us some. Because you are the helper – ' he raised one finger – 'and not yet helpless.'

'You're not helpless, Doctor.'

'*Mais oui, mais certainement.*' He brought the bottle around in front of him at the furthest extension of his arm, as though he needed to see it in the distance first; then seeing it so was surprised at the invitation and made a pouting of his lips and swung the bottle to him. While Jay made the coffee, the doctor sat with the bottle embraced against his chest like a baby.

The iron kettle took some moments.

'Here, drink this.'

'*Oui oui, attends.*' The doctor emptied the bottle, held it out from him and, with genteel manner, bowed to it then handed it over in exchange for the coffee. 'Now, be very good, very sober Doctor Pellier.' He tapped the chest pocket of his short-sleeved white shirt and then drew out the cigarette pack and brought it to his mouth and lipped one free, a second later lighting the match. He blew out the smoke in a straight line, as though it was a train track on which he sent his despair.

For a while Jay said nothing. They sat there in the night until he asked: 'Will Desta be all right?'

The train tracks broke as Pellier turned his head. His eyes were deep-set and his eyebrows heavy so it seemed he withdrew from the world he looked on.

'Why does she not move? Why does she just lie there?'

The doctor took another cigarette and lit it from the one he was finishing. *'Parce qu'elle ne veut pas souvenir.* Because she does not want remember,' he said.

'But what's wrong with her?'

The doctor lifted his shoulders, as though the question was too heavy above them. He sent the smoke to the side. 'What is wrong?'

'Yes.'

'She was raped by many soldiers, she was beaten. She has seen her father shot in front of her. She is HIV.' Again the weight descended and his lowered eyebrows furrowed deeper and he sucked the cigarette and closed one eye and blew. 'How one thing happens to make another. *La suite.* The Chinese come for the oil, the government makes the deal, *oui*? But some do not want the oil leaving the country. They think there is corruption. The Chinese are kidnapped. Many are killed. The government sends the troops; they burn down the huts. When none will confess who are the rebels, they are tortured, they are shot. *C'est ça.* The government must show the Americans there is no terror here. So the soldiers become their own terror in their own country. *C'est comme ça. La suite.* This is how it happens, not just here. The terror makes the terror. *La merde du monde.* What is wrong with the girl? You cannot answer what is wrong. You cannot and I cannot. We are not from this world. We cannot imagine.'

'But will she get better?'

'For what?' he asked. 'For why? You don't understand because you cannot imagine. Africa does not . . . does not . . .

I don't know the words . . . it does not translate. It is not simply, how do we fix it, *tu sais?* Some of it is unhelp*able,* because it is humanity. It is humanity itself that is the problem, yes?' As he spoke the doctor became more animated. He pointed his cigarette at the words; he tilted his head back and blew the smoke directly upwards as if his audience was above. 'You. You have a simple view maybe. You disagree.' He glanced at Jay. 'I am older, not wiser maybe, but older and so more experience, yes? And experience says there is a little, *tout tout petit,* a little bit only, this small,' he held out an inch of air, 'that we can do, but still humanity will have war, will have greed, will have *catastrophe.* So why? Why we bother? *Hein?* Each of us follows our own mystery. And you, what are you, *mon ami?*'

'What do you mean?'

'Who are you? For what are you here? You would not go home with Bridget.'

'This is my home.'

'*Mon cher,* this is not our home. Not for any of us of this skin. For some it is maybe our medicine. Okay to say that. *Mais n'imagine pas.* Africa does not need you.'

'Yes it does.'

'*Non,* no no. Why think this? Is it not clear: Africa needs money. She has people. She has millions and millions of people.'

'I am going to stay here.'

'You have no money.'

'I am needed here.'

'Are you?' Pellier blew a smoky doubt. '*Quelle confiance!* What assurance! What it is to be young.'

'I know I am needed here.'

'Any could do the same job. I could get someone in the morning from any school in Addis.'

Jay was stung and the doctor regretted his tone at once

and leaned forward then and held out both his hands inches apart, as if his thought was suddenly very clear and packaged and he wanted to pass it carefully across. His voice was old flannel softly delivering the words. '*Mon cher*, you have a conscience same as me. We are here because that is what we have. You see? That is the currency, yes? But in truth there is enough conscience. There is enough guilt in all the world for Africa. *C'est vrai, hein?* But not enough money. This is the real world.' Pellier scowled. 'Not that I care for it. But . . .' he shrugged, he blew. 'I suggest: go back to Europe, go back to Ireland, beautiful country, go to university, make money, change minds, this is the real work needed, not washing sheets, feeding children. Leave this to the Africans. You want to change the world, listen and learn how. To change the world you must change one mind. This is the advice I was not given but wish I was. *C'est un bon conseil.* Go back. Change one mind. I am sorry I am too old myself to take it.'

He leaned back to look at himself when younger, and Jay did not disturb his wistfulness or ask again about the girl.

The following days the conversation stayed with him, as though indeed something had been parcelled and handed across. But Jay tried not to think of it. Doctor Pellier himself showed no signs of having had any night conversation or drinking in the kitchen and had closed the flaps of himself thoroughly once more. He came and went with the same brusque manner, the same dismay on his face.

Desta lay in the bed silently in an impossible stillness. Every time Jay had an opportunity he came down the stairs to walk along the women's corridor, and as soon as his foot stepped on the tiles his heart quickened. He walked past the doorway of the ward she shared with eleven other women and he gave a sidelong glance. And always she was lying in the same position, her head propped on the pillow, her gaze straight ahead. If she saw or recognized him, her face did not acknowledge it. He passed and busied himself in the supplies closet at the end of the hall and stayed there long enough so that when he came back again it would not seem he spied. She had not moved. In the afternoon he did the same thing.

In the quiet of the evening when Dembe and Bekele could watch over the sleeping patients for him, he came back down the stairs. He stood by the door. Some of the women were sleeping, others awake. They gave him a moment's curiosity only and turned into the places of their private grief. This time Desta looked directly at him, but she did not speak.

Jay came to her bed.

'Can I get you something? Can I get you some water?' he asked her, then asked again by gesturing drinking and saying the word in Amharic.

The woman in the bed next to her was forty years old but weighed little more than her skeleton. She tapped her lips and Jay went and brought her water and held it for her and she lay back again and made a low moaning, then rocking herself inside the sheet.

Desta said nothing. She only looked at him.

He lowered his eyes.

She kept her brown gaze directly on him. He found a place on his arm where the skin had dried and he rubbed free the flakes. Everything he thought to say seemed empty. *Are you all right? Can I get you some food? Are you in pain?*

When the weight of embarrassment grew too heavy, he just nodded as though something had been said, and left the ward.

But the next evening he was back. This time he brought her the water without asking, giving it also to the woman next to her, and another three beds further down. The nurse for the women's ward whose name was Rejoice allowed it. 'You are maybe a little joy for them,' she said.

'Here is some water, you must drink it,' he told Desta.

He watched her. He watched the movement of her long arm, the slow grace of her even in such defeat. He watched the way she touched her lips together to moisten them before she drank. Her eyes were very beautiful, but he could not look at them without feeling sorrow. She passed him back the beaker, lay again on the pillow.

'I can get you more. Would you like more?'

She shook her head very slightly.

'Do you mind if I sit?' he asked, and then took the stool and sat beneath the window where the night was starred.

He held his hands together propped between his knees. He sat like that some time, the way people do everywhere in the world of hospitals. Then at last he said: 'I don't think you can understand me, can you?'

She looked at him, but she made no response.

'I . . .' He looked across at the woman in the next bed who was sleeping fitfully. He turned back to Desta. 'I want to do something for you,' he said. 'You don't understand me do you? I want to do something for you, and I know I can't really. I know it's stupid even and you have the doctor and the nurses and but . . . I am upstairs all day and I am thinking: what can I do for her?'

He stopped. He looked at her.

She had turned her gaze into the night.

THIRTEEN

The sea when they came to it was high and blue and thrilling.
A vigorous wind combed the dune grass as the van bumped
down off the road and followed a Mercedes in over the sand.
The workers stopped talking. They peered forward, looking
to the windscreen as though it was a film showing marvels.
Towers of waves came and collapsed, and the foreshore was
painted in a creamy froth that blew away like bubbles. The
beach was empty but for ten or so cattle that had come
through buckled wire further up and now stood in perplexity
on the first soft sand and dunged freely.

The Mercedes drove a curve and stopped and a man got
out and put his hand to hold his hair from the wind while
he waited for the workers. The sun was already high, and
the day boisterous with its own brilliance. The immense blue
of the sky, the shone quality of the sea, how the air was
filled with noise, made everything seem inspired. Some of
the Poles had never seen the Atlantic and now stooped out
the sliding van door to stretch in the revelation of the shore.
It returned these men to childhood, and looking about they
smiled and punched at each other and some ran a few steps
in the sand. Others stood, looking westward.

'Here!' the man called. He had to cup his mouth and then wheel his hand in the air to bring them over to him. 'Down there, along here and down there,' he shouted, 'you pick up the plastics, the bottles, bits of rope, everything.'

The workers looked at him. He reached into the car and popped the boot and took out emptied heavy plastic fertilizer bags. 'See, pick up, put in bag. The beach,' he shouted into the wind. 'Tidy up. Tidy up for Important Man coming.' He handed all the bags to the first man, who passed them out carefully as though they were precious. 'Pick,' he said, 'go ahead. Go. You, what is your name?' he asked a strong young worker with short fair hair.

'My name is Jerzy Maski,' he said carefully.

'Good, good man. You have some English. Now, you go this side, you take half the men. You understand?'

'I understand.'

'Excellent. And drive those cattle back will you? The cattle.'

'Yes. I understand.'

They moved off. Because it was dangerous for swimming the beach was not used and was rarely tidied. Upon it, the tide threw every imaginable sea wreckage, and bottles, plastic containers, netting, sheets of ripped plastic were brightly strewn along the sand. It was as though the wide arms of the bay welcomed all that the world discarded, and things came ashore there that had been thrown overboard a thousand miles away.

The Polish workers moved in a broken line, their bags swollen up with the breeze, so in the distance it seemed it was the sea wind that flew them like kites.

This is what we do. This is not my life. This is not what I am for, to pick up the rubbish of the beach.

And I do not like this sea. Look at it. It breaks up everything and throws it back here. I do not trust it. I want to be home in Jaslo. Is that so terrible? Does it make me less

102

a man to not want to be here picking rubbish off a beach?
For what? So some important fellow comes and says yes you
can build seaside houses here? For the rich. I will never be
rich. I will never live in this country after. I will go home to
Jaslo. The Irish want houses everywhere now. Maybe they
will want houses in Jaslo too. I will go home and build them
and that will be good.

And there will be a girl.

There will be a girl and I will build my own house and
have my own life there. In home.

That is what is meant to be. Not this. This is not my life.
This is another's. I am Polish. I am here for a little time only,
remember this. Do not forget this. I am a man now. A man
must go where the work is. For a little time only, remember.
Yes, bend down, pick up rubbish off beach but remember:
a little time only. All things change. Who is poor today is
rich tomorrow maybe. Maybe one day Irish come to build
in Poland. No one can know what happens. Maybe good
things are coming. Maybe they come now even when we
don't know. Maybe they are on the way. Maybe a new life.

Maybe not.

I hate this stupid sea.

Aloud to himself the Master read of the old man who dreamed
of Africa when he was a boy and the long golden beaches.
The Master imagined what it would be to have lived along
that coast and listened to the surf roar. He imagined as he
read the smell of Africa.

In Jay's dream, the sea. The sea high and full and roaring and
he alone on a beach before it. The waves were three times
taller than him and yet he knew he had to go out into them.

103

Why, he was not sure. He watched the fine high spray that combed up off the surf, briefly shown in moonlight before it vanished into the wind. He stood in the tremendous noise, looking into the blind dark of the waters beyond and trying to find the courage to move forward. The ocean broke at his ankles. His arms crossways, he held onto himself. He lifted one foot out of the water, hop-stepped, dipped it again, hopped, moved a little further out to meet a spent wave. How high above him was the dark sea. The walls that rose were briefly veined in pale light and then fell with such terrific violence there was a double crash, ka-boom, and wild whiteness running off everywhere. Only the nearest parts of it could he see. The night made the immensity and force and mystery of the ocean terrifying to him. How small and insignificant he seemed standing before it. A curve of water, a pull in the tide and he would be taken swiftly, lifted and thrown and then sucked under. The thought froze him, but he needed to go out into the sea nonetheless and in a moment was pitching himself forward, hurtling, his teeth bared, kicking the tops of the waves until the sandbar fell away beneath him and he plunged down. He saw the ocean from under as darkness only. He was in complete dark, and whom it was he had come to rescue was nowhere to be seen. He opened his mouth to call out and the sea rushed in. He thrashed and his moans were made mute in the gurgle and whoosh. He was drowning. He was in the dream of drowning in the ocean of the night then he felt a hand and he shot upright and was sitting in his bed, soaking wet. There was no one awake by him. His heart hammered. He lay his palm against it and felt the wet clamminess.

Then he got out of the bed and went to the sink at the end of the room and ran the water and doused his face.

He leaned on the metal sink some moments, then he went out of the ward and down the stairs to see if she was all right.

She was sleeping.

When he was next to her, he whispered, 'You will recover. You will get ARVs and you will be all right.' He leaned over then and touched the back of her hand where it lay on the bed sheet. She did not move. He stroked once very softly the back of her hand. He did not tell her anything more. He did not say that he loved her, nor that he had thought for the first time in three years to try to pray again.

He lifted away his hand and held it in the other. Then he went away back along the corridor where the neon tubes flickered between lighting and dark.

And the light flickered on in the underground cell where the prisoner was sleeping in what he thought might have been night. He was curled on the mattress on the ground and knew that, in the world he was in, light meant danger. In darkness none came. He watched the light pulse inside its wire cage, brightening, and he sat upright and tensed his body and waited. He heard the footsteps on concrete coming. He had never seen the corridor but in his mind pictured it long and bare and bright with many doors. Sometimes there were voices, sometimes the heavy slam of a metal door, and sometimes booted footsteps, like now, approaching. He stared at the door. Scored on it were different marks, some simply jagged lines of no import, slashed lineaments of frustration or anger, put there by prisoners unknown. Others were attempts to mark a name and date, as though the history of brutality must still be written though the only page was that door. He had written nothing himself; he had left no mark. If they took him now and his life ended, nothing would remain of him there. This he had decided. He would not acknowledge he had been there. For he was not. In all his waking hours, in the dark that they kept him, he tried to

105

escape through imagination and memory. He tried to be constantly in an elsewhere where the world was better than this.

But when they came for him his imagination broke.

The key was loud in the lock. The mechanism was heavy. The two men who entered shouted for him to get down.

He was sitting, but he knew he was to kneel, and to put his hands behind his head and not to look up.

He did it now without delay. He did it as though it had become second nature, this pose that was almost reverential, a kind of petitioning with the elbows like wings sprouted from the head. His hands were chained, the chains ran across the back of his neck and one of the men pulled on them, testing, and lifting the two hands up at the same time.

'You stink, Ali,' he said. 'Stand up.'

Because of the chains at his ankles, the prisoner could not rise from kneeling to standing directly, and made instead a series of small half-steps, and the man hit him on the top of the head and said, 'Now, will you, come on!'

He stood and the hood was put over his head. It smelled of fear. It had covered the heads of many and woven into the dense coarse khaki fabric was the putrid scent of terror.

'This way, come on. Shuffle on, Ali.'

I am in London.

I am in London and it is April. I am in London in a black cab and looking at the crowds on the streets we pass. It is ordinary life. It is marvellous ordinary marvellous life.

FOURTEEN

'That's good now,' Ben said. A part of the sky had come together. 'The thing is all the pieces are the same but different. That's something isn't it? All the same and you just have to find the joins: that's what I like about it. That's what I'd say if someone asked me, not that anyone would say you because t'isn't rocket science as the fella says, There isn't thousands beating down the door to ask why Ben Dack likes making jigsaws,' he chuckled at the thought, blue eyes shining in his round face. 'No sir there isn't. But, but.' He raised a finger as though to hold back the questions of his audience. 'Philosophy of life according to Ben? Connection,' he told them. 'Collage. That's the word isn't it? Collage. That's the thing, all broken up and still put together. So say this piece here,' he lifted a sky-fragment, 'this piece here is me and I go here, top left of the puzzle. And you are, say, this, this, well, piece that looks like, what, Africa, say, and you are strictly bottom right. One hundred per cent bottom right, so you go over here. But the thing is. The thing is there is no "here", no bottom right at all if you don't have top left.'

He paused, arrived at this clarity and allowed himself a moment at that pinnacle before adding, 'Of course you need bottom left too, and top right, and middle upper right and upper left and mid lower right and mid lower left, who could be a she, and God knows, dead centre, who could even be a dog, say. Because it could. Could be couldn't it? A dog that somebody loved. It could. Absolute. No question, I'd say. That's part of the collage isn't it? It is in the Philosophy of Ben Dack Volume One, isn't that right, Josie?'

Holding a jigsaw piece he walked across and kissed the top of her head where she was knitting before the muted television. He raised his smiling face and then saw the logo 'Breaking News'. Then the programme cut to the newsroom and even before Josie had lifted the remote to raise the volume there was a picture of flames and black smoke.

'Dear God, oh dear God,' Josie said. 'Ben, look.'

And whether from the quality of her voice or a sense felt then that something had happened, the Master and Jerzy came from the lesson in the next room and stood behind the couch and wordlessly they all watched the telling of the explosions at Heathrow Airport.

'You have heard?' Doctor Pellier asked. 'Three bombs London. At the airport. It is the sickness of the world back again.'

'In Heathrow Airport? But Bridget would be . . . when did it happen?'

The doctor lifted and let fall his eyebrows. He had not thought of her. 'She was flying to London? Of course.' He blew out his dismay as though he had been struck in the stomach. 'It was in the evening. I will find out.' He went away and Jay put his hand on the wall to steady himself. Then he slid down slowly and sat on the floor of the corridor.

What is the meaning in anything? What is the use?
Why don't you just burn the world up?

Why don't you just decide that's all the use that world was, I'll make another. I'll learn from my mistakes. I'll make a better one.

Because in this one you've messed up.

You've messed up badly.

Has anyone told you that?

Hasn't anyone's prayers said that? You've made an almighty mess. Because you've taken your eyes off us. You've looked away and you've let people starve, you've let people get AIDS, millions of them. You've let others bomb innocent ordinary people who are just doing their everyday things.

You've killed them.

You've killed them for no reason. They're just here one day and then they don't come home.

Why do you let that happen?

Answer me.

Why?

Is it just Chance? Is there nothing but that, no meaning, no purpose, nothing?

You made a world for nothing. Is that it? Just a meaningless star in the galaxy with millions of creatures with no purpose at all. Millions of creatures that have this delusion that you are there? You're the God delusion, is that it?

Why do we even have it then?

Why do we even dream there is any you? Why are we even persisting in you after all these centuries, when you can't do anything for us?

So you are either a joke, you have no power at all, or you are a killer. Those are the choices as I see it.

As I see it you are doing nothing for us.

You have done nothing for me.

You've not even been listening, have you?

Jay got up from the floor and walked out the door of the hospital into the hot street. He walked up through the thick crowds by the Mercato where the vendors were packing up what was unsold and calling bargain prices to any who paused. The way was littered and scavenger birds flew brazenly among the people and tore at remnants and fought with raucous cries. He hurried past in the throngs that seemed always moving in that city, not sure where he was going, only that he had to. If he stayed still, grief would destroy him. *Was Bridget dead now? At this very moment was her spirit travelling somewhere? Right now, right at this instant, was it flying through the air? Was it already there, wherever there was? Some crowded place where all his dead were? Was it anywhere?*

He could not bear the thought that she had suffered, that there was pain, and he had to keep pushing away that part of himself that was logical and looked directly into the facts of things.

He went past the market and down a side street. He followed this to its end and then turned left into an alleyway and walked through the cool deep shadow and out again into the white blaze of sunlight. A thin young figure in loose khaki shorts and oversize T-shirt with the word Evolution on it, he was barefoot and brown, his hair cropped, his expression set in a glare. Randomly he took streets, crossed traffic, passed among the diverse multitude that stirred there, walked a blind route to nowhere. A dusty ancient dog followed him. When he noted it he tried to turn it back, and even while hurrying along called over his shoulder, 'go home, go home', and then the Amharic word *'hidmo'*, which they used for the various fenced compounds and shanties alike. The dog followed still. It followed when he took a ragged narrow street of close dwellings where the tin doors were open and some men and women stirred in the inner shadows to peer out at the footsteps of the stranger. It followed when, without warning, he broke into running and ran as though

110

pursued down the hard-baked street where two small children were sitting in the dirt opposite each other and crying hard.

He ran to escape what he could not. He ran though his breath caught at his throat and burned and in that city built at eight thousand feet no air seemed to reach his lungs. He ran and thought that running was the natural expression of that country; that if you did not move you fell beneath the weight of sorrow. And that the sorrow, though heavy. came following still and that your only choice was to try and outrun it.

He ran until he fell. A roughness in the cobbling caught his toe and he tumbled headfirst and crashed his shoulder hard, and he lay panting. The dog when it caught up lay panting beside him.

'You're all right,' the Master said. He wore the same jacket he had worn for years now. His hair was still sprung off his forehead, his eyes still netted in wrinkles when he made his closed mouth smile.

'You're all right.' He was not breathless, but he leaned down against a window ledge and propped himself. He took out a handkerchief that frequent washing had turned a shade of off-white and he dabbed his forehead and then looked at it.

'That's no longer white, is it? he said. 'It's like myself. It's an African White, I suppose.'

Jay sat up; he held his shoulder where the hurt was.

'You'll be all right,' the Master said again and, turning to one side, tucked the handkerchief into the pocket of the other before rubbing hard the top of his head.

'You're dead,' Jay said.

'I told you, death is overestimated,' the old man said, rubbing away at his head still, as though he had fallen onto his crown. 'Did you ever think,' he paused; he raised his thick eyebrows, 'that all the people we thought were dead were not dead? Did you ever think they were all fully alive maybe right now, but just not where we could see them? That's what I think sometimes,' he said. 'I think your mother is not dead. I think your grandmother is not dead. Or at least not in the way we are thought to think of the dead. Not in the ground, or even floating around with wings on. I somehow could never get that right, you know? I could never get the notion of people with wings. It seemed too, too fanciful, or something. Something some artist had dreamed up because it made a nice picture. But it never seemed real to me, you know? So no,' the Master said, and looked out directly in front of him as though he were teaching a class, as though it were as in the old days when he came to a point and slid down off the wooden stool to make it, stepping around the classroom as he spoke but keeping his eyes on some point in the distance just above the pupils' heads. 'So no, I never got that. I've thought instead that she's out there, she's out there somewhere and I'll meet her again sometime and we won't have wings or anything like that. We'll just be. You know? And I can't go looking for her or anything. I could never find her until I got to the Next Life too because that's where she's living. Not dead.'

He turned to Jay and looked directly at him. 'I don't think you're dead,' he said.

'I'm not.'

'Well that's good news.' He smiled his wrinkles deeper. 'That's a relief. I feel better.'

He made himself more comfortable on the sill. He was wearing brown corduroy trousers and a crinkled check-patterned shirt open at the collar. His shoes were toe-scuffed badly and these he looked at now as though considering the great distance he had walked in them and how much of them had frayed away into the world.

112

'Do you ever think about when we went fishing?' he asked.

'Sometimes.'

'We never caught a blessed thing did we?'

''No.'

'I used to picture the fish below in the water, all heading directly for our bait, you know, and then getting a signal, a kind of Diversion Ahead, and every blessed one of them turning to swim past our lines.' He smiled at the memory. 'But the thing is,' he said, 'the thing is that even though we never took one home, not one between the two of us, we knew they were there, didn't we? *We knew they were right there*. Even though we couldn't see them. And that's kind of how I feel these days. Like I'm quietly fishing all the time, like my line is out there and going further and further out each day and there isn't really a tug or anything but I know. *I know.*' He did not explain further but seemed to let the line run, and he watched it and a couple of times blinked at where the sunlight angled onto the far side of the passageway and burnished the reddish stones.

'How do you know you're doing the right thing? That's a question isn't it?' the Master asked at last. 'How do you know? And is it enough to, say, do this one good thing and by doing that does that mean you are doing the right thing? Because it can seem so small, can't it? One small good thing, what's the use of that, a voice in the back of your head says. And sometimes that's the voice that wins.' He shrugged. Then again he had the classroom before him. 'But I don't think the other voice gives in. It comes back. All the time we have something telling us go ahead, do the good thing. Believe in it. That's the thing. It keeps coming back because that's our nature, we want to do good. And that's a kind of proof to me.'

'A proof?'

'Oh yes, definitely, because we want to do good, because,

113

despite everything, and I mean so much evidence to the contrary, we still believe in it, that's the proof.'

Jay looked at him. He knew that he was not there, but for as long as he put aside that knowledge, he was. He loved the old man. He loved the look and smell and sound of him. He loved the old clothes and the broken shoes and the pockets of his jacket that held the broken pieces of chalk. He was comfort and consolation and while he remained all puzzles seemed briefly to fit together.

'Come on now,' he told Jay, 'you better be getting back.'

Reluctantly Jay stood. He pressed his hand to his hurt shoulder.

'It's not broken, you'll be all right,' the Master said. He waited a moment and looked at Jay and smiled at something he saw. 'Remember now, don't overestimate death,' he said; then they came out of the passageway into the full white brilliance of sunlight and Jay was on his own, followed at a little distance by the dusty dog.

When he returned to the hospital, Michel Pellier took his two arms and drew him within the smokiness of himself. '*Qu'est-ce qui* . . . Where have you been? I have been looking for you. The news is good,' he said, 'Bridget has called. She is alive. *Mon ami*, she is alive! In Cairo she had a stopover. *Six heures*. She went into the city, to get a map for you. She wants you to know that. *C'est important ça. C'est ça la raison*. She was delayed there. Always late Bridget, she says. She got the map but she missed the flight. She missed the flight! She took another one to Frankfurt. She is in Germany.' The doctor held Jay by the two arms and shook him as though to make the understanding drop like a penny in a piggybank. 'She is alive. Bridget is alive!'

FIFTEEN

Bridget is alive. She is safe. She's in Frankfurt.

The Heathrow bomb brought the world back. It brought Jay back to those parts of it he tried to forget in the busyness of everyday. It returned him to the bombing at the BBC three years before, the moment of it, when the huge sound had knocked him down in the street, and the front of the building blew away. It returned him to the thought of Ahmed Sharif, the mystery that might have been his father, and for the next few days as he heard further details of the airport bombing, it was the ugliness of the world, the terror, anger, injustice, these things, that burned in his mind. Until now, he thought he had escaped. He had thought the terror was over, that it had gone away, like a disease of the skin that in the night slipped mysteriously back beneath the surface. But here it was. Here were the same scenes again, the same sirens and flashing lights, the same television images of bodies on the ground. He watched only moments of it on the small television that Doctor Pellier set up in the corner of the lounge. The commentary was not in English, but no translation was needed.

Jay turned away. He didn't want to be in that world.

115

He didn't want to think about hatred. Instead he wanted to be glad for Bridget, to think of her freckled face as it was when he first saw her getting onto the ferry leaving Ireland. She would be back there soon. And when he thought of this, he had the strangest sense of Ireland as a place removed, a place where the people maybe complained of the weather and the prices but lived by and large in a damp green peace. Maybe it was because of its geography, its position on the edge, or because it was where his childhood had been, it had an innocence he himself had lost. That this was the natural feeling of the emigrant he did not realize yet, nor that it too was a stage on the bridge between boyhood and manhood when you could look back for the first time and achieve the first perspective on yourself as another, back there, before the coming of experience. He thought of Ireland now as a place in a book, and in its chapters the names of towns and people had about them the ring of childhood, *Kilfenora, Kildysert, Ballyea, Doon, Mary McInerney, Tim Tom Halvey, Mick Dooley, P.J. Cooley.*

Long ago and far away. Jay put them back on a shelf in his mind. He filled a bucket with disinfectant and worked the floors. He mopped the black-and-white squares and in slap and splash sounds came along the hallways, a dream figure between worlds. He tried to make the work take his mind, but was unable to until Dembe and Bekele came to help and their footprints on the wet floor caused him first to give out and then to assuage their hurt eyes by offering turns at the mop. In a threesome then they washed their way about the hospital. They were at the far end of what was called the Old Ward when Desta appeared.

She came barefoot in hospital gown and walked with slow grace steering the wheeled drip. When Jay saw her, Dembe and Bekele were together racing the one mop swiftly along the wet floor.

116

'Dembe! Bekele!'

They stopped and smirked and one pulled the mop from the other and then at once grew immensely shy as the girl came towards them.

Jay was lost in words, not knowing which to say. He was a foreigner to himself. Even the smallest thing – whether he should smile, and, even *how* you made a smile – was profoundly awkward. His hands seemed enormous to him, his arms exceptionally long. He watched her approaching and then looked past her at the thin twin tracks the drip made alongside her footprints on the wet floor.

She came to them, her face concentrating on the movement and what she kept guarded inside her.

'Hello,' Jay said. 'How are you?'

It seemed to him that he had forgotten language, or the words he knew were worthless clumps he had let drop on the floor in front of her. He was embarrassed as soon as he had spoken. He moved his hand over the crown of his head, the short spikes of his hair standing.

Desta spoke to him then. She spoke quickly three or four phrases he could not understand. She looked directly at him. The awkwardness he felt multiplied and with each instant his body betrayed further its oddity, and his arms grew longer, his hands more huge. He crossed his arms in front of him. Desta paused and spoke again. What she told, she told with urgency and earnestness and her brow furrowed. He understood nothing. When she paused he was staring at her. The pressure of emotion was such that he feared what he might say. Here now the clumsy company of his feelings swelled out their chests and pressed forward. He felt the air taken up. She was looking at him.

'Dembe, quickly, a chair. *Wanbar.* Get her a chair,' Jay said, and the boy ran. 'You should be resting,' he told her. 'Resting, sitting.' When she showed no sign of understanding,

117

he said it again, this time squatting slightly to the words, making believe a chair.

And whether in response to this or not, she spoke at once another flurry of words, one hand holding the thin support where the drip fed into her.

'What is it? What is she saying?' Jay asked Bekele.

'She says.' Desta was still speaking. Bekele screwed up his eyes as if they grew knotted in the complexities of the translation.

'Yes? What? What does she say Bekele?'

'She says . . .'

'Yes?'

'She says . . . "Good."'

'Good?'

'Yes, good-good. She says this.' He smiled his teeth up to Jay. Dembe ran back carrying the chair.

'Here, here sit.' Jay placed it for her and she did sit and then told of something more.

'What does she say, Bekele?'

Like the other, he too listened with a tight face and narrowed eyes, as if seeing the words come from a great distance. When Desta stopped, Jay said, 'Well? What? What does she say?'

Bekele smiled. 'Miss says . . . "Good."' he said.

Jay sighed loudly.

'Says very good,' Bekele said, 'Says very very good. She says you.'

'Me?'

'And good.'

Neither of them had enough of English or her dialect to tell further.

'Tell her . . .' Jay said, and then was stopped by the impossibility of saying, by the inadequacy not only of finding language they understood and could translate but also by

118

the crowded congregation of his own emotions. What was it he wanted to tell her? She was still looking at him.

'I don't understand,' he said. 'I can't understand you.' Then he palmed back the beaded line of sweat at his brow, and he told her, 'I will learn your language. I will learn your language so that I can speak to you.'

If she did understand, Desta showed no sign of it, but the way she looked at him, steadily, was as if she wanted him to understand something. She wheeled the drip about and went back along the corridor.

The Amharic words he learned at first were random. Words he overheard and asked for their meaning, sometimes with great difficulty extracting the sense from different patients. There were easy words, *Migib,* food. *Injera,* flat bread. *Kolo,* roasted corn. Then the more difficult: *Ayzore,* meaning urging someone to be strong, *Buda,* a spirit that could take possession of you.

Diligently Jay noted them. He did not think that learning such an ancient language was foolhardy, even though the strange forms of its grammar were difficult. He *liked* the foreignness of it. He liked that it was *other*; that it came from the distant past and in so being did not belong to the world he had come from. When he said the words to himself in practice he liked their sounds, and liked how they seemed to draw him even further into that place where he was.

In his room the Master peered at the screen. Each evening now he returned here, to this site where everyone who came was searching. They were a vast invisible multitude. Each evening he entered his username 'Mater' and reran the search engine, and while he waited he read the names and studied the pictures of new faces posted across the top of the site. He said their names aloud. He wanted to give them reality, to not merely glance and dismiss them, but rather, as if they had newly joined his class, he announced each one. In those moments they were present, and in the old man's heart-logic he believed it must matter somewhere. So in that small attic room in the west of Clare he called their names. They were from Austin, Texas, from Tulsa, Oklahoma, from Lyon, from Birmingham, from Bonn, and one from Athlone in the middle of Ireland. He named each one and then said no more.

For Jay the search engine found 'no results'. No sightings, no listings.

The Master would have said he did not expect any, but he ran the search as habit now, and because it meant he was looking and that was an energy better than waiting and because it somehow bound him to this world. He could not escape the image of the thousands of others across so many countries sitting at screens after work and clicking the mouse to run searches, and once this came to him it was not long before he took the step of entering the site www.LookingfortheLost.com

There, a community of voices met.

'I'm Peter23 and it's going on six years now since our Patty disappeared and I have to say today I just broke down because I thought I'm never going to see her again. And of course I had thought that before but today it really hit me and it was like this voice saying, "No, actually you're not. You're not going to see Patty again and you have to start facing up to that." And I'm wondering is there a point you reach where it's better to just stop?'

'Hi Peter23, my Joan is gone now thirteen years. And I'm not giving up. Marjorie7.'

'you don't give up you don't give up you don't give up ever. James68'

And to these, he added 'I understand why you might want to give up Peter and even why you would give up. I wonder sometimes if our capacity for hope is limited, like our capacity to believe. I don't know. I like to think we are forgiven when we fail to hope or believe because it is part of being human I suppose. We are these creations with failings. At least that is how it strikes me. Mater.'

'Good evening, Mater. There you are. I do like your angle of perception as always. So, question, do you think the Creator intended us to fail? H-47.'

The Master did not respond directly and another flow of voices passed back and forth on the screen, the words scrolling down as Peter23 was variously advised how hope was to be renewed. He was counselled church and prayer, to sit in Patty's room and think of her, to hold one of her possessions, to imagine her turning on a street corner and beginning her journey home. Among these came: 'My answer, Mater, is this. H-47's own version. If He did not intend us to fail there would be no need of Hope, Faith or indeed Charity. Don't you think? He knew we would fail to keep believing. He knew it *and loved us for it*; H-47's Homily 235. Forgive the usage. But please, all, do not chastise your-selves for the hardships of hoping. Your suffering is immense. What solace can be offered?: only that some of the lost will be found. H-47.'

Another flurry of voices crossed. Then a white quiet fell, the screen empty. The blankness was like a hurt, like a wounded withdrawal across many time zones. Once across the screen came,

'Are you still there, Mater? H-47.'

He was, but he sat with hands cupped by his chin and did not respond.

On the screen: 'Mater? I do imagine that you are there, are you?'

121

He did not write back. Again the same site member tried: 'Curious business this, truly. My moniker is my old boarding school laundry code, H-47. Used to be on everything. Often wonder who was H-46 and so on and so forth. Nearness and distance and so forth. Digression, apologies. You there, Mater?'

The Master was lost in sorrow and absence. He could write nothing. Then another member logged on and began to tell of a daughter missing for one year tonight.

At last, how much later he could not have said, Ben called from the foot of the stairs and the Master came down to give Jerzy his English class. He wasn't sure why he was giving it other than that it was a favour to Ben and he owed him many. Jerzy was polite and quiet and had the studied earnestness of those who tackle a foreign language as adults. They sat in the side room and Jerzy opened his school copybook and took a pen from his coat pocket.

'Hello,' the Master said.

'Hello good evening.'

'Good evening. What did you do today?'

'Today I work on beach.'

'At the beach. New houses?'

'Yes. New houses at the beach.'

'Good.' The Master pressed down the seat cushion on either side of him to sit a little more upright in preparation. 'Do you like it?'

'Like? Like the beach, no. I do not like.'

'Why?'

'Why because no, not for Jerzy. No beach. No.'

'You don't like the sea? To swim?'

'No.' He shook his head.

'I see. And what do you like?'

Jerzy stared at the old teacher, and said 'I like . . .' and he searched in his vocabulary for what he might tell. He knew

122

words like mountains and rivers and had even written down 'valley' in his copybook when asked the same question the week before. But what he said was, 'I like . . . lady.'

And to himself the surprise of saying it was so great, and equally seeing the surprise in the Master's face, that Jerzy Maski burst out laughing then and put his hand across his mouth. And the more he tried to hold his laughter the more he laughed, and the Master laughed too, and from the sitting room Ben Dack could hear it, and paused in placing a piece of the sky.

When he thought he had enough words, Jay came to Desta in the evening. She was sitting on the edge of her bed. The drip was no longer connected to her, and she sat quietly looking across the ward where other women had come. She did not move. She had a stillness Jay could not imagine for himself. She seemed able to simply sit, her eyes steadily focused far away. Whether what she had seen, the horror of the killings, the terror, or her own experience at the hands of the soldiers, had blinded her to anything else, and in fact the world in front of her was nothing, Jay didn't know. He was struck only by the presence she had, this deep stillness that he thought was beautiful.

He entered the ward and watched her some moments and one of the women nodded to him a quick smiling nod and he waved his hand. Then he put his hands behind his back and approached the bed. He spoke in Amharic a greeting.

Slowly Desta turned her head. She looked at him, but the expression on her face did not change.

In broken Amharic Jay said, 'I am see you. I am learn more words. I know saying some things now.'

Desta did not reply. She simply looked at him, her brown eyes full of misery. Jay watched his words evaporating into

123

the hot air. Yet, he wanted to make her sorrow go away and he had in him then that prime force of love, that clean consuming desire to bring joy to another. But not only had he no concept of how, when he stood before her, he had no faith it was possible. She was for him, in one person, that continent. She was become his Africa, and in her he saw the need and hurt and shameful sorrow but also the powerful proud and enduring grace and beauty of that place. She was both her own person, this slim girl with high forehead and erect head, slow serene manner and remarkable eyes, but also the African he most wanted to help.

'I am happy you are good,' he said to her.

She looked at him.

'I am happy you are no sick now.' He tried to smile but the thing his face made was hardly that.

Why does she not say anything? Does she not understand?

The woman in the far bed who had nodded to him called out something, and Desta's eyes moved past him to look over at her. But what she was saying Jay did not grasp. She shouted across and then flapped her two open hands in quick movements as though they were birds or butterflies. Desta did not reply to her, but looked away at the far wall as if she had no opinion of what the woman said and no interest in anything that happened there.

'I am . . . happy,' Jay said after a time, but she did not look around. And because he felt lost then, because his own feelings were urgent and new, and because his language was inadequate to them, he reached out to stroke Desta's arm and firmly he took her hand.

At once she let out a cry and pulled it away. She shot forward off the bed and looked fiercely back at him.

He held up both his hands. 'I am sorry, I am sorry,' he said in English, and then the single word in Amharic.

But these made no difference. She stood as if to ward off

124

blows that were coming. She held the arm he had touched shielding across her breasts.

'I am sorry, sorry, sorry,' Jay said.

Then Doctor Pellier was at the door. '*Qu'est-ce qu'il se passe?* What is happening? What? Tell me.'

But Jay showed only the darkened blush of his face and hurried out of the ward past the woman who had nodded and who now looked at him the way she might have at a *buda,* a spirit, or at a man who was on fire.

SIXTEEN

Blindly the prisoner moved in shuffle-step down the corridor. Inside the hood where the smell of terror was there was an umber glow that brightened to yellow as they passed beneath the lights. *Six, seven, eight.* He counted the way. *Twelve, thirteen, fourteen.*

'Steps!'

Steps. Three.

He could not say why he wanted to count the journey but it helped him to feel that he was somewhere, that this place existed, and was of concrete and iron. For if he could think of this he could think his punishment was finite and would one day end. If it was not real, if it was a nightmare, or already he was dead, then it could continue forever.

In the room they pushed him into a chair. There were four of them, he thought, but he could see only the boots of two and only then if he peered down along his nose. When they caught him trying they hit his head hard at the back and he felt his brain crash forward and hit against the wall of his skull and then he stopped trying.

'Listen, Ali. We want you to tell us about Heathrow.'

'What about Heathrow?'

'You know.'

'I don't. I don't know anything. How can I know anything when I am in here? I am in here so long I . . . how long am I in here?'

'Look Ali.'

'My name is not Ali.'

'Listen, I'll say it slowly, tell us about Heathrow?'

'I told you I don't know.'

'You do.'

'Why don't you believe me? What? What happened? Was there a bomb?'

'You tell us. Was there?'

'Tell you what?'

'What do you think? We know you were in London for six years. Six years. We know you know their names.'

'Whose names? I don't know anything. How can I tell you? I don't know. I have been in here for . . . how long? Tell me, how long?'

'A few months. Tell us the names.'

'A few months? No no, it is much longer it is . . .'

'Listen! Shut up. Shut up shut up shut up! Nothing, not a word, you hear. The next thing you are going to say is going to be a name.'

'I don't . . .'

'Shut up! Shut up shut up! A name. You're going to say a name. Then you're going to say another. How easy is that going to be? That's going to be very easy. You can think for every name there's a few yards. You can think every name moves you a little closer to the gate. How's that? You understand that, Ali? You say a name, you get a little nearer to getting out. You got that?'

'I don't . . .'

'Shut up! You nod your head. When you speak you speak a name. Simple. That's how we're doing it. Nod, name. That's

128

how it is today. Got that? Nod. Then name. See? Easy. Names in London, England. Your bomb-friends. Ready? Nod, okay . . . I'm waiting . . . Still waiting . . . You understand English, don't you, Ali?'

The place was to be called Duneville. There were to be a hundred and twenty houses built into the sand dunes. Thirty-two Polish workers were to make them. In warm sunlight Jerzy worked at the vast network of foundations that had already been dug out and reinforced on the Clare shore. The days were blue, and the Atlantic pounded in white foam. He worked hard and fast, and tried not to stop to look out at the sea he found frightening. He had never learned to swim and never wanted to go to the north of Poland to see the Baltic. It was a cold, unforgiving sea, his mother had said, and Jerzy had accepted this as fact. He preferred to be inland. He didn't like the sense of being near the edge or the un-predictable nature of the ocean. Already he had heard of Poles and Latvians drowning since coming to Ireland. They went fishing by the rocks and the tide came and took them away. They had none of the local knowledge and fished with the innocence of small boys, imagining the free fish they would bring home and eat and then text to Poland.

No, he did not like the sea. It meant nothing to him to be there on that western beach, that today had a photo-grapher from Ennis walking out into the vast empty apron of sand, setting up the shots that would be in the brochure for Duneville.

'A terrible place,' Jerzy said in English to himself. 'The sea is wild and terrible.' None paid attention to his prac-tising, the others were older than him and had already worked in five or six countries and learned a way of living without connecting to the place. They never learned the languages.

They had heard of Laslo's clever deal to get Jerzy to stay, and they thought English so difficult it would take him so long that all the houses of Ireland would be built before he would master it. They said Laslo knew this; it was a trick. Before Jerzy knew English he would have forgotten his homesickness.

But they had underestimated him. They had not considered that he would come to Ben Dack's house every Tuesday and Thursday evening and go into the side room with the Master and take out the school copy and sit clutching the pen in a hand whose skin was white and dry with concrete residue. For Jerzy had become a builder by circumstance only, he would have preferred to go to university, to have become an architect. But when he thought of this now he dismissed it. *Over one million men have left Poland. How many building in Ireland this day might have been engineers, architects? Thousands*. One of the older men who worked only the barrow because he was not skilled with blocks had been a computer analyst in Warsaw. As a barrowman here he made five times the salary. 'I am five times more valuable in Ireland,' he said one evening when they were drinking and you could not tell if his eyes were proud or sad.

Still, Jerzy wanted to be home. He wanted to stop dreaming of his mother alone in the house, fallen down perhaps with her hip broken, her cry small as a bird's.

The sun beat down all day long. The sea crashed. He worked shirtless on the site, a muscled gleam of tanned skin and blond hair. He liked to concentrate on the work, and to see the progress, as if each block that rose carried him not upward but eastward, back to Poland. Sometimes he imagined his last block. He imagined for each of them there was a finite number they would lay and that this figure was already determined. Five hundred thousand three hundred and twenty-two blocks, perhaps. Perhaps more. And one day, in some place in Ireland, in Kilrush, in Killaloe, in Killsomewhere, for each of them there would be a last block tapped in and trimmed, then *home*. For some it would be years in the future yet, that day when they would straighten against stiffness and put down the trowel and discover they were no longer young.

How many blocks are in living? He finished the line, and stretched his back. Then he saw the dark figure on the shoreline.

It was a thin figure. Too dangerous for swimming, the beach was empty and the figure was clearly visible even at great distance. It was a dark silhouette approaching the water. Where he had come from, Jerzy had no idea, but the moment he saw him he felt a shadow crossing inside him. He watched him come to the apron of surf. *Is it a young man? Is he wearing shoes? Does the water not come up onto his feet there?* The figure was standing still now, facing out into the sea.

Jerzy looked around, but the others were working on, oblivious. Was he the only one who saw the man? The sunlight was strong; he held a saluting hand to shield his eyes. There was the person still, well down the beach, inside the line of the water.

'You see this man?' he called in Polish to an older worker who had hidden from the others his failing eyesight so he could continue earning.

'Slacking off! Get back to work,' the man teased, squinting, shaking his head.

'There is someone at the sea, down there,' Jerzy said. But because this was unremarkable and the men were each in the private places they kept their minds while building the blocks, none paid him attention.

He watched the figure. It stood in the sea fully dressed and without moving further. Jerzy turned to his trowel. He

131

cleaned the blade. He considered the next line, then turned to glance back down the shore. The figure was still there.

Jerzy lifted a block and carried it along the planking. But before he had laid it he knew he was going to walk out onto the beach.

'I am taking break,' he said, but the others supposed he was heading to the bright plastic Portakabin with the Polish newspapers folded on the floor, and they did not pause.

He jumped down the last level of the scaffolding and headed out onto the shore. The figure was a good distance away but still clearly there, standing in the sea. Jerzy's boots twisted in the sand. The wind was strong and the waves high. He did not like to look out into them. The depth of it was frightening to him, to see the water tower up and crash. Instead he looked directly at the silhouette and walked towards it; he tried not to think of the sea, and he tried not to think of his mother, and yet both were strangely there all the time.

As he approached he could see it was a woman. She was about his age. She was wearing a black cardigan and black jeans. She folded her arms across herself and her hair that was long and dark blew wildly. She was in the sea nearly up to the knees of her jeans, but did not go further nor step back.

When Jerzy came closer he realized he had no plan. So he passed behind her along the edge where tide turned back, his boots sinking to the ankle-supports. It did not seem he had been noticed, and Jerzy thought he would walk by and pretend nothing. They would simply be two figures on that seashore without connection. He would just nod and walk on.

But he didn't. He took three, four steps past, and then he stopped. He stood and looked out at the same sea, not a dozen feet from the woman.

She lifted one foot with effort from where the sea floor was steadily burying it. Sand and a little weed seeped back. Then she lowered her shoe into the sea again.

Jerzy waited behind her, not knowing for what he was waiting or why, but in some manner connected to the scene.

Then, the woman took from her cardigan pocket small pieces of paper and she began to throw these towards the waves. There were many but, as she threw them outward, the sea wind sent some back and they fell into the shallow waters. She had more. And more still. She pitched them out wordlessly and Jerzy watched as they briefly flew. They sailed the top of a retreating wave, becoming small white boats of language bobbing outward in swift tow until they found themselves rising the inside curve of a great breaker and vanishing into the crash.

One missed the sea entirely. It blew behind and Jerzy picked it up. It was a torn piece of white paper with a phrase written on it in black ink.

There is nothing, there is no

He held it and called 'Excuse. Hello.'

And the girl turned, startled to see someone. Her hair blinded her face and she pulled at it sharply.

'It came . . . it came . . . back,' Jerzy said, apologetically, and offered her the piece of paper.

Pulling up one leg with both hands, and then the other, she stepped back to him. She took the piece, read it, and walked back into the sea where she threw it hard against the wind.

'It is cold?' Jerzy said. He moved back when a longer wave washed in, and moved out after it.

She did not turn to look at him.

'It is cold, the sea, yes?' he tried again, and again she did not answer.

And not because he wanted to and not because he knew any reason other than that there was something not right and that whatever it was had drawn him there and even though he did not know what to do, he stepped out into the sea until he was standing alongside her.

They stood like that, side by side, some moments, until Jerzy said, 'Yes, very cold.'

The woman made no reply. And so they stood in the numbing sea. Gulls flew along the breaking line of waves where the words had drowned.

The sun poured light into the sea, a shimmering path, but neither man nor woman moved nor spoke, they the only two figures in the water on all that hoop of bay.

Then, without announcement, the girl turned and walked out of the sea and up the dunes and away.

Ben Dack turned down the volume on the radio. 'What I think is this,' he said, inching the lorry through the city traffic. 'There's things random and things ordered. And sometimes the random is ordered too, or maybe all the time it is if you look at it a certain way and long enough. How he's now in our family as it were, this man I'm after telling you. Like it was just chance that one day I pulled over and picked up his grandson and then dropped him off and that was that until I was in the hospital and making the visits to the wards and that only because of Josie and I was along for the company because the company of saints like Josie isn't bad company for Ben Dack to be keeping, you see. Sort of a shine you might pick up, if you get me. And so then he's, the Master that is, in our life. And he's kind of part of our family like we adopted him or he adopted us and we're part of the same thing only at first we didn't know it because how could you you hadn't seen it coming but now you're thinking this random thing this chance meeting is maybe the way the world is, you know, random family of man, that we are all part of. Random family rather than planned family, not that even planned is planned if you get me. Because you don't know what's coming do you, genius or what, but just newcomer as it were. There's a baby. Meet him or her and off you go. Cripes you see, because this met that and bingo as the fella says, without getting technical, so he could be she or she he and there's no guarantees, the random fit we'll say. And who you meet is part of who you are. That's how I see it. Stands to reason. How we are living on the planet as it were. You get me? That's why I love jigsaws, but that's another story. That's why I love the lorry. That's why I stop for the hitchhikers. That's why you always have to be open to the possibility,' Ben said. 'Absolute. Philosophy of Ben Dack, Volume five, three words: You Never Know. That's it. You Never Know. Philosophy of Ben Dack, Volume six: You sometimes get inklings.'

He stopped the lorry at a red light, looked over at the two Chinese students that were next to him in the cab. Then, as the light changed to green, a young woman with short brown hair and a freckled face stepped out, and then seeing the red light stepped back onto the path. But Ben gestured for her to cross, and because she was running late she did with a quick apologetic smile and a short wave of her own and then Ben Dack put the lorry in gear and Sister Bridget disappeared into the crowds.

SEVENTEEN

In Addis, the foremost voice of the company in Jay's head told him:

You're an idiot. You're a stupid selfish thoughtless idiot who can't even do that much right. You don't even know the first thing, not the first thing about how to tell her anything never mind love. You don't love her. You can't love her. You haven't even had a conversation. You know what, a hundred words? Brilliant. You know bread and water and homestead and all these other random things but you don't know how to even talk to her and you won't ever. You won't ever be able to because she is not even in your world, she seems like she is but she's not. How can you know what it would be like, what it is like for her? You can't unless you are so arrogant that you suppose you can come here, you can come to Africa and wave a wand and make everything all right for everybody. You can't. Get that through your head. You don't have any wand. There is no magic. How dare you even think that you love her. You don't, you can't. And even if you did she wouldn't want that love, what would she do with it? Might as well give her sunscreen, might as well give her a disposable camera. Here, this will be wonderful for you, this will make everything in your life better. See I came from Europe and I brought you this wonderful thing, now forget all the horror, forget everything you've seen. What kind of idiot are you? You don't love her. You don't love her. You've imagined you do because you want to be part of something you're not and because she's beautiful and because she's the most hurt person you've found. That's all, that's all your love is. It's something you dreamt up. Forget it. It's this thing running around in your head and you're letting it. You're letting it take over everything so now all you're doing is thinking of her. You're thinking of her so that she's with you. You want to believe that there is something, that there is this something between you and the way to do it is to keep thinking of her. You keep saying her name, keep thinking Desta Desta, *and the whole thing is just one huge fantasy and when it comes to it, when it really comes to it, when she's actually there in front of you what do you do? You terrify her. You become part of the very world she is trying to escape. Why did you touch her? Why did you reach out like that? Did you see her eyes?*

He was out in the night in Addis. The grey dog followed him. He was in a fever of guilt and loathing and recrimination and desire and he could not stop moving or he would burn to ash. He knew this section of the city was dangerous and knew he was not to be there but he had come out of the front door of the hospital into the street with furious haste and kept going. He hurried as if on an urgent errand. Those he passed he did not look at. When silver cars slowed and drove with smooth menace for some moments alongside him, he looked down at the ground. Men in the back seat called out to him or waved him over or just stared and he turned off the street, down a random other.

The night was warm and close and he was already filmed with sweat. He crossed down by the Mercato and past a building where a digital clock was counting down to the Ethiopian Millennium. Seven years after the rest of the world, the year 2000 was now only three months away. It was an oddity of that country, which followed the Julian calendar still, and with deliberate pride acknowledged its own difference. To Jay it was apt. This was another world. This was not the one he had known, and frequently he had the sense that it bore no connection to elsewhere. It was most often forgotten by the world until prompted by disaster.

He hastened on in the dark, the dog trotting behind. He came upon figures in doorways, or propped on window ledges. Shadows with watchful eyes. Jay knew not to look, not to give greeting, to hurry on. He was back in that place now he had thought he had left forever. He was back in the place between boy and man where his mind bubbled with questions, where everything was stirred up and his emotions seemed to come in furious formless rush, burning his cheeks, shining his eyes. He was not how he thought a man would be. He had no clarity, no directness, no ability to decide and act. Instead there was only this turbulence, these voices. He knew he seemed petulant and foolish and was these even as he chided himself for being so. He was the boy he had been when he walked out of the church of his Confirmation, and so too he was an older youth who could look back on himself mercilessly.

I love her.

You don't love her. Don't even begin with all that.

I love her.

Stop.

I do.

Stop thinking it. Because you'll convince yourself. You have that much imagination you'll believe it's possible.

I love her.

Listen carefully now, I'll say it slowly. You are an idiot.

139

He had no destination. He was soon beyond the city centre and those parts he knew and was walking to put distance between himself and shame. But it kept following.

She was raped by soldiers. And you, you had to touch her.

I wouldn't hurt her.

You did. Did you see her eyes?

He passed a line of shanty compounds each of tin and painted timber where dogs barked at his approach and figures stirred to watch trouble pass. He went on. He came out into an open plot of ground where a wire mesh fence had been broken down and in the darkness he could only partly see towards the far side. He was crossing here when the four men appeared.

They came out of the dark and were about him before he knew. There were two in front of him.

'Hey fellow,' one said, and cocked back his head.

'Hey fellow,' smiled the other.

Jay hunched his shoulders, turned to go the other way.

But another man was behind him. 'Hey fellow,' he said.

They were a ring. 'What you got fellow?' the first said.

'I have nothing. Here see,' Jay pulled out the insides of his pockets. 'Nothing.'

'Nothing?'

'Yes. Nothing. I have nothing.'

'Ah,' the man said, as though he understood a mistake had been made and he half turned away but then spun back around his with his right arm extended and his fist flew into Jay's face.

He did not see it coming. The shock came before the hurt. He did not remember falling to the ground but he was on the ground and a kick came into his stomach and he doubled over and yelled out and another kick came. This time it landed at his throat and took his air and his head spun back

140

and the ground tore his face. He thought to shout for help but the blows were fast and he retched over on himself. There was a pause suddenly then, as if they left him free to vomit and might already be gone, might already have felt some victory in the curled figure voiding himself in the dust. But as he coughed the last spew and lifted his head a little, another of them kicked him. In the small of his back he felt a laceration of pain and he cried out and this brought another kick to the side of his face. His head spun like a ball. They said not a word. The silence and the dark were their permission and within it they half-danced to find the vantage for another kick. While he moved they attacked. He raised a hand; it was kicked back. He brought his face up off the ground and a hand fisted the hair at the back of his neck and dragged him upward. He knelt there in a blur of pain and dark, the smear of violence taking away the stars. Then the youngest of them who had so far only watched came forward and took out a knife.

Jay saw it, but momentarily it seemed he had lost some immediacy of connection, he saw the object but not its meaning. He saw this thing in the man's hand, the blade thin as a finger so it was more spike than knife, and he saw it coming forward at the level of his face where he knelt, his head half hanging, his eyes heavily pursed in grit and blood. He saw the hand holding the blade lowered but he did not look up to see the face of the man nor those of the others.

Time was forever then. The six steps the man took across the baked dirt of the lot were the slowest moments. They were slow enough for thought and fear, for Jay to think *get up now,* for him to think *get up and run,* and yet also *I can't get up I can't move.* And in that eternity while he hung there, the strange and deeper quiet falling and the dust of the kick dancers dispersed, he had a sense of his own end. *It will be now,* he thought. And he had a brief wafer of gladness on his tongue. He would swallow in a moment, his life would pass and he would spin away into the dark above and go to find all the ghosts who were already waiting to welcome him.

He lowered his eyes. He breathed a thin breath of hurt and let sigh away the thought of any meaning or purpose for there was none. He had nothing they could rob but his heartbeat.

The man's bare feet he saw. He saw the spike-blade held not six inches from his face.

And some part of him did not surrender then. Some frayed tatter of spirit that yet was undefeated made him suddenly cry out. He jerked his head forward and propped himself with his hands and then was standing, swaying, in the blurred dark. Blood was in his mouth and he spat a thickened glob and the men made comment he did not understand but seemed in tones of admiration and delight and anticipation. They stepped back to widen the circle in which he was caught. Upright, pain announced in all parts of him. There were spears in his side that were his own ribs. The pain sang through into his back. His throat he thought kicked crooked; he held one hand against it to secure it there. The blood pooled and he spat again and the men again made comment but Jay couldn't hear clearly. His hearing was under water. When he shouted out then he heard only the muffled boom of himself that clamped with sharp nails into the soft tissue of his brain. By instinct he had raised his fists and swayed then in a pose old as Cain, facing the other who stood with a scowl-smile of bared teeth and widened eyes.

Only vaguely Jay was aware of the others behind him. Only vaguely did he have any sense of how things might proceed, how in such moments a life ends. He held one fist up before his bloodied mouth, the other before his chest. He had no plan or purpose other than to stand and show that

142

he had not entirely surrendered, that he would make one last show of refusal, would offer one last chance to God to show himself or to make any meaning clear.

The three men called to the other by his name, Yefat. They goaded him that he was afraid of the boy. And Yefat responded, telling back what he was going to do and holding the spike-knife in the air and gesturing short stabbings at the dark above.

All this played back and forth while Jay stood, his head raked with nails, his breath thin, his ribs tearing something inside. If he could have thought then he might have thought to try and run. If he could have thought, he might have thought the moment would break and maybe they would just stand and laugh to see the crazy broken hobbling of him scurrying away into the dark. Maybe this would be enough for them, he might have thought. But his mind was flooded with fizzing blood. It was flooded with the dark hot stuff of shame and guilt and despair and he did not run. He held his fists up.

One of the men picked a small stone from the ground and threw it at him. It clacked against the side of Jay's head, and the man laughed and the others did. But Jay did not look away from Yefat. The men goading him further and another stone flew. Then, as if such things have their own clockwork, as if it was decreed that now in that warm Ethiopian night, in that empty lot with the broken wire fence, a life would end, Yefat came forward.

The knife he held low by his side.

Jay had his fists raised. He made effort to open his eyes wide to try and take away the blur in the darkness. Then as Yefat approached he swung a blow at him. The man stepped easily out of it. Another great arc of nothing Jay made and this time shouted out as Yefat watched the blow pass. The men made no sound at all now. Jay swung and swung again.

He came forward wildly flailing and whether by surprise or fearlessness Yafat did not step back and was hit on the side of his head and on his shoulders. But the blows cost Jay more and his face twisted and he was aware of stopping, of suddenly not being able to bring his fists up to strike again. He was aware he wanted to, and that somewhere between his brain and his arms there was a delay, that he could not bring his arms up but was right there in front of this man, was close enough to smell the spices of his breath, to see that he was little more than youth.

Then he looked down and saw the spike had entered him.

Jay looked down and saw Yefat's hand on the handle at the place below his ribs where pain was just now come. He saw it and he saw Yefat twist the narrow blade inside him, and then he saw no more and fell to the ground.

EIGHTEEN

That day there was no wind. The kite would not fly. The Master ran across the tufted grass on the hill and tossed it into the blue but it would not rise. He tried twenty times. He took off his jacket, gave the kite short leads and with his uneven stride ran crookedly to the west. With rough jagged motion it followed, but fell as soon as he stopped for breath. He studied the sky for cloud movement, but there was none, only the same perfect blue that had been for weeks now and had turned the country into another place. He ran back to the east. He tried running down the hill but still the kite would not rise and when he stopped it banged against his shoulder and he stumbled and rolled over and pulled the kite in under him. A strut snapped.

It upset him. His feelings these days were always so close to the surface that they needed little prompting to break through, and now he sat on the grass in his shirtsleeves and a pulse of emotion jumped in his chin. He held the two thin broken pieces of the shaft together as if they might mend.

What use am I? What use is an old man who can do nothing?

Don't be pitying yourself, he heard his wife say.

I am pitying myself, I am pitiful.

You're my same sweet old Joe, she said.

He lay back on the grass but she was gone and loneliness came to him across the hill. He couldn't get his spirit to rise. He could only think now that more sorrow was coming.

He felt he had been betrayed by the world. It had brought him back and left him empty. His return was meaningless and suddenly now with quiet sad resignation he wished himself dead. He wished he could follow his spirit and be gone. The kite had not flown, and though it was a simple thing and he had told himself it could not matter, he came down the hill with a profound sense of loss. For the first time, he felt Jay was dead.

He carried the kite in through the kitchen where Josie paused, flour-handed, over the bread basin.

'Early back today Joe,' she said. 'Too hot for anything isn't it? I'm baking myself as well as this bread.'

'Yes Josie. Early back.'

'You want tea, Joe?'

He didn't answer, and drifted past her and out of the room.

Upstairs his grief deepened. Can a man die of sadness, he thought. Can it just seep into him like black ink and fill more and more every day until he drowns in it?

Jay.

Jay.

After a long time, he took down *David Copperfield* and opened it to where he kept the picture. He took it out and looked at it and the boy that was there, then he placed it face upward on his knee. He thought reading might free him of sorrow for a time and he took out *The Old Man and the Sea* but read only four lines.

*   *   *

146

Then he knew he could read no more and that it brought no consolation or escape and he had only to sit there and let the black ink fill.

That evening on the site he wrote: 'Some days you wake and there is this hole. It's right through you. Today is one of those. I think the thing that keeps me living is that I believe I will see him again; that he will come home, and that somehow whatever was broken will be mended. Somehow he will be all right, and I will do a better job of minding him or not even minding, just helping him grow on or not even helping, just witnessing. He's nearly a man already now. And I think of what he must look like and I can't really. That upsets me so much. Just that I can't quite picture him except as he was and even if he comes back he's not going to be that boy any more. And then on a day like today there is this great hole where hope should be. You can't escape the thought that actually no, it's not going to happen. You're going to live on waiting and the days will pass by without anything ever happening, just the struggle to keep breathing. You will just get older and then one day sickness will come for you and that will be it. From that comes such weariness that I just want to lie down under the weight of it. I want to lie down on the hill and close my eyes and be done.'

He typed slowly, stooped, and squinting a little. His mouth was dry, his cheek when he lay it in his palm felt like old paper. He did not weep, nor did any emotion rise in him. What sources were in him had stopped. He tapped out the name 'Mater' and then clicked on 'Send'.

Later, he stood up and went to the skylight and opened it and stood inside the unlidded sky. Cloud obscured the stars. Night was black not blue. From the rooftop he could see the light of no other house, just a black hole where the valley was. The quiet of the country made it seem not country at all but a terrain between worlds. His head above the roofline, he might himself have been partway to another place. And so it had been with him for a long time now. For a long time he was yearning for the sky. There was some part of him that reached upward, even before Mary died and Marie; before even his parents had died there was this longing to be up there. The kite-flying he first did as a boy was perhaps the beginning, although he did not think of it as anything other than a thrilling experience when the wind pulled the cords tight. As a boy he did not gave a moment's thought or interpret anything unusual in it. But when he became a man and – one June afternoon repairing the struts on the kite that had been left in the stone cabin, taking it to the back hill and letting it up – found the delight still with him, he knew it was more than just a pastime. He loved to watch it fly. He loved the different faces of the wind and to watch the kite climb and meet them, moving along a plane of fast air, arriving at a high stillness where the sail was tight and full and seemed to want to escape the cord and fly on up beyond the visible. The sky he loved more than the land or the sea. With another life he might have been a pilot not a teacher, but in the time he had lived and with the parents he had, the schoolmastering was most honourable. The flying was for his dreaming not his living. *Now if I just go. If I could just float up and diminish. If I could just close my eyes.*

So the old Master stood and looked into the dark and wished that he were gone. But into his mind, then, came an image of the sea, great tumbling waves in the night. The image was so sudden and clear that it puzzled him and made him at once uneasy. The sea, wild and ferocious, tumbling: this is what he saw. What sea it was or where he couldn't tell; only that he was seeing it, a heaving sea in the dark and the waves a dim cream churning. Whether it was vision, whether purposeful or random, whether it held meaning or was just prompting from the back of an old man's mind, the

Master couldn't tell. The sense of a turbulent sea was all there was and it did not leave him for some moments until he said aloud, 'You old fool, it's just the novel. It's the old man. It's just from that.' And he stooped back inside and closed the skylight, and still he thought Jay was dead, and still the idea of the sea was in him, and he slumped back in the chair by the computer and stared at the screen.

Remember, remember.

If the prisoner can remember he can escape. When they turned off the lights in his cell he was supposed to sleep but he could not. A strange reversal happened whereby his mind woke fully as the dark came. He sat on the thin mattress and held his knees and his brain fizzed. It brought him moments from the past, some startlingly clear, others with the edges dissolved. These he worried at with the teeth of memory, trying to pull free more details, to return himself there. *I am only what I can remember of myself. I am the sum of memories I have. That is all. When I forget, I am forgotten by the last one who remembers me.*

So, his work was in the dark. A moment flashed across his brain and he tried to stop it in flight. Here: one time, for an article on the poppy growers and the drug trade, he had been in the main square of Tirin Kot, in Uruzgan province in Central Afghanistan. *Remember the sunlight there, and the young translator. What was his name? What?*

Little more than a boy. Always smiling.

His name? What was his name?

Remember.

He thought hard on this and tried to reassemble the boy from his smile. He tried to see him in the Jeep when they drove out to the poppy fields together, then he remembered: *Nazeem.*

149

That drive they took, the brown expanse and the dust pluming, the mountains.

In another life he might have been my son.

If I had another life.

He worked at the memory as long as he could. He tried to remember what happened that day and carry on from where the vivid quickly faded. He tried to think of the day before that one, and the day after. What time did he wake up? Where was his bed? What did he do that day?

Whether because of the beatings, the hosings, the solitude, his mind was become frayed; he could not remember. And it tormented him. He slumped over against the wall and beat his forehead against it. He was back in a cell under the ground. He was a puzzle with pieces disappearing each moment.

How long will they keep me here? How long will they keep coming back and asking the same questions? How long can I keep saying I am innocent until I start to say I am guilty?

He returned a thousand times to the moment he was taken. He was on a street in Frankfurt in Germany. There had been an explosion earlier. He came out of a café and for a second he had the sensation that there was something odd; then he was taken by two men, one on each arm, and was being rushed forward. He was brought to a blue van but he did not want to step up into it and he dragged his legs and his shins cracked on the step. Then he was inside and blind-folded and struck every time he tried to speak. He remembered telling himself: *pay attention. Make note of everything. Remember every detail.* He remembered separating from himself, telling himself to think like a journalist, *this is first hand. This is what happens. This is what you will be writing.* And in this way he had tried to overcome the fear, to be the observer of his own suffering. *Notice that we have been travelling for half an hour. Notice that the road is straight, probably the autobahn. What did you see of their faces? The one with the cropped hair. The one who smelled of citrus.*

But then when they brought him to the room and began he could no longer think like this. The pain and the fear were everything.

Now he would not remember back there. He himself had removed those pieces of memory.

Instead he thought of when they moved him, when in blindfold he was taken and put on an aeroplane. His hands and legs were chained. The plane took off from where he did not know and landed later for one hour before flying again.

He remembered that. He remembered the plane must have been on a distant corner of the airport for the hatch was opened and he could hear the planes taxiing. He could smell grass. And he heard one of the guards make a joke about Guinness and he thought: *This is Ireland.*

He had never been there but once he had loved an Irish girl he met in England.

He thought of her now. He thought back sixteen years and how his heart hurt when she left him. He thought it was because she could not reconcile their two worlds even though she had loved him.

Marie.

NINETEEN

Dear all, see, I made it to Ireland. Don't know what to say about the bombing. But I am in Ireland and it's actually not raining. Of course it is not raining, I'm here! It feels strange to be away from you and I am thinking of you all. Please tell everyone. A special hello to Jay. Got your map. Bridget.

Doctor Pellier turned the postcard over and looked at Ireland. It was a fantasy, this too-green place.

He drew on his cigarette. How would they tell her Jay was gone?

The last cow to calve that year was stubborn and unpredictable and Mick Daly had had kicks from her in the past. He called her Eunice because he had an aunt he despised with that name. He had been studying Eunice for three days now and swore she wouldn't drop because she knew he was watching. That was the make of her, he'd say. She had a sidelong suspicious look about her. She moved always on the edge of the herd; when he followed them down the road to the sea-fields she went up into the ditch grass and straggled when the others moved on. Until he came with his length of black drainpipe and thwacked the side of his Wellington, she would linger. Then with a quick step of fear and pretend submission Eunice would trot on, a little half-kick of her hind legs to tell him to come no closer. She had given fourteen calves, none easily.

The evening before, Mick had seen her standing apart and not grazing and he thought she was sickening for it and he had come down the dune-side of the grass not far from the last golfers and squatted half-hidden to study her. The long wild ribs obscured him. The tide was in and briefly he had scowl-squinted over at the crashing sea. He disliked it, he saw no attraction in it and considered only the danger to his cows and especially the calves that had less sense than rabbits. The golfers he disliked more. He thought one year he would let his bull escape onto the golf course and meet all those red jumpers. He spat the thought sideways into the grass and resumed his watch on Eunice. She had stood a long time, and let the others drift up the field in the slow dreamlike way of cows. Mick had thought she was ready then, and maybe would calve there without trouble this time. But he never had any such luck. Twilight came with the first stars over the sea and he had stood up stiffly and told Eunice she was a useless bloody cow. He had come down the slope and opened the gate. Then he went back in to the field to separate her from the others and bring her back to the cabin for the night watch. As soon as the gate was opened others in the herd, confused in the clockwork and thinking it must already be milking time, began at once to come in slow file. But Eunice did not; she stood and watched. Mick had to turn the others back, waving his arms and with a sharp tone making almost a barking of *goback goback goon goback backback backback.*

The cows stopped, they looked at him, they did not go back. They stood in puzzlement, delayed long enough for

Mick to run up around behind Eunice. He was a short stocky block of a man and laboured to race in the grass. His face reddened into his red wool of hair. The length of black hose in one hand, the other pressed against some jingling coins in his pants pocket, he tried to get above Eunice before she knew it.

But she knew it already and before he was halfway around she trotted in the opposite direction.

His curses followed her. He stood and caught his breath out of the sea air. The herd was still standing facing the open gate, but not yet knowing whether to go forward or back.

Eunice went up the field toward night coming. She went by instinct to darkness and privacy, and watching her Mick Daly thought, *She's definitely having it*. And he headed up after her, turning back the herd first and then making a wide arc up the ten-acre field, as though he was not interested in Eunice at all, as though he was touring his farm or hunting a golf ball. They saw the golfers all day and didn't scare, so why would she head off now unless she knew she was due? Mick didn't trust nature. He had seen enough of her mistakes. He didn't trust that he would get to go to bed and sleep and wake up and come out to the field and find a bull calf standing. *She'd tramp it more likely. Or bust through the wire and drop it in the sea.*

In the near darkness now he went stealthily. She had gone into the coarser dune grass that went ungrazed and was standing with her back to him. He tried to steady his breathing. He tried to make no sound as in the heat of his Wellingtons he high-stepped over the grass. Then, when he was close and still she had not moved, he slid the hose-length into the side of his pants and he held out his open palms. He carried some awareness of birthing and its terror and knew enough of the female to choose the time for tenderness and so whispered to her then. He whispered no words but a *shush shush* over and over and with each one stepped a little nearer until he was next to the heat of her and could see her wild eye and knew a moment before it happened that she was about to puck him with her head.

He went over as if he was nothing. His ankle snapped and he cried out and Eunice turned and bucked and trotted down the field and out the gate.

Still the Master sat before the computer. The postings on the site came sporadically, and down the screen more stories of the vanished. H-47 did not write that night. To the Master's earlier entry there was a brief back and forth of offerings, advice to pray, to not despair, to think hard on the boy being out there. To none of them did he reply, and soon the other stories came and the site filled with the newest of the lost. He watched. When a child was added he said their name out loud in the room. That was all.

He was there when Ben knocked. 'Josie says you're not yourself,' he said, sitting on the side of the bed, 'and she's a good judge. Indeed she is.' Ben rubbed his two hands over the balls of his knees as though they needed polishing. Then he saw the photograph. 'You thinking of Jay? Of course, stating the obvious: speciality of Ben Dack. Part two: it's made you sad.'

'I think he's dead, Ben. I hadn't thought it until today. Until today I thought he's out there somewhere, he's in the world. But today.' He was looking straight ahead at the roses in the wallpaper where the join split the blooms from the stems and realizing he had never quite seen them that way before. 'Today I couldn't believe any more. I think he's dead.'

'Oh cripes no. No no. No no no. That's.' Ben smacked both knees and stood up and looked about him as though to see where grief was leaking in. He came around in front of the Master. 'Now listen to Ben Dack,' he said, and he raised a finger to make the point he wasn't sure of yet. He stabbed the air twice more as though at a button marked Start. 'Right,' he said. 'Now,' he said. 'Listen,' he said. 'Point: you've had a bad day. Point: normal, one hundred per cent.' He jabbed a fat finger. 'Point: doesn't mean anything. Means not one thing. Means you're a man. Normal. Loneliness normal. Sadness normal. Point is: you don't know. You can't know. But.' He held the finger upright to pause his thought. His eyes flicked left to right reading it. 'But. Next Point is: action. You try again. Computer, excellent. Searching, excellent. But tomorrow morning. Tomorrow morning, second approach, another phone call to London. I have the name of that man. Missing persons. Point: we renew. We re-engage, Joe. You get me? We keep the search . . .' he nearly said 'alive.'

'He's dead, Ben.'

'No he's not. He's not. Don't even say it.' Dismayed at the failure of his speech, Ben grasped one hand onto the Master's shoulder. 'Even if you think it, don't say it, because. Because point is, Joe, I will be believing still. Point: I will be believing for you.' Surprised at the sudden emotion, he let go and smacked his hand into his fist and his round face reddened in an abashed smile. He patted his check shirt smooth over his belly. 'Ben Dack, Champion Fool of Ireland maybe, as Josie says, but only when she's mad at me.' He smiled again. 'Are you real at all, says she. Are there men like you in the world still? says she. Indeed there are, says I, walking every corner of it. And oh then heaven help us, she says.' He scratched the top of his head vigorously then. The Master was staring past him at the wall, the sorrowfulness still pervading. Ben Dack clicked the fingers of both hands restlessly against the silence, but for the first time in a long time could think of nothing more to say. Then he heard the car arrive in the yard below. 'That's the young lad I'd say,' he said. 'Smart fellow I'd say, is he?'

'I'm sorry, Ben, what?'

'The young lad, Jer, that's him now below for his lesson. He has a car now. He's keen, you know, he is. Learning good is he? I'd say has the look of a teacher himself or something. You're making a big impression there, you know?'

The Master did not acknowledge this and Ben said, 'One hundred and fifty thousand of them here, more maybe, and imagine how many hundred thousand more scattered. So what is it like now, Poland, that's what I'm wondering.'

There was a moment, then he asked, 'Will you come down?'

The Master's head was lowered, as though he had taken a blow and expected another, but in a thin voice said, 'I'll come down.'

In the sitting room, Josie and Jerzy were standing watching a primetime report on the London bombing. She had pressed him to taste the bread she had baked and he had taken a wedge of it into his mouth. As his teacher came in he nodded and chewed quickly and swallowed and then said, 'Very good bread thank you very much', and made almost a bow with a kind of courtesy Josie thought had vanished from the world.

'I'm over to Finucane's,' Ben said. 'I need to get Gerry to look at the lorry. I'll be back before you're done.'

Master and pupil went into the side room where the lesson began with the usual preamble.

'So how are you today?'

'I am very well thank you, and you?'

'What did you do today?'

'I went to work. I worked these, I work these days at the Atlantic Ocean.'

'At the sea. We just say, "at the sea or by the sea",' the Master said wearily. He lowered his forehead into his palm.

158

'At the sea, yes. I went to work building. I am builder, a builder sorry.' Jerzy paused and waited for the next question. He could see the Master was burdened and he feared it was his slow progress and so he continued, 'It is the end of Ireland. At the sea. Where I am building many houses. Many people want to live by the end sorry sorry edge the edge of Ireland. But I prefer the middle. I prefer Poland. Not the sea. I do not like the sea. I do not like it because of the . . . because the wafs are . . . because, I do not know for sure why but still no. Maybe because it is the end, edge . . .'

Suddenly the Master looked up at him, his wiry eyebrows raised, his face pale with revelation. 'The end.'

'No no I know, edge. Sorry.'

'No the sea.'

'Yes.'

'Say that again.'

'I am sorry?'

'You said his end is at the sea.'

'No, no I do not think,' Jerzy shook his head.

The Master looked through him. He looked at the epiphany the way you might a great white bird emerging from the wall and beating wide wings, flying a clean arc above their heads before suddenly landing on the table. The sense of it was askew. The laws of the world did not allow for such and yet it was there before him. Was it only in the nature of madness to see visions? Was it simply confluence of fluids, erratic pulses in the synapses, imperfect mechanisms of brain in the aftermath of serious injury such as his? What visions could belong in the real? Were they not just projections, actualized wishes, confabulations of the mind that wanted them to exist and so created them? Were visions not in the credible world, not actual? Could nothing *come* from outside of us, nothing be manifest that was not made of our own desire or hurt or fear or longing? He could not be seeing what he was seeing.

159

His head was wrong. He could not have heard the young man telling of the sea and then instantly had an image of a drowning in the same sea he had imagined earlier. He could not have seen it so clearly as to make a chill pass up along his neck and fizz his eyes with shock. But he did. He saw the sea and the high waves and the figure of a young man stepping out into it. He saw it in front of him even as he sat there in the side room with the copybook open and the young Polish builder looking over at him. He saw it in seconds, a frantic electric moment charged with foreboding, and he stood up quickly and was already moving to the door, already he was heading out and through the sitting room and past where Josie turned from the television to see what had disturbed the lesson. And already Jerzy was following and the Master said 'come on come on quickly', and whether she could see the whiteness of the vision on his features or she trusted in the improbable, Josie rose and followed. They came out into the yard and the mild black night and the Master said to Jerzy, 'Will you drive?'

'Where are we going, Joe?' Josie asked him. 'Where is it you need to go?'

'He's drowning,' he said to her. 'He's drowning in the sea.' And he did not look back to see whether she believed him or not, whether she feared for his sanity or considered stopping him. He pressed forward in the front seat next to Jerzy Maski and peered out into the dark they blazed alight as they went.

TWENTY

Whether the one he thought he was to save was Jay, or whether it was a stranger and – he believed in the complex of higher mathematics by which an action in one place makes function another – that this would save his grandson, the Master did not say. Like all most common madness his insight was profound but acute. He was certain he was to go to the sea. He was certain there was danger of drowning, and maybe it was already too late. Maybe when the vision first came to him in the room upstairs he should have left immediately, but was too dulled or too focused on his own sadness to have understood. Of inter-pretation there were many variants, and they ran in his mind while the car bumped forward over the uneven bends that ran to the sea. Jerzy was a new driver and unlicensed and tried to take care but the Master urged him on, 'Come on come on, next left now. Now. Here,' and he crunched the gears.

'It's all right, Jerzy, it's fine,' Josie said.

'Where are we . . . ? What is . . . ?'

'The sea! We have to get to the sea!' the Master told him.

'Yes but . . .'

'Right up here. Right, right, yes. '

They turned right, down what was more track than road and the car took a whipping of brambles.

How did he know what beach to go to? He didn't. Knowledge was not part of what had happened to him. He went to the beach that was nearest, the one where they were building the houses, because he believed that if the vision was real and if he was in some way *meant* to have received it, then whoever had sent it – if *sent* was right, logical extension of the implausible – then it would be the beach nearest to him. In madness there is often logic, he knew, but he was not mad. He had had a vision of the sea. Someone was drowning. He did not know more.

'This way? The buildings are—'

'This way, yes, Jerzy, good. Just over there, pull over. Good man. Thank you thank you.'

They arrived at the site and the Master got out of the car and the others followed and crossed by the ghostlike shells of the half-made houses down to the sea. It was a clouded night and the piece of moon part-veiled so the division between waters and wet sand was barely distinguishable.

'Are you all right Joe?' Josie asked.

He was standing, looking into the dark, lost. Epiphany was gone. He shoved his hands into the pockets of his tweed jacket and squinted out at the sea.

'Joe?' Josie looked at him with concern. 'Can you tell me, Joe?'

He had thought it would be apparent; he had thought he would get out of the car and whatever he had come for – whatever had been sent – would be obvious there before him. There would be no need for explanation, only action, and he would not be the very foolish very old man he felt now.

162

'Joe, love?'

He stared at the sea. The ordinary world came to him as an assault. It was a long bay and would take an hour to walk; if someone was drowning *where* were they drowning? If they set out to the east and walked in that direction the person could be drowned to the west of them before they had time to even get halfway. Was there any point in dividing up? Could he actually have *saved* anyone? The sea was immense and unforgiving.

In the dark the smallness of himself, the agedness, all that was faulty, every weakness of joint, aches to which he was long habituated – knee, elbow, knuckles – and the great weariness that was never far, these were overwhelming now. He was as ridiculous to himself as he would have been to any if he told himself as a ludicrous tale. There was no one in the sea before them. They could make out only the smallest portion. The tide was going out and the clock of the waves continued with the same measured uncaring since first the world moved.

There was small wind off the sea. He faced it, the others stood on either side looking at him.

'Joe?'

He did not answer Josie. He had the image of his own father ghosting across the very front of the shore, and he followed him with his eyes and the others looked at the figment but saw nothing and in each of them was the fear that he had lost his reason.

Then the cow came trotting down the beach.

Eunice loomed out of the dark. She came at quick-trot, full tight udder in sway, eyes wild. She bellowed hugely, a sound that out-noised the sea and told the night she had yet to drop the calf. She came to them and, in whatever terror-dream she was, did not see them until she was upon them.

The Master waved his hands at her and Jerzy likewise and Eunice turned and bellowed, and in that same moment they each saw the man.

There, in the dark mid-distance of wave, in the certain mesmerism of the night-sea, was a figure.

The cow turned into the sea in his direction, then found the salt at her hooves and back-kicked and spun and bellowed again, and the Master threw up his hands at her in a gesture not unlike a magician's and she went in splash-trot back from where she had come.

The figure was chest-deep. It may have been considered wreckage or timber or debris as much as man had they not been looking for one. Jerzy was first to point him out and said something in Polish. The Master called and then Jerzy called too but the figure went on into the sea. And before anything could be said, before he might have found the language to tell that he was terrified of the sea and that he could not swim, before he had time to tell himself he shouldn't and that here coming was the reason he had always feared the water, here was what some part of him had always known would be his death, Jerzy Maski threw off his shirt and ran into the waves.

The Master called his name.

'O sweet God,' Josie said, and she took the old man's hand in hers and murmured the beginning of prayer.

Jerzy jumped the first wave, and then the next, and it seemed at first that he would cross the way without touching water. He would hurdle to the place where the other's head was just now going down in ink. But Jerzy's foot hit the crest of the next wave and he went headlong. From the shore they saw him vanish for the first time. Jerzy went down through the surf and when he came up he was trying to run against the sea. He was already beyond his midriff and each wave breaking made him cock back his head as if still he could escape. He pressed on, his face skyward to night when the waves hit, working his arms like oars to get to the place where the other had gone under. In the rising falling dark of the sea there was no sign of another. Jerzy was shouting something in Polish. He was shouting but he was not looking back and the Master saw his head disappear as suddenly the undertow took him.

He was gone.

The Master stepped out into the water to see better but saw nothing.

There was only the dark and the sea and the remorseless sound of the waves. There was the brute cold simplicity of death, the fact of it, the ocean taking the two men in a mouthful without boast or victory, a soundless swallow, and the surface unbroken once more.

'God almighty,' he said.

And in the utter abandonment and hopelessness of man in the face of mystery, on that shore where any meaning or purpose was beaten beneath the perpetual pounding of the sea, he shouted out.

'Agggggggggghhhhhhhhhh! Agggggggggghhhhhhhhhh!'

He shouted as loud a cry as his lungs bore. Josie put her arm across his chest and another behind him and she held him as he cried out again. He cried that he might express out of him the desolation that wolfed his heart, and cried too with that raw primal urge, to draw down the Creator to the imperfection of his creation.

For an instant Jerzy's head appeared in the deep. He was up and his fair hair gleamed and it seemed he tried to pull up in both hands the arm of another, and then he was gone and again there was nothing to break the surface.

And because he had reached an end, because he felt his spirit was gone and he needed to know if his death was now, because he would rather die trying to save the young Pole and the other too, and because he thought again there may be a mathematics beyond his teaching, some relation that connected A not to B but to J, he stepped away from Josie, threw off his shoes and ran into the sea.

TWENTY-ONE

He was drowning.

Jay could not breathe and his lungs were filling and he had
a sour taste that his brain did not tell him yet was the taste
of his blood. He had fallen and the ground had become the
sea and the place where the knife had entered him bled a
slow ooze that came through his fingers. He had singing in
his ears. He had a high ringing that blurred the words the
others said as they stood back and watched and then left
him. The edges of his vision were smeared.

He was drowning.

He gurgled on the thick clotted liquid that kept filling in
his mouth, then he was blind and the ringing continued still
and he was telling himself to stay awake and not die there.
The pain was gone and with it the lower part of his body,
and he was very still as the world about him was fading,
that empty ground with the broken fence, that hood of stars.
All fell away and he went under the sea, drowning in his
own blood with the blind dark of death coming, and the hand
that he had held against the wound he put out into the air
as though to reach another. It floundered in a void and
soughed back. He thought to cry out but could not. He tried

to find how it was you took breath, how you brought air into you, but it seemed he had forgotten and the effort to remember was moving beyond him.

There was such stillness then as he had not known. He had a vision of the waters closing over him like cloths, enwrapping him, binding him, to be taken elsewhere into another world. And he was going. He was glad to go and felt only absolute surrender. He was seeing his life leave him like a thing left down, seeing all of his days slip away and slowly dissolve, and he did not care. Tenderly the cloths were folded over him and around him, and he had a last thought that was a strange nearness of the Master to him, as though now at last they could meet again. In moments he would see him. And by this, his last feeling, he was filled with joy and he angled back his head to better see and then offered himself to death.

TWENTY-TWO

The one who found him was an old man. He heard the dog
and thought it was a cow. He thought it a cow-noise of a
kind and came to see that it was a dog that lay by the body.
It was near to dawn. The old man approached with caution
for he knew that evil had many tricks and the lures of thieves
were innumerable. He saw the dark stain of the blood on
the ground and he looked about him for where others might
be hiding. Then he said to the dog, 'Are you dog?'

It came to him. He gave it the scent of his fingers and
waited in that mute moment of acquaintance, looking about
still for the murderers-in-hiding. When none came, still
standing he studied the dead figure curled on the ground.
The old man had seen death in many guises and believed in
traffic of spirits between this world and the next and he was
fearful to intrude on any transport of souls that might be
happening. He stood, the ragged dog whimpered beside him.

'Dog, what do you see?' he asked. Then the old man sniffed
the air and as if he caught there the remnant scent of life,
he approached and knelt and put his hand on the young
man. Then, from a tied bundle he bore, he took out two
long cloths and he bound one around the man's waist where

169

the wound leaked and with the other he enwrapped him completely. Then, squatted alongside, he shuffled his bare feet in the dust for better position, and pressed his arm in beneath the body and then bore it up, laying the head over his shoulder as a mother might a child. Then slowly he stood, steadying and swaying and steadying until he stood upright with the body in his arms. 'Come dog', and he walked out of that place; a thin arm was hooped over his other.

> *Jay, are you not dead?*
> *If you are, then I am.*
> *Are you?*

The old man took him to his place that was made of tin and cloth and plastic. He entered and laid him on a mat and un-wrapped the cloths and removed the bloodied shirt and looked at the wound. His understanding of life was that it was an energy not unlike fire and that in some it persisted vigorously beyond all circumstance and ordinary prediction. He had seen men and boys blown up in landmines and live still. He had seen ones shot with machine guns, tattoo of holes in their chest, who had grinned Death back from them. The diseased, the burned, the drowned: he had seen some of all live and could find no explanation other than that the spirit-fire was yet unquenched.

The young man had breath still. He was weak, he had lost much blood, but he lived. The old man dipped a cloth in water and brought it to his face. He saw it was not the face of an African and he told the dog, 'He is a strong *ferange*.' He went to make a paste of earth and this he applied to the wound. Then he sat and waited.

The sun rose. In that tented shelter the heat grew colossal. Flies did not fly. The oven of day made the tin roof scorch, the blue plastic sheet softened to near melting, but the old

170

man kept the cloth flap closed. He was himself a figure of wiry strength and his body glistened as he sat. He was not a doctor and he did not administer herbs or other medicines. He believed it was between the young man and Death and he had brought him there only to give him a fair chance. The day burned over them. 'He has to make again the blood he lost,' the old man told the dog.

The fever started near sunset.

The old man considered this proof of fire rekindling and to aid it he gathered cloths, some sacking, a jellaba, and laid these over the young man in the cooling of evening. He watched the shivering and the sweating and he heard the delirium and he did not understand any word spoken but he wondered what life this was that would not die. He wondered what place it came from and how it came here into his country and what crooked lines the world draws in the lives of men. He gave the dog some of what he had scavenged that day in his travels. He sat.

The fever burned on through the night. The old man brought a cloth dipped in water and pressed it to the young man's forehead and when he did he thought the spirit surfaced near life again and he watched the eyes in case it should appear. But it did not. The next day the fever continued and with it the delirium. The old man did not want to leave and divided the small food he had in two parcels and then these again in two in case it would be four days before he would know if the other lived or died. Either way he would be witness. He broke up the *injera* pancakes he had into quarters, but found he had five, and ate the fifth to have an even number.

In the middle of the second night for a brief time the fever released the young man and his eyes opened. What he saw was not in this life. He stared with wide eyes as do the drowning, and he waved his right arm over and back, over and back again, thrashing at an invisible sea.

The old man did not move or speak. He waited.

On the third day when the young man was still and his breath so thin it seemed he took it from the furthermost edge of the world, the old man unbound the cloth and examined the wound. He washed away the mud poultice to see there was no infection, only a clean incision where the knife had entered and healing was not yet apparent.

When the body moved the wound opened like a mouth. The old man dressed it again, and again sat back, and he told the dog who was at his feet, 'I know you are hungry but we must wait.'

Then he tented the thin bones of his fingers together and looked on like one looking into the deeps of the sea for the swimming there of a remarkable fish.

TWENTY-THREE

The sea was blind dark and deep and cold and the Master fell forward into it before he could dive. The cold took his breath. Already he was past the sand bar and there was no footing and he plunged down and kicked hard and thrashed with his arms over and back to try to find a stroke that would bring him back to the surface. He shot up into the air and threw back his head and gulped at the dark. His chest would not open enough; he felt the sea pressed upon him and his heart ached and still he trod the swell looking about in that ink-black for the others. He was beyond the breaking of the waves and pulled further outward on the tide. Into the dark he called out 'Jerzy! Jerzy!' But he could hear and see nothing but the ocean, and was floated about on it like a thing of no consequence. He swam a dozen strokes to his left, his swimming so long out of practice and his body so compromised he made no progress. He could neither go in nor out and realized he was at the unproven mercy of the sea. But he did not panic. He believed himself so saturate with sadness, so deeply grieved that he was owed compassion; that for the foolishness of man leniency existed, and existed in infinite measure and this not because of but often despite man. He believed it could not be that three would drown here, and he was happy that if one had to then it should be him because it would mean his grandson too was dead.

And like a plot then that needed turning, the sea lifted a wave and on it appeared the fair bobbing head of Jerzy Maski. He came up and roared into the night. He roared the sound that in all languages was the sound of the life force refusing to die. It was a long guttural cry of a single syllable, a matching aaaaaaghghghgh of defiance, a rough roar of both denial and affirmation at the same instant. He threw back his head and cried out and the Master heard him and called back and tried to swim towards it, rising and falling in the swell, pawing in imperfect dog-paddle, kicking legs that were weakening with exhaustion.

He had sight of him when Jerzy went under. The sea carried the Master outward as quickly as he tried to swim across. Then he feared he would be the rescuer that needed rescuing and he stopped. He turned over and lay on the water and looked blindly upwards into the face of night. He put his hand up to the heartache in his chest and he tried to find breath. Above him the piece-moon slipped through the clouds and silver light was freed. He thought: *if I am to die now.* He thought: *tell me if Jay is alive. What is the use of an old man left here? Tell me.* In rapid succession his mind flickered, but most clearly this: the day his own father took him fishing in a blue boat far out into the sea.

He lay in that ocean of memory, exhausted beneath the vast dark.

Then he heard Jerzy call and he rolled over and could see him not ten feet away holding another against his chest. The Master renewed his stroke and kicked and came to them and he saw it was not a man but a young woman.

'Is she . . . ?' Jerzy spat and gasped.

174

'We must . . .' the Master pointed to the shore. 'The tide . . . tide, strong.' A wave washed his face; he spat. 'Very slowly. Slow, yes?'

'Yes.' Jerzy nodded, then asked, 'Is she killed?'

'I don't know.'

With the meaning or meaningless of their act unclear, they stayed together and paddled with their arms, carried forward sometimes by a wave, toward where Josie was praying on the sand. It was a long time, ahead of them the pale line where the surf broke. When at last they arrived inside the wave line, they were borne swiftly forward and could tip-touch the ground like dancers harnessed from on high.

Another wave and they toppled, the harness severed. The woman lay face down in the shallow water, her long hair entwined. She appeared lifeless and was about to be dragged back by the retreating tide when they lifted her and staggered to the sand. Josie rushed to them and they lay the woman down and collapsed, kneeling and gasping on the pain that was air that could not get quickly enough into their lungs.

Jerzy recovered soonest. He turned the pale figure of the woman gently and moved the sand-heavy hair from her face and recognized her. She was the one who had been standing in the sea, her expression now tranquil and her skin gleaming. 'Is she killed?' he asked again.

Josie moved forward. She knelt in the sand and pinched the nose and put her mouth over the cold mouth. Nearly sixty years of age, Josie had the kind of clear focus and intent that women have in crisis. She worked the breaths in mechanical fashion as she had learned a lifetime ago, turning to the side to inhale, trying to count evenly and keep her composure while nothing at all happened.

And continued to happen.

And Jerzy said, 'She is killed', and he banged his fist down on the sand and then leaned forward and pressed his forehead there and said something in Polish that might have been curse or prayer. The Master was on his hands and knees. 'She's not dead,' he said, 'Jerzy, she's not dead,' and Jerzy lifted his head, likewise paused, both of them watching in exhaustion.

'He's not dead. She's not dead, you're not dead,' the Master said firmly, and it was partly unclear of whom he spoke and whether he was telling it or being told.

In the whispering and sighing collapse of the sea, Josie kept at the breathing, blowing into the salt mouth, working the chest until at last to her pressure there came a gagging spasm and the drowned woman spewed back the sea. They all three turned her to the side. They watched the life come back into her, air exchanged for water, and they this strange trinity mysteriously bound.

The woman opened her eyes and stared at the uncertainty of being back in the world.

It was an expression familiar to the Master, in parts dismay, puzzlement and relief. 'You're alive,' he told her. 'You're in the world still. Just lie there awhile.'

Then he took Josie's hand and held it tight and none of them spoke. The sea retreated and left silver on the sand. Though the men shivered they were unable to move; it was as if the scene had happened too fast and their minds were some way left behind in a fuddle. It was then that they heard the suck-sounds of cow hooves in the wet sand and out of the dark came Mick Daly, leaning on an ash branch and hobbling badly behind cow and calf.

'She came back,' he said. 'You must have turned her back from the water. She came back and found me. Knew she had busted my ankle. Had the calf right in front of me.' He stood a moment, and was so taken by this that it was a moment before he considered these figures before him and what they were doing. Mick Daly couldn't keep the smile from his face; it spread into the wild wool of his reddish sideburns. 'Fine bull calf too,' he said.

And this struck the Master so bizarrely, so wildly improbable, that he laughed. He laughed loud, his head back. The laughter came like dry hasps of cough, suppressed and yet squeezed through, laughs that were shudders, that convulsed him forward, laughing that would not be denied as hope returned and rushed into the old chambers of him with the news: *it will be all right, things will be all right*. And it felt to him then, his mind full of the crash and foaming of insights, of the first attempts to understand in the after-vision, as though the place had been found where a lever fitted that moved the world.

TWENTY-FOUR

Jay?

'Jay?'

A dull, muffled sound.

'Jay?'

Again, the sound that he wasn't able to distinguish yet as his name, it seemed to come from somewhere far above him.

'Jay, can you hear?'

He opened his eyes and Doctor Pellier was leaning over him with the brown smell of tobacco.

'You are awake, *c'est bon,*' he nodded and came closer and quickly in turn drew down the skin below each of Jay's eyes and peered in. 'You will have pain, it's normal, some discomfort as the morphine passes, but *quand même.*' He stood back, fished in his jacket pocket for cigarettes, found a crushed pack, lit one. '*Bienvenue,* welcome back,' he said, blowing the smoke high to the ceiling.

Jay studied the dream in front of him.

'*Tu as eu de la chance.* Yes, very good luck,' Pellier said, 'a clean incision, the knife was clean at least, yes? This was good luck. And the old man who found you, again good luck. Another would be dead. *C'est vrai.* But you, you do not die.'

179

The doctor considered this as he sucked as much of the cigarette as he could into him.

The room in the dream was familiar. It was the Boys' Ward, and a wheeled iron bed that had been set up by the far wall. Jay turned and saw the rest of the room was as it always was; his home for the last three years. He saw the other beds and the young patients, some sleeping, others propped on elbows to look down the room and see what was happening. Standing behind Pellier was Dembe and Bekele, to whom the doctor always gave the job of watching out for Sister Eucharia so that he could extinguish the cigarette in time. Everything was as it should be, except that Jay was in the bed.

'We have been very worried, you know. Seven days you were gone.' He puffed and shrugged at the same time, as though to doubly underscore his point.

Jay reached out his hand. Pellier was momentarily uncertain of what was wanted and thought for an instant it was the cigarette and he withdrew it from his mouth and hesitated and was about to pass it over when he understood. He transferred it carefully to his left hand, and then he took Jay's fingers firmly. The grasp was immediate and intense. Jay clung onto the doctor's hand and squeezed and, behind Pellier, Dembe and Bekele smiled white teeth.

The doctor was surprised by emotion; it came quickly into his eyes, and holding Jay's hand he felt the awkwardness of it; he feared the sentimental with that part of him that remained outside, that part that was doctor always dispassionately observing. So he shook the hand he held then as though in greeting.

'Yes,' he said, 'yes, very lucky,' and he blinked rapidly and then stood back, smoked left-handed, then withdrew the butt with his right.

'How did I get here?'

180

Pellier stubbed out the cigarette, then dropped the butt into his jacket pocket. He was suddenly comfortable again. 'The old man. He brought you. He knocked at the door. He said, "This one does not die." I asked him where he had found you and he told me the place. He said you had strong dreams. He said *esprit* – spirit – strong.'

Jay swallowed dryness and Bekele was at his side with water. He drank; the dream was over. He was alive there in the ward. 'Thank you.'

'You are good-good?' Bekele asked.

'The old man, I asked him if he wanted something, if I could pay something; *bon,* he said, no. He said maybe the dog would stay with him.' Pellier fished again for the cigarette pack. 'There was a dog.'

'Yes.'

'*Eh bien,*' he shrugged, 'it stayed with him.'

'And?'

'And *rien,* nothing.' He found the pack and had lifted it out when Dembe made a whistling sound through his teeth and the doctor quickly slipped it back as Sister Eucharia entered the ward.

'Well, Jay, you are awake.' She was a kind elderly nun with a thin frame but firm uncompromising grey eyes.

'Yes, Sister.'

'You gave us a fright.'

'*Oui oui,* I said,' Pellier told her, and at once turned his breath into his shoulder.

'I am sorry, Sister.'

'You'll get better quickly now,' she said. And the way she said it was both prediction and quiet command. 'Here, I brought this for you.' She put the postcard from Bridget on the bed, and she smiled and said, 'You know we were all praying for you? Isn't that right, Doctor?'

'Oh yes,' Pellier nodded, '*absolument.*'

Then she turned to leave and as she was going asked, 'Is there the faintest smell of smoke, Doctor?'

Theatrically he sniffed the air to the right and left of him. '*Non, non non,*' he said, '*des fleurs, je pense,*' and she was gone.

For several days, Jay remained in the intolerable heat in the bed at the end of the Boys' Ward. He vaguely began to remember what had happened, stepping his way through the night scene and towards the men coming about him. He could remember to the instant of the knife entering him, but he could not remember the old man or anything thereafter. When the doctor came to check on him on the second day, Jay said, 'there is something I need to do.'

'Not yet,' Pellier said. He was changing the dressing.

'I need to apologize to Desta.'

Pellier didn't stop bandaging. He didn't show the least sign of knowing or caring.

'I made a mistake and I need to tell her.'

The doctor worked on, the sweat glistening off his forehead.

'Can I walk?'

'No!' Pellier raised his head. 'No, I forbid it.'

'When can I walk?'

'When your doctor says.'

'But when? Tomorrow? The next day? When?'

Pellier shrugged, it was obvious. 'When you are healed.'

'Well, when will I be healed?'

The doctor threw his hands from his hips chest-high. 'Irish are so stubborn. *C'est vrai,*' he said. 'Who can say when? It depends. Lie back, be good patient, and heal. That is my directive to you. It is simple, do it!' He had more to say and he bore it in three furrows on his brow, but he kept his lips firmly pursed then and he did not tell what he knew about the girl. He shoved one hand into his jacket and took out a cigarette pack that was empty and he grunted and picked up his case and left.

That night, sleepless in the warm close dark, Jay slid his legs to the side of the bed and, holding one hand across the bandaged wound, he stepped down. Briefly his head swam, as though he was in the sea, and he leaned to the side for support. Steadied then, he moved to the end of the bed frame. One of the boys near him shot up sharply in his bed and stared at him as a ghost. The boy watched with wide fearful eyes some evil witnessed in his past, but he did not say anything and then lay back with slow resignation, into the sleep where terror was harboured.

Jay moved from bed to bed. His wound stung, as if a phantom knife remained. He came to the door of the ward and squeezed it open very slowly and then stepped out into the corridor. He went along it, feeling with one hand, holding the other against himself. He went up the stairs pulling on the handrail and then entered the hallway to the Women's Ward where Pellier was sitting in a chair in the hall as though waiting for him.

'Stubborn Irish,' he said. He had a bottle on the floor beside him and a glass in his hand. 'Stubborn as Africans.'

Jay did not know what to say.

'Sit!' Pellier commanded. And, exhausted by the effort of the short journey, Jay was glad to squat down and sit with his back against the wall.

Pellier took a quick drink and grimaced, either at the inadequacy of the wine or human nature. He said nothing for some time.

At last Jay began, 'I was just—'

'Shshsh!' Peller said sharply. 'You don't speak. Only Pellier speaks.' Again a long pause settled over them, then the doctor said, 'There is a village in France. In the *sud*. Near the *Côte d'Azur*. It is called Valbonne. There Pellier should be. He should be the doctor there, not here. He should stop there in the *place* for his *café* in the morning and watch the pigeons. He should sit in the shade of the trees and look at the lovely women there. *Mais pourqoui Pellier n'est-il-pas à Valbonne?* Why is Pellier not there?' He offered the question both of his upturned palms. 'Because he must be here. Because for his . . . his . . . *le mot?* His sins. For his sins he must be here until one day he will wake up and he can go back.'

He tipped the bottle to the glass. 'You have a cigarette?' he asked.

'I don't—'

'No! Pellier speaks,' he said. 'You have no cigarette, you have no sins. Pellier will tell you a story about the girl.'

'About Desta?'

'Shshsh! *Silence!*' He held the glass from beneath in the fingertips of both hands as if it were a chalice before him. 'Desta. Desta.' He looked into, then through the liquid. He sighed.

'I have no son,' he said, then quickly amended to, 'Pellier has no son. Maybe Pellier would have been a poor father. But he would have tried to . . . *conseiller*. Advise. Pellier's advice: go home. Go to Europe and learn. You are intelligent but you can learn more. You must go to university some years. Love some women. Live. Pellier says. This is the message you have been sent.' He drank the glass empty. 'You have no cigarettes? No, you have no cigarettes.'

'You were going to tell about Desta?'

'*Qui parle?* Who speaks? Shsh! Only the father speaks.' He placed one hand on his neck and slid it inside the opening of his shirt as if, while abstracted, he sought his own heart. 'Desta,' he said. 'You know she is pregnant?'

Jay felt he had been struck.

184

Pellier continued. 'She is *triste*, sad, but more than sad. There is no word. Who can say it? Who can say what it would be to see what she has seen? There is no cure for this. Pellier can give medicines, but not for this. Pellier knows. You know what she wants?'

'What?' Jay's voice was small.

'She wants to go and kill all the soldiers because then she will have killed the father.'

His hand remained inside his shirt, his head lowered. The dimension of the grief was enormous and robbed any possibility of speech for some time.

'I think I love her,' Jay said at last, and Pellier shook his head and let out a long loud sigh. He held up both hands as if to stop a train of feeling that was coming then.

'*Non non. Non. Et encore non.* You don't say this. *Absolument pas,*' he said. 'You don't get to say this.' He went to pour from the bottle by his feet but it was already empty. He frowned at it.

'It's true. I do think I love her.'

'The sadness you love. Pellier knows. The loneliness, the hurt, the strength; these, yes. These maybe you love. And you are *jeune homme* and you think you can love her to happiness. Like Africa. You can love away some sadness but this sadness you cannot. *C'est toujours là.* Always there. She will not believe your love. Listen to Pellier. Listen to your father.'

There was in the doctor's face a bright intensity and Jay did not reply. He sat on the floor feeling his wound sing. Some minutes later he understood why the doctor had been sitting all night in the hall. The door of the Women's Ward slowly opened and Desta stepped out. She carried the blanket from the bed like a bundle at her shoulder. She stopped when she saw them.

'Stubborn as Irish,' Pellier said.

185

Jay stood, and again felt the sea in his head. He reached out to the wall for support. Then he tried to draw a deep breath to keep himself from shaking. But he shook anyway. He stepped forward and she looked uncertainly a moment, but her head was erect and her eyes full of pride and resolve.

When he stood before her, Jay thought she was more beautiful than in his imagining.

'I am sorry,' he said. Then he said it again in Amharic as Bekele had taught him.

She looked directly at him. Then, with slow purpose, she raised one hand and placed it against the side of his face.

He could not speak.

The touch lasted a moment only then she withdrew her hand and went to walk past. The doctor got to his feet.

'No no. No go,' he said and held up his hands. 'Desta must stay, stay here.'

She shook her head and Pellier grew more animated, waving his arms and raising his voice. 'You have to stay! Desta sick. No go!' He danced back and forth in front of her, swaying a little with the wine.

She stood and watched him, then she looked at Jay.

He wanted to say something. He wanted to tell her he was sorry for all that she had suffered, for the sum of unutterable cruelty and torment, for the desolation of her family and all the grievous failing of imperfect humanity. He wanted to tell her he would give himself to repair it if he could. He would give himself to be proof of another side of man, and that he would love her and love the child she was carrying. He wanted to ask her to give him that chance, and in return he would ask nothing for himself. She did not have to love him, only allow him to love her. So it pulsed in his heart, this pure stuff of a selfless loving. He did not think that he barely knew her, that they had shared less than a dozen words, that the loving was an invention founded on pity.

None of that reached his mind. In the state he was in he did not care what the reasons for love were, he did not examine its psychology nor consider the reality of how it would be, how they might live and where, what life might be theirs. In the blind white innocence of it, he knew only the force of the emotion and its completeness. It was the first time his heart was taken over, occupied, filled with the kind of absolute feeling that in later life is thought of by old men with mixed reverence and embarrassment. If he could he would have put down a cloak beneath her. For although he could not have worded it then, what he wanted was nothing less than to remake the world for her in more perfect form.

What she saw of this in his eyes she didn't show. She stood some moments before turning back into the ward.

Pellier collapsed back into his chair. He exhaled loudly, then began a new search in his pockets for cigarettes. When he had found the empty packet he looked at it in puzzlement, then turned to Jay who was still standing.

'My advice,' he said, 'take out your heart and jump on it. *Oui oui*. Make it break before it does.' Slowly he shook his head. 'You have no cigarette, *non?*'

TWENTY-FIVE

The following day, Jay woke thinking of things he could do for her. There were no flowers to pick, no gifts to buy. Although he had stopped playing it, he still had the timber flute he had brought with him from Ireland, and now took it out and tried to finger the tunes. He sat up in the bed and, because of his wound, blew very thinly while fingering the stops. But this was enough for the boys in the beds there to raise their heads and listen. They had no familiarity with those rhythms, and yet quickly found in jigs and reels what Pellier that afternoon called a '*cousinage*'.

'I can't play very well,' Jay said.

'*Pas vrai*,' Pellier frowned. 'There is feeling. *C'est ça le but*. What else is art for?'

'Is she . . . ?'

'Yes. She is there still.'

'I thought I would play . . . for the women in the . . . Women's Ward.'

'*Bravo*.' Pellier shoved his hands deep into his jacket pockets. 'The heart will break but *tant pis,* never mind. Who listens to Pellier? Not even Pellier when Pellier's heart was broken.' He walked away.

In the evening after the meal trays had been taken, Jay played for the Boys' Ward a soft subdued version of those jigs and reels he had remembered. Music like Jay's was not in their lives and while he played they remained absolutely still, because the notes were like a fragile substance that floated with delicacy on the air. They did not applaud but rocked their entire bodies up and down on the thin mattresses and said the Amharic word for 'more'.

Later, when Jay went up the stairs to the Women's Ward, Desta was sitting on the edge of her bed. She was not engaged in any conversation or activity, but sat looking away into the horizon as had now become her habit. Her stillness, her ability to occupy a perfect quiet, was astonishing to one so restless as Jay. The women patients looked at the young man with the flute and some smiled and others scowled depending on their experience of men. All considered him, and awaited his first actions like an episode in which the true nature of hero or villain is revealed.

Jay stood just inside the door. The bandaging of his midriff was tight and his breath shallow. He blew to warm up the channel of the flute and the hollow sound brought an anticipatory murmur from some of the women. One said the flute was like *washint* that was played by shepherds in that country. Desta turned to look at him.

He played. He played 'Sweeney Astray' and 'The Skylark Sings' and 'The Mountain Top' and 'The Clare Reel'. He played even though his side ached and his fingers sweated with the heat of the ward. He played from the memory of his life in the classroom of the Master's two-room schoolhouse when all were being taught the tin whistle. Then he had played to see the smile in the Master's eyes as he clapped the time. Now he played with his eyes shut so as not to lose concentration by seeing Desta's face.

He played the jigs 'The Gold Ring' and 'The Humours of

Ennistymon' and then the reel 'Come West Along the Road'. He played them, aware of how foreign they were in the world that was Ethiopia, and yet how familiar to him. While he played he suffered the notes in a wave of nostalgia that rose even as he tried to push it down.

When he stopped he opened his eyes. There was complete silence.

The women looked at him as though in the charm of the music they anticipated a magic that would accompany it. Perhaps this is what he thought himself. Perhaps he had imagined some transformational moment. But none came. No one spoke. Desta turned away to reconsider the faraway horizon once more.

After an acute, awkward moment, Jay turned and went back to his ward.

Suffering an anguish familiar to the unrequited, he fed himself a soup of longing and loathing. Thorns of self-disgust he added, so that soon an indigestible repugnance was his. How repulsive he was. His nose was enormous, his hands great flapping knobs of nothing. His forehead, scarred from the sunburn of his first weeks in Africa, was patchy and uneven under his fingers. His cheek where her hand touched was rough with his not-yet beard.

What did she think of him? She could only despise him as he did himself.

Twisted in the bed covers, he was wild as a bird in a blanket. When he could take no more he rose in the night and went out and to Women's Ward where Pellier was again keeping guard in his chair and studying in an abstract way a ladder of smoke he sent heavenward. He had his back to Jay but did not turn around to look as he said: 'It is a curse, this love, *non?*'

'I could not sleep.'

'*Bien sûr.*' He indicated a second chair he had brought. Jay sat. He hugged both arms across his wound.

'You want a cigarette?' the doctor asked, and then withdrew the pack saying, 'Of course no, you don't. You are too pure still. Another night *peut-être.*' He lit another cigarette from the butt, stabbed that out and pocketed it in his jacket. '*Tu as de l'imagination. C'est vrai.* Great imagination. To be able to imagine what kind of life for you and she, *non?* Love and im- agination, terrible combination, fatal really. Yes.' Rolling his lower lip he blew the smoke over and back until it was gone.

Jay said nothing. He held onto himself

'The music was good. A good stratagem. But not enough now. Too late now, I think. For her all that is too late.' He blew a loud sigh. 'But you will still imagine. That is the beauty you have. Imagine the world can be . . .' he paused. He put the cigarette in his mouth to free both hands and he held them a little apart as if right in front of him was the spinning world and he was on the point of reaching out and grasping it. Then he did. '. . . stopped. And *guéri,* cured, fixed. This is your kind of love, *mon cher.* Is it not?' The doctor nodded. 'Pellier knows, worse kind,' he said, and took the cigarette from his lips and flicked the ash. 'Find the heart, *et le casse,* break it. *C'est un bon conseil.* Really. I tell you the truth, it is the only hope.'

Jay did not reply and shortly the ward door opened and Desta appeared as before, a bundle at her back and her bare feet stepping near silently into the corridor. She stopped when she saw them.

'See, she escapes again,' Pellier said. 'Impossible.'

Jay stood up and went to her. 'Please don't go,' he said in Amharic, just that, 'please don't go.'

She studied his face, but if she took in its kindness truth or goodness she did not show it.

'Please don't go,' Jay said, and in English told her what he could not have known or promised, 'It will be all right. It will be all right.'

And she did not move forward or back until Pellier coughed and stood and said, 'A terrible thirst, *excusez-moi*. I must go and get something. You should . . . the chairs, *asseyez-vous,* sit, sit, doctor's orders. Send her back to her bed soon.'

He left them in their own awkward company, each variously burdened and fearful and yet standing there and not moving away. They were of an age. They had each known the death of parents, loss of home and hope, and the loneliness of survival.

Jay held out his hand to indicate the chairs, and she took hold of it, startling him. Holding his hand she looked at his eyes, and he felt the company suddenly quieten and sit down inside him. She released his hand and went to Pellier's chair.

'I want,' he said in English, 'to help you, to be of some good to you. I want to do things for you.'

She sat impassively. He could think of no way of reaching her and then put his hand over his heart and gestured the giving of it. 'Love,' he said.

She watched, her eyes deep and still and sad and he could not tell what she had understood.

'I will not touch you,' he said, and shook his hands and his head. 'I will not.'

And he thought then that he felt something begin to flow towards him like the first trickle of a stream in the dust. He thought he saw tenderness amidst the sorrow in her eyes, and impulsively and for no reason other than the hope of making her smile, he hummed a jig he had played on the flute, and he danced a step of no dance while holding onto the ache in his side. But she smiled. And so he threw up his arms in the air and clapped them together and hummed on

193

still, jigging the tune faster, trying to be ever more comic to keep that smiling happening.

When he stopped, she put her smile behind a hand. He sat next to her, catching his breath, and with the perfect innocence of lovers was at one then with all those who in a moment of their own exuberance and passion have thought they have healed the world.

But already her smile was gone, and she folded her hands into each other and turned her head to the side, as though her own grief chastised her.

Jay thought he should dance again, but the ache at his wound pulsed and he was forced to wait.

Without a word, Desta stood then and he rose next to her. But already she was walking away from him. She went down the corridor though he spoke her name. She carried the bundle and entered the Women's Ward, and did not look back.

'Well, one thing's clear as a bell,' Ben Dack said, 'you can't be killed.'

He had come directly to the hospital when he'd heard, seen the undrowned girl and Jerzy Maski put in beds side by side for observation through the night, Mick Daly have his ankle set, and had then driven Josie and the Master home. Now, as they sat in dressing gowns in the kitchen, he wanted them to tell him the story again and again, but couldn't keep himself from interrupting. 'You can't,' Ben said, chuckling, 'you're like I don't know what. And Josie, my Josie, she saved him didn't she?'

'She did, Ben,' the Master said.

'Of course she did. One hundred and one per cent saint. Guaranteed. A three-person rescue though, by cripes. That's something. That's something else. Tell me now again, she was out how far? Because it was dark wasn't it? It was a dark night tonight, those clouds came in earlier and, well, its something, that's what it is, something. We'd be right to have a celebration. And we will. We will! What have we got? Have we anything good?' He crossed to the cupboards and began opening doors, but became at once perplexed by the crowded array of packaging, and Josie rose and said gently, 'I'll make something, Ben. You sit down.'

'Will you? Will you, Josie?' It was the gift of Ben Dack to be continually surprised by his wife's goodness, as though each time he thought he must have reached the end of it, or his deserving. Each time it moved him; if he had been told that it was he himself who was remarkable, that in fact kindness and goodness were more commonplace than supposed and it was only familiarity that caused them to go unnoticed, he would not have believed it for a moment. He was certain his Josie was a saint. 'Wonderful wonderful wonderful.' He smacked his palms, the width of his smile making buttons of his eyes. He pushed both hands deep into the pockets of his baggy corduroy trousers and turned as if to head off somewhere, found the space of his own kitchen small, and turned back again, and then to the Master said, 'Let me just shake your hand again.' He did, pumpingly. 'Because jeepers. Absolute. No question. Honest to god, honest to god heroic. Now tell me again: she was gone into the sea, the poor girl?'

'Joe is tired, Ben,' Josie said above the frying of the sausages.

'Of course, he is. And do we have anything, any bottle of anything? What goes good with a sausage? Would you take a drop of something, Master, something with a bit of . . . we have Paddy's, I'd say don't we Josie?'

'Just a cup of tea would be lovely, Ben, thank you.'

'A cup of tea ordered, and that much Ben Dack can provide.' He spun about and headed towards the cupboards again, as if commencing an expedition and having every hope of success. But at once he grew puzzled by coordinates and scanned the countertop for where things might be, then, considering the components necessary for the task and making a mental inventory, he took down three mugs, paused, studied the area once more, realized he was lost, then asked, 'Where might we have tea bags, dear?'

'The tea is made, here you go, Ben,' Josie told him.

'Perfect. Tea is made. Perfect,' he said. 'Will I pour?'

'Do.'

'Right. Ben to pour. There you go now, as ordered one tea,' Ben said proudly. 'Now milk and sugar. Milk and sugar? Josie, we . . . ? There they are, that's right. Perfect. There you go.'

The sausages arrived, and with them eggs, and the three sat in the late night around the kitchen table and said no more of the rescue. Then the Master thanked them both and excused himself, and Ben shook his hand once more and Josie told him to sleep deep and dream well.

He went up the stairs, the exhaustion meeting him at every step, and when he came into the tiny bedroom he thought he would collapse. But the events of the night were too vivid and perplexing, the various pieces still floating unattached in his spirit, and though his body ached and needed rest, his mind was far from sleep; he sat at the small table and turned on the laptop. Its bluish light ghosted his face. He entered the site and by habit ran the search. It was impossible to suppose the sea-rescue in any way connected to his seeking of his grandson, it was outside of reason and logic and all accepted laws of causality; but so too was he. He was his own First Proof of the Improbable. He was Senior Professor of Mystery, and like any in the blind depths of suffering could continue only by holding to a thin thread of belief: things had meaning, there was an order, even if it defied understanding. This was the position he took, but like any in the face of mystery what he still craved was an instant of clarity. *Just a glimpse. Why did I have that feeling, that sense of the sea, and that I had to go there. I saw it; I actually saw it. Why? Was it just chance that girl was there?*

The search engine returned with no matches found and his spirit sank a little.

It's not that simple is it? It's not going to be that simple.

He pressed the heels of his hands into his eyes. He lowered his head and was aware of the shallowness of his breath and the low murmur-beat of his heart.

The girl was saved. The girl was saved, that's what counts.

He regained himself and sat upright and clicked the icon to enter the 'Searchers' room. There was a posting ten minutes earlier from H-47. It said, 'I had some good news today I'd like to share with you all. You see, I am not a parent like so many of you, but I come across quite a few children without parents down here. They seem to just end up as it were at the mission and we take them in for a time and whatnot and sometimes they go off again and sometimes they stay quite a while. We're a kind of station along the way I suppose, and, well, to get to the point – H-47 rather fearful that H-47's point is often unpointed, I don't do sermons any more – but no, there was this boy. I'll say his name was A, and he was quite young and seemed to have been living by stealing whatever he could until he became very ill indeed. And well, he's been with us for some months, in and out of the hospital, and recuperating with us here, and today we got the news he's got the all-clear.'

The posting finished. Then a moment later, there was another. 'H-47 again, I'm so sorry, I should have said he had been diagnosed with leukaemia.'

The Master wrote back immediately. 'I don't know him but I can feel your happiness and am very glad. MATER.'

'Mater, so nice to hear from you. Indeed yes, I am decidedly happy. And that is not a word I have recently attributed to myself, so the bounty is plentiful. It's so important to acknowledge, isn't it? Simplest things. I used to fear I was terribly terribly sentimental and this was an affliction no serious person had. But in my latter years I seem to, well, lose the baggage of judgement. So, yes. Now what is new in your world?'

'A girl was saved from drowning here tonight,' the Master began. He typed single-fingered and stooped over and wrote the events of the evening clearly. He wrote at length and told of his earlier vision of the sea to his doubting his sanity and right on to his finding himself in the dark water. He wrote it without colour or comment, a sequence of actions, and at the end he paused and then added, 'That's what happened. I don't understand it. But that's what happened. MATER.'

'Allow me to say back to you I also am so very glad,' H-47 wrote. 'What an evening! What adventures! Only in my later years have I come to understand and even welcome mystery. Not everything fits, you see, in our comprehension, but allowing for mystery I find allows for there being something greater. Apologies, temptation to sermonize a constant weakness in H-47. No, but really, absolutely wonderfully glad. And for the Good Lord gifting me insomnia or I would have missed all this.'

The Master replied again and the night-correspondence continued on the theme of mystery. They wrote to each other back and forth deeper into the small hours, sometimes in single lines, ('I was dead and came back. MATER.' 'Astonishing. I myself am dying but don't think I will be back. H-47'), sometimes in long passages that wound around topics as various as fishing, the importance of boredom, the music in our memories, the flying of kites, the sense of a plot, the satisfactions of endings, and novels, even Charles

Dickens. It continued all across that dark piece-mooned night, a kind of answering to both that, although they did not know each other or would ever meet, brought deep consolation. For hours they made steady traffic of thought and feeling, each one by the strange impersonality of the Internet freed to be more personal.

The first light rising in the fields of Clare outside, the last exchanges took place. H-47 signed off; he said his day's duties had already begun. Each knew they would look for the other on the screen again, and there would be further correspondence, but neither wrote it. The Master thanked H-47 and, some moments later, received thanks back. Then he closed down the lid of the laptop and the light to which he turned his face was day.

TWENTY-SIX

In the morning Jay woke from a dream of butterflies. He had never dreamt them before and lying in the bed he tried to decipher them. They were inside him, he decided, and with that decided also that he was healed enough to return to work. He had a lightness of heart. Later, he thought, he would find the old man that had saved him and thank him. He would bring a bone for the dog. He was filled with such. Like a chalice he bore his strange luminosity out of the ward and down the corridor.

He met Doctor Pellier standing with his back to the wall outside the Women's Ward. He was not smoking. He was standing with his head tilted back, his face upward and his hands buried in his pockets.

'*Désolé,* I am sorry,' he said. 'She has gone.'

She had left in the night, shortly after Jay had seen her. One of the women told him.

'For what is medicine?' Pellier said.

'What? She's gone. What are you doing? We should be after her.'

'*Pour rien*. For nothing if it does not mend the spirit.' He shrugged. 'She is gone, I am sorry.'

Jay walked away from him. He went up the stairs as quickly as he could and he took the small bag of his things and came down and rushed out of the front door.

Where was the place where was she from that's where she'll go. Where? Where think think. The east. It was east of here. She will go there. Won't she? But Pellier said she wanted to kill all the soldiers. She wants to kill all the soldiers because that way she will have killed the father. Isn't that what he said? Wasn't that it, the soldiers? Where? Where then? Where would she go to kill the soldiers? And how? What would she think?

Think.

Come on.

You'll find her you'll find her you will.

He came out into the brilliance of sunlight and shielded his eyes and hurried away into the noisy crowded streets of the city. There seemed as always ten thousand pedestrians, a great flux of people and sound. Addis Ababa pulsed with such a surreal mix of lives: here was a barefoot boy carrying a kicking goat against his chest, next to him two men immaculate in business suits and white shirts; here stern watchful policemen with rifles, there two men in running singlets holding hands. There were old women bent forward under bundles of firewood, water, bulging sacks upon their heads; there were well-dressed women with bright-coloured parasols, others alongside them in *hijabs*. There were white-bearded old men with dusty garments and ancient knotty *dula* walking sticks, these next to young boys in shiny football shirts. The mass moved constantly, a restless traffic of feet.

At the first crossroads he tried to intuit which way she had gone. He stood next to a young man carrying the single-stringed *masengo* and bow to soon begin his day's playing. He wore the traditional woven cotton *gabi* over his shoulder and looked at Jay directly as though Jay were a messenger who was about to announce something. Jay hurried away into the flow of people, scanning all directions, in the first frantic haste of that searching.

He reasoned she might have followed the main roadway, and he hurried along. He was not unaware that the last time he had been in the city he had been stabbed by the man Jefta and he bore a tight apprehension even as he searched in the crowds. His right hand he kept pressed to the bandaging. Because it was apparent he was not Ethiopian, children came up to him asking would he buy single packets of tissues, would he buy these good shaving razors, would he buy a hen's egg, would he buy a hen? They ran alongside him some of the way, then found another prospect and left him alone.

An hour Jay walked in the city, then another. He passed the impossibly green lawn of the Sheraton Addis Hotel, and went on until he was out by the individual compounds of wire and tin behind which were the flat-roofed houses. At one point two trucks of government soldiers sped past him. A man came out to look at their dust, then stared at him as though he was some part of the story.

He walked on, out of the crowdedness and onto broken dust roads where there were young men sitting on the ground in a cluster of their unemployment, having exhausted talk they now watched the day pass. He walked into hunger and out through the other side of it. He walked into the noon and the afternoon, and he did not find her. Then he thought *she has left the city.* And he stopped, tired and hot and empty. He sat on the roadside and lowered his head onto his knees. Paused, his wound pulsed. He sat there and hugged his arms about himself. Then it came to him: *Nazret.* The name of the place she came from was Nazret. It was to the south and east. He got up, suddenly refreshed, and walked towards the ragged outer limits of Addis Ababa, and by the time the sun was setting behind his back he was out of that city, not yet knowing that he would not return.

The hunger came back and brought with it weakness and with that the fierce dogs of doubt. What was he doing? How could he find her? What would she say if he caught up with her on the road?

Night came swiftly from the mountains. Darkness deepened all his feelings. In darkness he loved her more; he doubted more.

The road was thinly trafficked. Car lights came from nowhere and threw his shadow in front of him and then diminished it. Smoothly an oil tanker came past. *Would she have hitched a lift? Would she trust anyone?* He did not think so, but in truth he couldn't know. He walked on in the fierce loneliness that was his, head low, shoulders high and curved forward against all – whether inquisitive, well-meaning or lawless. At one place he was joined by a herd of camels led by men with sticks and thick knotted hair. They did not seem to notice him, and led their herd crossways to the road into nothingness. He walked as the road cooled beneath his bare feet and stars studded the profiles of the mountains. He walked because he did not want to rest and because suddenly the country there seemed full of unseen peril. What animals waited in the dark, his mind imagined? And between reality and imagination he would find no sleep. So he went on and came into Akaki in the between-hours when only one old man with a goat walked down the centre of the street. They passed as ghosts, their eyes meeting as if to ascertain they were not dreaming, but said no words.

Jay walked by broken-down tin-roofed dwellings where

he did not think any could be living, yet he heard a child crying and the voice of a mother stirring from sleep.

With the sun rising, he had come to Debre Zeyit. He was so weak he knew he could not continue without food and at a door he knocked. A woman opened it and squinted at the strange beggar who wore the dust of the road in his hair and on his face. Jay opened his bag towards her and gestured the offering of anything inside for food.

The woman mistrusted, and she looked behind him for thieves and then behind her for her husband. Then she glanced in the bag. She pushed aside the flute and took out the T-shirt that had the words Evolution Tour written on it. Then she raised a hand to tell him to wait and she went inside and shut the door. When she opened it again she had some *injera* pancake and a small bag of roasted corn, *kolo*. Jay took them and thanked her and gestured drinking and she went inside again and brought him a large glass Coca-Cola bottle filled with water. It had a cloth bung for a top and appeared very old. He drank from it and she watched him and watched behind and down the street for the thieves who might be coming yet. Then she took back the bottle and went quickly inside and shut the door.

He walked all that day and on towards the night. Before sunset he saw fish-eagles flying above and he followed their flight some time before they seemed to vanish in high air. He passed huge fig trees and sought for the fruit but found none ripe. He rationed the pieces of corn, sucking each one slowly for flavour. The land rose into the mountains. Rain was coming at last, but not yet. A truck labouring on the road had four children pushing it and when he caught up he thought the two boys looked like Bekele and Dembe and he gave his help. When the engine fired and coughed a blue plume, the children fell back laughing. He smiled at the marvel of their smiles and thought not for the first time how incongruous it was that in that country were the world's most magnificent smiles. The father waved for all to run and jump on and he did then, and sat on the rattling flatback beneath a most deeply blue sky. The father did not want to risk stopping the truck again, and so it shook and coughed on, climbing the mountain road until it came near Nazret. And there they met the soldiers.

There was commotion. The truck stopped and the engine died. Jay and the children got down. Two soldiers were standing with guns cradled, and some distance behind them there was a small crowd and two Jeeps and more soldiers.

The father got out of the cab and threw up his hands and said something to the engine. Then he went to the soldiers to enquire about the delay.

He came back to his children, shaking his head and sucking breath between clenched teeth as though the air was thickly soured.

'What is it? What?' Jay asked him.

The father shook his head.

Jay went past him then. The soldiers raised their guns and told him to stay back. Some in the crowd further up the road turned to look, and in that moment he saw Desta dead on the ground.

TWENTY-SEVEN

If there was clemency, the prisoner did not feel it. He felt only the randomness of fate.

The light in his cell was turned on when he thought it was night. The door lock sounded and the bolts slid back and then two men were standing there and he thought his life was going to end now. He thought *they cannot torture me any more, they will kill me now.* And he did not resist the hands that grabbed his arms and led him into the corridor. He saw the line of cell doors for the first time and then one of the men said 'hey' and pointed and the other said 'Christ' and quickly drew out a grey cotton bag from his pocket and roughly put it over the prisoner's head.

Blindly he moved on with cuffed hands and ankles, shuffling in short clipped unstrides that are unknown in nature but are man's invention so that not even a step is free.

'Here,' he heard. Then two hands turned his shoulders. 'Go on Ali,' one said, 'in this way.'

There was the sound of another door opening and then one of the men said: 'Steps!'

He banged into the first. Then he realised they were rising, and the manacles made them difficult, each one a kind of crooked climb as he put his weight to one side and hoisted his leg.

There was again a door, and then, for the first time it seemed in half a lifetime, there was the air of day.

He was outside.

He could smell the freshness and he angled his head back to suck breath from the opening of the bag at his neck. What he smelled was summer, even there in the concrete yard that he crossed he smelled the warm, tangled scent. The sensation was as intense as a sudden memory blowing open a flap in his mind and he stopped. One of the men said, 'Hey! Hey Ali, come on!' and pulled him onward by his shoulder.

It was summer. He was outside in summer.

I am going to be killed in summer.

He shuffled on across the yard and he heard the heavy sliding of a van door and then, 'Bend down, step up. Step here. Here!' Hands grasped one of his calves and guided a step. He got up and hit his head on the doorframe and one of the men laughed and the other said, 'Sit. Sit.'

The door slid closed, the smells of summer gone.

The engine started and he could smell the diesel fumes and he did not know if he was alone or not and he said, 'Is anyone there? Is there anyone?'

'Shut up.'

'Where am I going? Where are you taking me?'

'Shut. Up.'

'I have a right to know,' he said, then he felt the muzzle of a gun pressed against the bag at his temple. He pulled back.

'Now Ali, shut up!'

'My name is not Ali! '

'Bang!'

The van drove out over cobblestones.

Where am I?

It doesn't matter. What does it matter? They are going to kill you. What do you do? Think of something. Anything. Think of something, something you remember. Think. They say your life flashes in front of you. Where is my life then? What is flashing? Nothing.

Think. Remember.

Then he felt a small dart of pain that was gone before he even knew it was pain. Then he remembered no more.

When Ahmed Sharif opened his eyes in the next life he saw the sky. He saw a blue sky and white clouds only and he stared at it for a long time, unsure if it was above or below him.

He watched the sky until he heard the traffic. Then he lifted his two hands together to touch his own face and he discovered he was no longer chained.

He opened his arms as wide as he could, lying there on the ground, not far from where traffic was passing, and he laughed. He laughed hard. He laughed so his body shook and his eyes watered and turned the laughter to crying.

At last, he stood. He looked at where the manacles had been on his ankles and he bent down and rubbed the calluses on the skin. Then he blinked the tears and sleeved his face and he looked at what was written on lorries and shop fronts and he realized he was in Poland.

TWENTY-EIGHT

Though they had known each other for many years, they seemed unlikely companions, the two men standing out on the middle deck of the car ferry, crossing from northern France to the southeast tip of Ireland. One of them was Father Gustave, a thin man in his late twenties, pale and energetic, smoking his restlessness into the sea wind. The other was a strongly built man of sixty-one, with blue tattoos covering every inch of him, including his shaven head and face; his name was Whatarangi. In the summer night he wore a heavy red-plaid jacket, thick trousers of coarse cloth and fisherman's white boots. Lately he had taken to a pipe and, whether lit or unlit, he liked the perch of it at the corner of his mouth; it kept him from his temper, it allowed him to suck back in the anger and bite occasionally on the stem. Besides, he thought it apt for the book he had been slowly, painfully reading for the past three years; *Moby Dick* had taken Whatarangi's imagination. In the small room upstairs in the priest's house where the blue man lived now, he often thought the walls to be the creaking stressed timbers of a whaler sailing from Nantucket. He spent whole days thinking himself in the sea. Ever since a heart attack had stopped him dead on a street in Frankfurt when, mistrusting his tattooed face, none had come to his aid, Whatarangi had understood he would never get back to New Zealand. He thought his life was borrowed now and the whale could come for him at any time. 'I am mostly salt,' he told Father Gustave solemnly when the priest said pipe-smoking would kill him. 'Smoking is nothing. Salt is what kills. Fifty years of salt fish, salt potatoes, bread and salt on butter. Salt. Little white sails filling up the channels of my blood. Smoking helps clear the salt.'

Gus had known him in Frankfurt before he had returned to the priesthood, when they lived in a condemned building with others transient through Germany from all corners of Europe. Gus had hidden there some years in the strange high places of hashish and marijuana after God had betrayed him and let his father die. He might have stayed there in the puzzle of meaning but for the moment on Friedrichstrasse when he found Whatarangi collapsed in the street. He had prayed for him and told the passers-by he was a priest and to call the ambulance, and when the prayers had made no difference there on the pavement he had bargained that he would return to the priesthood if his friend was spared.

Now, they stood and watched the night-sea flow past. Neither had been in Ireland before and had little idea of what it was like. Whatarangi thought it would be like Nantucket. He thought there might be whales, and he sucked hard on his pipe, on the remnant tobacco and salt air slipping into a waking dream-state where the world was inverted and the island they approached was New Zealand.

Gus thought of his mother. He thought it is only in the experience of death that faith is tested or understood. It was only when the priest came and told him that his mother was dead that he realized he had to believe now that heaven was actual. He felt her absence more than he had her presence, and the

212

guilt common to sons was his. Before him the night sky met the sea, a bleed of ink, and into it he stared with contrition and tried to consider an afterlife where now his mother was meeting his father. He tried to truly picture it – what did she walk on? Was there ground, was there grass, was it cloud? Was there no walking, only floating? Were there wings? How did she move, how did she enter heaven? By the mythical gates or was there none? Did she simply arrive, a short Polish woman in a heavy brown wool coat and headscarf, shopping bag still clutched in her hand? Was there a great crowd of souls before her – she would have turned back, she had been frightened by crowds since the war. How did she enter? Did she have to seek out her husband or was there some means by which he knew she was coming and from the multitudes came forward to meet her? Would he have aged, would he be like her now or still the young man he was when he died? What was it like? How did it happen?

While the ferry pressed on against the night, Gus pressed at the frontier of heaven. He could not say for certain what he believed, and though he had not seen his mother often in the recent past, he felt the absence of her now as though a part of the known geography of the world had been removed. He smoked in a fitful manner and tossed flaring half-cigarettes onto the wind. Ahead of him, in darkness still, lay Ireland. He could have phoned with the news. He could have found the phone-number of one of the workers and sent the word, but he wanted to tell it in person. He wanted not to continue as an absence, and he looked directly above him into the blue-black to see his mother and father watching him. But he could not and, as though he might escape the sadness that he was bringing with him, he began to quickly pace the deck.

TWENTY-NINE

Jerzy was upstairs in the bedroom he shared with Laslo. His uncle had insisted that he not return to work for a week: he was a hero, Laslo had told him; he had saved the Irish girl *and* the old schoolmaster *and* a cow! He would still be paid but was not to even think of coming to the sea-houses. But the free time was burdensome for Jerzy; after a good rest he felt perfectly well, and now, when the others left the house at six in the morning, he was awake in an emptiness that made him uneasy. He tidied up the sink, he filled bags of rubbish and another of cans, he turned on the radio for a short time, but there was too much talk and not enough music. He sat on the couch, his big hands clasped between his legs, week-old copies of *Warsaw Gazetta* on the floor.

He couldn't read them. He had the strange sensation that they were completely alien, typeface, photographs, headlines about transport or emigration, all seemed *unreal* in the small sitting room of the empty house. Things when looked at in the bare light of that morning appeared dull and lifeless; had he ever actually looked at that place where they lived, the flattened worn carpet the landlord had put down in all rooms, the cheapest of furniture? All wore a sorry air of loneliness, and Jerzy got up from the couch and went into the kitchen – eight steps – where he found the sink tap dripping and went to get the tools to fix it. It was a ten-minute job. When it was done he turned on and off the water several times to be sure, watched carefully in case a drip gathered. But throughout this, moving forward in his mind all the time, was the image of the girl he had carried from the sea. The startling reality of *her*, the feel of her in his arms; how she had entwined about him in the blind waters so it seemed she was the one who found her rescuer: these were what dominated his thought. He knew nothing of her or why she had tried to drown herself, what had driven her, but there she was now, swimming in his mind.

He turned the tap on full, let the water rush too quickly for the sinkhole, then shut if off sharply. No drips. He stared at the tap some moments, then snapped his jacket from the door-hook and left the house.

He should go to the hospital, he should check on the girl. Then he thought his English not good enough and that she would not know who he was. He argued both sides back and forth as he walked around in the town. In the late morning, the narrow streets were frequented by a mixed population of the new Ireland, African women with prams, young dark-suited men on mobiles, coffee-breaking tilers, plumbers and painters with the strong features of eastern Europe, a scattering of town and country people. Jerzy walked up through the market, past the French crêpe van, the Indian carpet man, the jams and plants of Rainbow Farm, the egg man, the boot and shoe man, the woman selling angel cards and incense sticks. He went around by the side of Old Ground Hotel and crossed then into the cathedral of Saints Peter and Paul. He always took the back pew. He knelt and bowed and said the Hail Mary in Polish in his mind. He asked God to mind his mother, and then he quickly blessed himself and left.

He went down alongside the single traffic of Jeeps and newer cars that snaked up O'Connell Street and crossed by the monument that was to someone he didn't know. He followed the crooked elbow of Abbey Street on the way that led towards the hospital, but when he came to the bridge over the Fergus River he stopped. He shouldn't go to see her. It was an intrusion. The rescue had been chance and he had done his part and now it was for others to care for her. He stood on the bridge. The river ran swiftly below. He was to turn back, he was to go back up the town, but what force propels one life into another was already engaged in him, and he went on to the hospital.

The girl was already gone home.

He nodded his head to the nurse, 'Not here,' he said, 'yes, understand, I understand.'

He went back into the town and discovered in the midst of his disappointment that he carried a yearning now, as though it was something he had picked up, and that now moved into his bloodstream.

A thick curtain of cloud had come from the west, the sunlight paled opaquely, and the streets seemed drained of their earlier energy. He walked up through Ennis and out the end of it and back to the house in the estate. When he got there he saw there was an old car with a German registration in the driveway, and before he could put his key in the door, his uncle Laslo opened it from the inside. He had been brought home early from work and his grey eyes were brimming. He saw his nephew and he seized him in an embrace and held tight, and was holding still as in the hallway behind him appeared a giant blue man sucking a pipe and the brother Jerzy had not seen in three years. The moment he saw Gus, the knowledge came to Jerzy in a cold instant, it came without words like a chill wind and he cried out 'Mama' and he knew that she was dead.

*　　*　　*

The Master had taken the kite to the hill. The hot summer had gone and the day threatened the first rain in a long time. The wind was brisk. He had suffered no after-effects from the sea rescue, and went up the hill fields at a steady pace, as if late for an appointment. When he reached the higher ground that was too rough for meadowing and was used for winter grazing, the grass was to his knees, and he waded forward holding up the kite and pressing on until he came to the big rock where he liked to fly.

He was happy to be away from the house below. Since the rescue, Ben and Josie's neighbours called a little more frequently. Mostly they brought cakes and scones with their questions, and sat looking at him, further confirmed in their belief that he was an oddity. They were wary of him, as if his return from the dead signalled ill-luck not good, or they believed calamity would follow him now. When he did not indulge their desire for a detailed and dramatic story, invariably they began to tell their own, whatever they knew of drownings, of sea-horrors and, whenever they ran out of these, general suicides. The Master excused himself as soon as he could; he slipped away to see if H-47 was there, and when he was not, and if there was good wind, he took the kite out through the back door and went up the hill.

At the flying place he laid down the kite and put the two spools of twine on top to hold it. He leaned back against the rock and put up his face to let the wind tell him where it was. The sky was moving to the south. He looked at the white clouds a long time. He watched the direction of drift and commingle, the slow traffic of atmosphere and vapour, and he thought of Jay. *You are alive. I know you're alive because I'm alive, because I didn't drown.* He wanted to believe his grandson might hear him, or if not hear, then know; because if he knew, he would return, and because if he didn't have this thin faith then all the rest – his own

218

double return from death, his continuing and being cared for – had no meaning. And suffering must have meaning, he thought, and he thought then of the old man in *The Old Man and the Sea* whom he had taken as an image of his own father. When the old man in the book was suffering, and when he wanted so to catch the fish, he had said aloud, 'I am not religious', but then he had prayed and promised to make a pilgrimage to the Virgin de Cobre if he would be allowed to catch it. *He had prayed mechanically, wasn't that right? What? Hail Marys and Our Fathers. But more Hail Marys because Hail Marys were easier, he said. I remember that. And after the praying, he wrote: 'feeling much better but suffering exactly as much.' I remember that too.*

He went then to fly the kite. For once the lines of the two spools were not entangled and he unwound more or less equal lengths and then lifted the kite to let it feel the wind and then released it. It pulled back hard and fast and he had to move quickly with both wrists flicking over the spools to let it up and away. It climbed in seconds, swinging right and left, flapping, buffeted, its long tail playing. He double-handed it higher, snapping both lines in short quick pulls before unspooling another twenty feet. *This is a wind we haven't had. This is autumn coming.* It had been a summer of record, the heat and dryness running alongside the headlines for months, the country first luxuriating in the sensual delight of such warmth before the farming alarms began, before the lakes began retreating underground and the rivers slowed. It had been a season that burned itself into memory, a summer some remembered out of childhood, but others warned that if it came again would mark the beginning of the end of greenness there. *But now it is ending. I can feel it. The kite hasn't had this kind of wind. There is rain in it. There is rain coming. And look at the blackbirds. So many blackbirds today.* He watched the kite high above him against sky that was still blue and he felt then the dread of winter. He felt it with every year of him, as though the knowledge arrived in each organ and made it contract and shudder and feel its age. *Another winter.* It was not the cold but the dark that he dreaded, the blackness of the countryside at five o'clock that since Jay had gone made him feel a prisoner.

But I will survive winter. I will.

Then, perhaps because he was not as certain as he wished, and because he remembered that passage from the book, the Master prayed. He prayed Our Fathers first and then Hail Marys because, as the old man said, Hail Marys were easier. He prayed them mechanically and the words were little more than a mumble in the wind and could not even be recognized as prayers by anyone who might have come close to him. They were an old man's muttering. They followed one after the other as if from his chest were released butterflies, and he did not keep count nor did he burden any with specific petition. They were said with simplicity and innocence and continued even as the kite caught a sudden current of cross-air and veered sharply to the left, continued even as the old man let the lines pull him windily across that hilltop, moving him in quicksteps across the spongy grass with firm insistence, as though even while he continued praying it was the thing in the sky that was flying him.

The first rain-clouds were coming but no rain had fallen yet when like blackbirds the three men in dark suits with another behind them came up the hill. They were crossing the crest before the Master knew Jerzy and Laslo.

'I am coming to say thank you,' Jerzy said.

Both hands held up in the air with the twin lines, the Master looked at them over his shoulder.

'There is no need, no need at all, Jerzy,' he said, struggling with the fierceness of wind to spool in.

'I will not be taking lesson,' Jerzy said, laying the phrase

220

in English carefully as though it was a thing of stones. 'My mother has died.'

The Master stopped; the tension released, the kite fell. 'I am so sorry.'

Pipe in mouth, Whatarangi came forward and with a small bow gestured to be given the two spools and with easy expertise then tied in the kite.

'This is my brother Gus. He is priest. *A* priest.'

'Thank you for helping my brother,' Gus said.

'I am very sorry for your loss, Father. For both of you.'

'Yes.'

The Master shook their hands. The wind blew about them. 'This is Whatarangi, my friend.'

The blue man squeezed the Master's hand. 'It is a good kite,' he said.

They stood briefly in the company of the sorrow until the Master, thinking of what it must be to grieve in a foreign country, told them they must come to the house for a drink.

Ben Dack was home and on hearing the news made serious business of gripping the shoulder and shaking the hand of each. Some people are gifted in condolence; Ben Dack had tears of his own. In moments he had at the edge of his eyelids the sad passing of his own mother years before. He had a big heart and a large handkerchief. He went to the kitchen to get bottles and glasses and had to hug Josie by the sink. She knew her husband well, and had a fondness for that hopeless softness that some thought intolerable and others humanity.

'I feel terrible sad for the young lad,' Ben said.

'Of course you do.'

'I can't help but feel . . .'

'Of course not.' She patted his back. 'You go on in now. I'll cut some sweet loaf.'

'I'm a terrible fool,' he said.

'You are. But you're my fool,' she told him.

He brought in the bottles. He poured generous helpings and only water for the Master and then he offered the toast. 'To the faithful departed. May perpetual light shine upon them', and the others drank and then Ben offered the same toast again and had to stop then to explain what perpetual light was and where it might be shining.

The visitors drank quickly, and spoke a little more loudly, frequently in Polish; Laslo offered a toast in Polish and Ben and the Master tried to pronounce it and they raised their glasses, and then Jerzy in a surge of emotion took the Master's hand.

'Thank you,' he said. 'You are a good man.'

'What will you do, Jerzy?'

'I don't know. I think I should go back and then I think I should not. My mother is not there. I think: you should stay here, Jerzy. Then I think: why stay here?' He shrugged, his eyes were in glass.

'Never decide in hurt or haste, my own father used to say. Wait, to see what happens,' the Master offered. He took the other's hand and squeezed it, and before either of them spoke again, Whatarangi roared out, 'DAVID COPPERFIELD!'

The room stopped. Josie halted at the kitchen door with the tray of sweet loaf. Ben stopped with the bottle poised on the lip of Gus's glass. Jerzy was still holding the Master's hand.

The largeness of the voice stopped them all. They turned to the tattooed man who was puffing smoke from his pipe and peering down at the photograph inside the Dickens novel.

'David Copperfield,' he told them. 'Here! Hero of your own life!'

'That's the book all right,' Ben said. '*David Copperfield*, a good one too.'

But Whatarangi shook his head. 'This is him,' he said. 'Gus, look!'

And he showed the photograph, saying, 'He read it to me in Frankfurt, my teacher, this is him. This is Jay of David Copperfield, here in *David Copperfield*. And his eyes widened white in his blue face, and he smiled and nodded at this proof of plot, and his part in it, and Gus frowned in disbelief and Jerzy felt the Master's astonishment in the sudden weakness of his grip and Ben Dack, for once speechless, turned to Josie who closed her eyes briefly as if she had been kissed, and the room remained in that stunned amazement, as though something from above had landed amongst them.

THIRTY

The soldiers would not let Jay get close. Though he tried and said 'medicine' and 'doctor' their eyes were wild and they shouted and lifted their rifles and called him *'farenge'* and made clear they would shoot. He looked up into the birdless blue sky and roared.

Yohannes, the father of the children, came up to him, and whether he could tell there was connection between the dead woman and the young man, or it was simply in his humanity to comfort the suffering, he put his arm over Jay's shoulder and pulled him to him. Jay was staring at what he could not believe. He was staring at Desta's body not thirty feet away from him. Her blood was on the road. It made a dark stain, not red but blue like the deepest shadow. The stillness of it, the pool in random shape with road-dust thickening and flies hovering, sickened him. This is what he looked at. He looked at where her life had leaked away. The stain was so small. She lay on top of it in a strange pose, one leg twisted as if she half-turned back from the bullet in mid air. His hands in fists, Jay looked into the sky, then again at the stain.

The soldiers, frantic and fearful of rebel attack, kept an armed circle in place. Then, under orders to clear the road, two of them lifted Desta and bore her a little to the side and laid her on parched scrubland and weed. An officer among them shouted something in warning or instruction, and the people gathered there cowered. Then the soldiers returned to their Jeeps and truck and were gone.

Jay ran to the body. Women had already come about and were praying. They moved the hair from Desta's face. She lay flat and the bloody flag on her chest showed the two neat holes where the bullets had entered. They turned to look at Jay as he approached. He was the only foreigner, and this, coupled with the anguish he showed, made them consider him. He carried a story, it was clear, and two of the older women gestured for him to come through and see the dead girl.

He knelt. He was not going to cry. He put his hand down and tried to stroke away the bloodstain on the road. Then he cried out. It burst like a thing lanced. He lowered his head to her.

There were dream-days then, lost days he did not know were passing, when prayers were being said, when a monk with white beard and white eyebrows appeared, when there seemed constant movement through the one-room metal house that was once a cargo container and where he was now a guest. He lay curled into the corner. Yohannes and his children, as a mark of respect to the mourner, sat with him and made an offering of small hard orange-like fruits. Jay slept and dreamt his flesh turned red and woke shouting to the startled faces of a mother and grandmother and nine children. He attended the burial, but it too seemed unreal. It was as though his mind was made numb to protect his heart; if he could not think, perhaps he would not know how much he suffered.

Then, the rain came. It began with a single drop – a single loud *pat*. It clattered on the metal roof and deluged down as though a knife had been taken to the heavens. The sky was weirdly light and dark and the mountains were great black shoulders hunched against it. It rained all day and all night and again the next day so that puddles and drips and leaks and small floods were everywhere. The dust roads became swift brown mud ways. The children wore the weather like invisible clothing, coming and going without the slightest shelter, faces dripping, smiles always ready. Outside the container-house where Jay stayed, they played a game of water-football, where a third opponent was the deep puddles and the skill of the long-limbed players not unlike that of ballet dancers. They danced past the doorway. The rain did not stop. With a certain majesty, a man in a long, darkly soaked robe with a pink-frilled umbrella walked through the centre of the game. The game paused to let him pass.

The rain made time different. Traffic on the road was slowed to nothing. Half a day passed in a moment, the other half seemed to take several days. Jay sat outside in the continuing deluge wanting to be drowned.

When darkness fell, the grandmother of the house, a tiny crouched figure of glittering eyes in a million wrinkles, tapped his shoulder to come inside. They fed him doughy *kocho* or raw meat called *kitfo*. He ate in the same comatose state, as though vacant of feeling. Those gathered under the tattooing of the rain took their food in the custom with which he was already familiar, rolling it up in a piece of *injera* and feeding the package to one sitting next to them or across the way. They fed each other this way, and as he watched he was moved to be included and to be offered shelter.

At last, from the women, in the patchwork of phrases he understood and the tone of the rest, Jay had this story: Desta had come along the road walking. When she stopped to rest her feet, a Jeep of soldiers came. The Jeep stopped and one of the soldiers called to her. She did not reply and he called again and the others in the Jeep jeered him. Then Desta got up and walked to them and the soldiers made lewd comments and gestures and when she had come close enough she reached quickly and took the gun of one of them. They had shot her before she could find the trigger. They had shot her before the truck and the other soldiers came so they could say she had tried to ambush them.

With the rain still falling, he went to her grave.

He squatted by the rocks and told her it was him. He said nothing and imagined it was as if each grew settled in the other's company in the way of old couples when the urgencies of the world have left them behind. The quiet that was between them contained their history, and in it the history of all such lovers, and he did not try to break it. What grief and anger and hurt he carried slid away there in the channels of the rain. After a long time, he said out loud 'I loved you', and the sound of the words in the wet emptiness was a kind of confirmation and at once he felt bestowed on him something that he could not say yet was grace.

'I loved you,' he told her again. After a while he turned his face up to the rain and blinked it and he said in a firm voice 'I loved her', as though God was that near.

And before he stood up, he knew that he would leave that country now.

He had little to give to thank those who had welcomed him, but offered two of the boys the last of his T-shirts and a pair of shorts. The grandmother watched from the corner with a look, knowing and glad, as though she could see restoration of spirit or changed destiny. She took his head in the bony nest of her old fingers when he came to say goodbye and

228

she said in that language 'God goes with you', and then pulled back her hands to release him as though he had wings.

Out on the mud road where the rain had stopped and the air was cool, Jay had no clear idea how exactly he was going, but only that he must go back now to see the Master's grave. It had come to him when he sat in the rain by the stones and felt at peace with Desta. He needed to go back before he could go on, he thought. It was not that Africa had died in him with Desta. No. He knew if he left there he would return, but he knew he had leave.

I am not really African, or I am, and I am Irish too. I am the mix of bloods. Did You bring me here? Did You lead me?

How is Your memory? Do You remember what I said when I went along the road that first night? Do You? I told You to prove to me You existed.

Well, I am waiting.

Although You shouldn't have, You still have a chance.

Jay stood on the road and the children and the mother came see him off.

He had no money. He had a flute, he had a copybook and pen and a passport with a picture of himself as a smiling boy he didn't recognize. His hair was darker and wilder, he was thinner and taller, and a questioning look had replaced the smile. But he was the same person, only further across the bridge between boy and man. He also had the sense that he had become a burden on that heavily burdened country.

He looked at the sky cleared of rain.

I will take the first car that stops for me. Like I did with Gus back in Frankfurt.

I will give You that chance.

If chance is You.

He stood waiting. The children grew bored of watching him wait and brought out the unburst ball that was kept like a treasure in the kitchen corner of the container. They played sliding football in the mud road, yelling and squealing and celebrating goals with arms raised to the heavens as though even these were bestowed.

An hour passed, the road brought not a single car. A shepherd came with a small flock. A man and a cart.

Then nothing.

It was mid-afternoon.

Does it take a long time for our words to reach You?

Are You shut down? What Gus said, gone creating other better worlds elsewhere? We were Your first draft. Early work, is that it?

Another hour, the football game ended, some cars passed, none stopped.

Is she there with You yet?

A child brought him a holed bucket and offered it upside-down as a seat. The world was stopped, it seemed. It was such time as to make believe the Creator stroked his beard and considered the plot and all its possibilities, and rose from His desk and paced the room and returned and considered and then paced some more. If those we meet are meant in some way, as all lovers like Jay believed, then there was now an absence of meaning.

No car stopped for him. He looked at those drivers who looked at him, as if each might divine some connection or reason in the other, but mostly he received only the mistrust of the foreigner in that remote place, and the old noisy trucks and vans and cars passed on. At fall of darkness, he returned reluctantly to the container-house when the mother came out to invite him. Again they shared what they had, and gratitude at their generosity flooded through him. So in the dim light of the single candle he played the flute for them. The music bounced around in the weird acoustics of the metal house, but from child to grandmother there was the same smile.

Jay slept in the corner and he dreamt of going fishing with the Master. He dreamt in such clarity that when he woke he had a warm after-dream for company.

Again he gave his goodbyes and received embrace and returned to attend what would be sent along the road.

It was a yellow car, its windows open. From inside, a man in his twenties both bald and long-haired with huge black-rimmed glasses leaned out and in an English accent asked, 'Do you need a lift?'

THIRTY-ONE

When the plot turns, it turns quickly. It turns without regard for laws of probability or chance and pursues its course foreseen or outrageous with a sure swiftness, as if a thought clean and whole arrived in the mind and now the hands flew at the keys to write it down.

'How far are you going?' Jay asked.

'Impossible to say. Too far probably,' the man said, and raised one hand in the air and jerked it back again and made a loosening movement of his shoulders before angling his head back. 'You?'

'Same.'

The driver laughed and accompanied this by another series of rapid movements, neck, eyebrows, hands. 'Africa,' he shrugged, or what twisting of his shoulders must have been a shrug. He said his name was John and either Hammon or Harmond, Jay couldn't be sure. He said he had a Syndrome.

'Important to clarify right off. But don't worry,' he said. 'Some people are put off, but really it's just . . .' He grasped the steering wheel, composed himself, smiled over. 'I drive perfectly well.'

'I'm not worried,' Jay said.

John had the astonished, slightly scorched look of the European new to Africa. His car was English; he told Jay he had driven it from outside Oxford six months earlier, when he stopped in mid-study for his thesis on 'The Impossibility of Arrival, Place and Meaning in Classics of Travel Literature'. 'You read much classic travel literature?'

'No. I'm sorry.'

'No no, no problem.' He spun his head sharply to the side window, back, craned forward, reached up and snapped off his glasses, rubbed them on his blue shirt, and put them back on again. He was a windmill. His thoughts came not to him but through him, each with such accompaniment of actions and reactions, spasms, jerks, gestures, that the first response of anyone who met him was to be disconcerted.

'You are sure you are okay to drive?'

'Oh yes, no problem,' he said. 'By the time I had knocked down all those people in France I was getting the hang of it.' He looked across. 'Joke,' he said.

'Okay.'

'No you're perfectly safe.'

'I wasn't—'

'It's fine. Concentration is actually about one hundred and fifty per cent above normal. So some advantages.'

They drove on in the first quiet of two strangers after meeting.

After ten kilometres, Jay asked, 'Is this north?'

'South actually.'

'Okay.'

'Is that all right?' John threw both shoulders up and down twice and shook off an invisible something.

'Yes. That's fine.'

They drove into the mountains on broken roads where stones flew out from beneath the wheels. They spoke little but were each glad of the other's company in the loneliness of the landscape. The car was unsuited to the roughness of the long journey, had long since flattened all springs and shock absorbers and drove low to the ground, often scraping its underbelly. The engine was harshly tuned, and announced them long before they approached herdsmen, goats, and those single stray figures that seemed to be always walking great distances with fixed purpose. To one of these, an old man carrying sticks on his head, they offered a lift. He placed the sticks in ahead of him very carefully, and then sat into the back seat of the car where John had a box of foodstuffs and bottles of water. The man sat smiling, not thinking to close the car door. Jay got out and shut it, the man grinning all the time with expectation at the wonder awaiting.

'Where are you going?' Jay asked.

The man nodded and smiled.

They travelled on and came by the particular beauty of the Rift Valley, the land green and fertile and lush, the birds plentiful and astonishing. When at last they pulled over to take water, Jay opened the car door. The man got out. He took his sticks and put them on his head. He smiled and said thanks or blessing and turned then to walk back in the direction they had come.

After, sitting in the shade of an acacia tree, Jay asked again where exactly they were headed.

'To Awasa, first, I think.' John took off his glasses and blew on them, clearing the lenses hardly at all, putting them back on, squinting through them, wrinkling his nose then shaking his head sharply twice. He spoke rapidly, 'You know, this is a remarkable country. I mean I have read lots and lots about it. I am something of a, well, expert is too strong, more like – well – info-holic or something. I used to love getting books out of the library from when I was quite small. Always books about places. And that just became a bit of an obsession and the thing is, you see, I never went anywhere.

Never really wanted to. I can't see a thing actually,' he squinted at the tree bark as if he was trying to see inside it. 'But I've been lots of places, as it were. A lot of them in previous centuries,' he said, and waved his right hand at no flies. 'Have you read Isabelle Eberhardt's description of "The Oblivion Seekers"? in Morocco? Probably not. No, of course not. But well, it's riveting, you know: *"Finally the smokers are quiet, and merely stare at the flowers in ecstasy. They are epicureans, voluptuaries, perhaps they are sages. Even in the darkest purlieu of Morocco's underworld such men can reach the magic horizon where they are free to build their dream-palaces of delight."* Wow! I mean, really. Wow!' He stood up, shook out the energy that was flowing in his arms. 'Sorry, yes, to Awasa, and then to Kenya.'

'By car?'

'Isn't this the road to Nairobi?'

Through a strange majestic twilight of unearthly stillness and colour they passed. At the noise of the engine, ghostly pinkish birds rose off the lake waters by Adami Tula and flew across the reddish light. The landscape was as it ever had been.

They arrived to the city of Awasa in the dark, driving past shanties and compounds flickering with light within and came further on into the city proper and down towards the lakeside, following the empty streets until they came to a church with three golden domes on its towers. It was a church as great as any, and in that deserted night-time loomed proud against the stars. John got out and Jay joined him.

'Well, there it is,' John said.

'It's . . .'

'One of the most important churches in Africa.'

'I can imagine.'

'You can actually *feel* it, can't you? If you think what we have just driven through and then look, here, there is this,

236

in Awasa.' He made a sound like an in-breathed whistle, and threw his head back and then shot a shoulder up as a spasm passed through him. 'It's even better than reading it,' he said when he regained his composure.

Like pilgrims, the two of them stood before the great church.

'What is it called?' Jay asked.

'This is the Church of Saint Gabriel.'

They stood gazing for some time, both engaged in an actual form of John's thesis, both considering the relation of Arrival to Meaning, trying to fathom what it was to have built this magnificent church here, and how now it fitted into their lives. Jay understood there was a reason why John had travelled here and he hoped he would learn what it was.

'This is what you have to love here,' John said, and took off his glasses and blew nothing on them and squinted at what he could not see. 'Nowhere more surprising in the world, I think. Nowhere more suffering, yet nowhere with more smiles. Nowhere more poverty, yet nowhere more majesty. Yes?'

'Yes.'

John put his hand on the crown of his head, palmed the bare dome, rubbed at the long hair above one ear so it stood out at an angle. He shuddered then. 'Sorry,' he said.

'It's all right,' Jay told him.

They came back to the car and John drove them back down to the lakeside and pulled over.

'Here I think,' he said.

'What's here?'

'Our accommodation.'

'The car?'

'I can't leave it,' he said. 'If you want to go somewhere else I won't be offended.' He shuddered again, a mime of

237

puppet string pulled and cut. 'It leaves me when I sleep,' he said. 'I won't be . . .'

'The car will be fine,' Jay told him, 'Thank you.'

They let back the seats, and soon John was perfectly still in sleep.

Kenya.

Do I go to Kenya?

Is that the way?

What happens if someone steps out onto the road and goes whichever way he is brought? If he travels long enough, is he brought back to the beginning? Is that why the world is round?

Prove to me You exist.

I dare You.

In the morning they awoke with tapping on the window. Three boys' faces grinned in at them. They offered small hard bananas for sale and for a few birr John bought them all. The streets were already awake with people walking. Men heading to the National Tobacco and Matches Corporation. Women, as ever, travelling erect with bundles on their heads. Already there was the smell of goat meat being grilled for sale.

'Now to find the Abaye Alem.'

John had directions written on a piece of paper and drove out of Awasa to the south. The day was very clear and still, and seemed more than others a thing perfectly *created*. They passed a herd of hippos, another of goats. They came by a place where a scattering of round huts with grass roofs was a world unto itself that took no notice of them.

They drove on without talking.

John was searching for a holy man who lived not in a monastery but at a place not far from the road where a giant rusting Coca-Cola sign had been laid as a wall against tin sheeting, old window frames, and sacking.

'He says he has seen many miracles,' John explained as they arrived at the spot. 'Every few days another. You can stay here or you can come.'

They walked up to the dwelling with the shyness of those who know they will encounter the company of piety. The fence of the compound had been taken down. There were a dozen people already there, the monk on a rise of ground before them. He was a small old man with a great spool of white hair. When the foreigners approached and stood on the outside of the gathering, he nodded towards them. Among the ragged congregation were various men and women staggeringly ailing, some with diseased limbs, a man with a red stump for a leg, another with a hugely swollen eye, a woman with a swaddled child. They were those familiar to all countries at all times since Time, the misfortunate and stricken whose suffering moved them to the edge of life. Here a wafer of hope balanced on a tongue of prayer.

The Abaye Alem prayed with an uplifted smile. In that shattered place of neither chapel nor cross, he prayed aloud in his own language, his arms held out and his head raised to the blue of sky. He was entirely absorbed in his action, his praying was without pause, eyes shut in nets of wrinkles and the words rising in a kind of chant.

John knelt down, hugged his arms close to his body, bowed his head. Jay stood alongside him, then he too knelt.

The praying continued and after a time the Abaye Alem's voice dropped to a near-whisper, as if he spoke in the ear of God beside him. His head cast back and his eyes shut. He raised his two hands. If what he spoke were prayers, they were joined one to the other, and flew up from his mouth as if pulled on a cord. The old man was gifted in this, and whether he played the prayers or they him could not be said, but perhaps prayer was his instrument. This was his daily habit in that broken place without name. An hour, more, he continued. And some of those gathered before him murmured or fell forward or held out a hand in the air as if to take the blessings coming down.

But there was no miracle, or none visible. When the monk had reached the end of the prayer or knew otherwise that it was time to pause, some rose and left and wandered out across the sun-baked ground. Those able to walk went silently and serenely, perhaps for miles into that vast landscape. Others, having nowhere else to hope, stayed. The Abaye Alem never lost his smile and came among them. He embraced each in the clasp-and-nuzzle custom of the country, whether they were diseased or not. When he came to the two foreigners, he offered the same greeting.

John kept his arms wrapped around, holding onto himself; he bowed and the monk said something neither understood. The ancient man gestured with both bony hands for him to stand, and when he did John's arm jerked out, his neck twisted twice sharply, his shoulder jumped.

'Sorry Father,' he said.

But the monk, seeing his affliction, needed no apology, and took his head in his hands and held it till stillness.

And a calm did seem to come in John then and, like light breaking, Jay understood why he had sought the Church of Saint Gabriel and why they had come so far to be here. He glimpsed something of the desperate pilgrimage that had begun when John left Oxford and took the old car and began to drive south, stopping at churches, seeking holy men. He understood something of the suffering and the yearning and was moved and wished for him a miracle.

The Abaye Alem removed his hands. John was still.

Then the monk turned and took Jay's hand, and pulled him to him and pressed the wild white hair in against his neck. His embrace was like no other. It was strong and almost fierce and the head of old man burrowed in and his entire body clasped onto Jay. The holy man held on and would not let go. He smelled of dust and spices. He was of the earth and the air both, both there and not, and as he clung to Jay he said something. He said it against the flesh of Jay's neck, as though he was speaking not to but *into* him, and with urgency and conviction, the tightness of his hold diminishing not in the slightest.

He stepped back. His eyes were fired with joy, dark and smiling. It was he who bowed to them then. And when he lifted his head his smile was enormous, his cheekbones prominent in the thinness of his face, his top teeth bared. He spoke again to them and looked at each and again he bowed and then he raised his two hands, palms outward, as though from them something shone.

John blessed himself.

Then, in a moment he would remember years later, in a moment that would come back to him like a white bird flying – time and again in the course of his life – a moment when he felt with perfect clarity, when the certainty of what happened was inescapable and arrived in his understanding with profound astonishment and gratitude and humility, Jay felt what he could only describe by saying: *God is here.*

It was nothing less than this. It was startling and instant. He had not seen the bird descending. He had not felt the wing-beat or glide as the knowledge arrived inside him, but it was there, and was in fact a kind of Confirmation neither puzzling nor distressing nor burdensome, but light.

The monk stepped back from them, smiling all the time. He returned to the small rise before his crooked tin-house and, head back, eyes shut, began praying skywards once more.

They left there and took the road without speaking. John was still; Jay was quiet. They went south and passed through Yirga Alem and when the road forked to the left for Somalia, they bore right for Kenya. Here the lush land was no more, but with slow certain persistence was turning into desert. At four hundred kilometres to the border, the road worsened.

As they approached the border town of Moyale, John suddenly took some banknotes out of his shirt pocket and offered them across.

'Here, you have no money, do you?'

'No.'

'They will ask you for an exit fee, and maybe more.'

'I can't repay.'

'Take it.'

'Thank you.'

'There's no need,' John said, and still his hands did not jump nor his shoulders twitch and in him there continued a calm so ordinary as to be marvellous.

The passport control was slow and the officer fastidious. He considered each page of the old passport Jay had, examined carefully the picture of the young boy and looked at the cover several times as though to be sure there was a place called Ireland. Then he searched for a new page and stamped it forcefully.

Jay thanked him and walked out of the small office. John was standing on the wooden deck looking back at Ethiopia.

'Say goodbye. Say goodbye to the country of orphans,' he said.

THIRTY-TWO

Jay was everywhere in the Master's mind now. When the others at last could tell him no more, having told and retold him all they knew half a dozen times, he sought the quiet of his room upstairs and opened the skylight to the night and began to reread the pages in his head. He had the piece that was Jay stepping out from a forest in Germany and Gus stopping the car and picking him up. He had the arrival in the dance studio and the transient figures that lived there. He had the whole story of Whatarangi noticing the quiet intense boy with a flute and a book and his deciding to take *David Copperfield* and then bargain its return against reading lessons. The Master had vivid scenes of the giant tattooed man sitting cross-legged in the opaque light and listening to Peggotty and Little Em'ly and Barkis and all those with whom he was so familiar and who still were as real as life in Whatarangi's mind. He had the story in a shortened version of Nuno, and how he stole Jay's flute to sell it – 'because he was a thief,' Gus said, 'but a good thief.' And how he became blind and how at last they had persuaded Jay to bring him home to Lagos in Portugal. The Master had so much of it, his own imagination latching unto the slightest detail – the hooded shirt Gus said he wore, the broken-heeled runners – and, following it, letting it grow richer, more real in his mind, until he had the *comfort* of it. For that's what it was. He had felt first shock and astonishment and then disbelief and then a sudden dizziness as though a hand had stopped the world but he was still turning. The slow warmth of realization rose through him and he felt in the company of a miracle and he had sat down and stood up and asked that each thing be said again. He felt surprised by joy and then afraid of it and queried the details and showed the photograph again in case it was a mistake. But already in the pandemonium of that crowded kitchen, Ben Dack had been asking for the whereabouts of this Nuno, and although the story told was already three years ago, he was going to find out.

And maybe you are there.

Maybe you are there, right now, in the south of Portugal, because you think I am dead.

Maybe you are still at the house of Nuno Serafim.

Maybe this is the time of things returning.

Maybe you will come home now.

He stood under the skylight and looked out into the night sky. He thought of his wife and of his daughter and he allowed the hope to come into where had been only sadness. He thought of all things unlikely, beginning with himself and his own history. He thought *life is more unlikely than books.* He thought *God is more unlikely than life.*

Then he turned on the laptop to tell any who connected that he had good news, that his heart was risen, that it was like a kite catching wind.

Because she was late, because she should already have been back in Dublin the day before, because she was supposed to spend two days with Sisters Agnes and Cecilia after she had

244

been west to visit her parents' graves, Bridget was flustered. She was unused to driving and the gears in the rental car seemed stiff, and there were so many more cars in the country now and she really didn't like having to hurry, and then this rain. It was like rain in Africa: straight, ceaseless, purposed. She leaned forward as she drove, as if she was short-sightedly reading a message off the windscreen.

It's just because you're so nosy. It's because you can't ever leave things be.

She drove south off each of the roundabouts at Galway and at Ennis turned right for the west of Clare.

I want to see what it's like, that's all.

I want to be able to see for myself, and then when I go back I'll tell him I went there and how lovely it was and maybe it'll prompt him. Maybe he'll want to come home.

I can't be this near; I can't be in Ireland and not go there, simple as that.

No more about it.

But just dear God thank you for the rain very nice and please turn it off now.

She had not thought she would miss Africa as she did. Until the moment she was home, Bridget had not realized her home had moved. The green wet place through which she drove was as familiar as old photographs of herself, but just as distant too. The country was utterly changed. The rows of new houses stacked, ringed, single-named with Park, Close, Dale, Downs, Meadow, attached, seemed to her cold, even forbidding.

Of course I'm daft. Of course they're lovely really. And they probably have every kind of thing inside and the people who live in them probably love them. Only. Oh you're such an old biddy Bridget. You're such a I don't know what you are. But that's what you are. Things change. It's good. Look at all the good things. Look at all the money people have now, and why not, why not have our turn? Why not?

245

She argued herself south. She took the side of newness, of prosperity and cultural diversity, but she could not quite win. Inside her there remained an unease. Africa changes everyone, she remembered being told shortly after she had arrived. But the change was only measured now. Now she realized she was a different person; she seemed to carry with her not exactly the presence of the poor but the actuality, what it was like, how life was. She had the sense, common to travellers returning from profound experience, that Ireland was not quite real. It was all on the surface, and she thought of the remarkable vibrancy of Africa, the joy she had met, and she longed to be back there.

But first, she would find the house that Jay had lived in.

Is this the road he walked away on? Is this the way he came?

She took the turn for the village and tried to remember the way he had told her once.

He said he could walk from the school. He said it was just down the road to the cross and over. Or up?

The skies fell; great grey masses of cloud were laid one upon the other and quelled the light. The rain pelted. Bridget passed the blue two-room schoolhouse on the side of the road and stopped the car at the cross. Nothing came or went. In the fields, cows stood in the mindless mesmerism of the rain. Then she took a chance and went down the right-hand side of the crossroads and she imagined she was following him; she imagined Jay as a small boy going this way to school, his mother dead, his father unknown, and the world before him. She tried to imagine what he must have thought, what he must have feared and suffered, and how it had removed him from everything, from trust, from faith in anything.

The road lay alongside a farmhouse built right next to it, and she knew this was not the one because there was no garden, but yet when she saw the high hedges grown wild with the fuchsia through them, she pulled the car over onto the ditch and got out. The rain smacked on her cheeks and thickened and she thought *what a comedian You are* and found the small gate where the hedges tried to meet. She pushed her way in and came inside the wild garden. Jumble of late blooms, of roses and astilbe, of Michaelmas daises, and orange heleniums, and pearly everlasting. Tangles of things fallen and grown together, of rain-awakened weeds writhing up out of the summer-cracked ground, lay before her. The house behind it was paint-peeled, the walls dark-streaked where the clogged gutters spilled. It wore the sorrow of memory. In the long grass, the handle of a spade stood aslant where a flowerbed was no more.

Bridget came up the moss of the path in the rain. Sadness overwhelmed her. When she came to the front of the house she peered in at the window and saw the room as it was on the morning Jay had left it: the empty seats, the bookshelf over the fireplace, the glasses and bottles of his Confirmation party untouched. She bit her lower lip and lowered her head and pressed her forehead against the glass.

THIRTY-THREE

The journey was over eight hundred kilometres; it took them three days. Twice the yellow car broke down, and twice John fixed it the same way, with water and waiting. In the immediate aftermath of the visit to the monk, neither spoke of it, and for hours John had no sign of any tremor or spasm. They had travelled in a hush, each in the privacy of interpretation. But when the car broke down the first time, in his upset some of John's symptoms returned. His shoulder jumped, he jerked his head, but Jay did not comment. Later, passing a family gathered at a trickle stream, his hand flew up off the steering wheel and he managed to turn the wild motion into the action of smoothing back the long ragged ribs of what hair grew above his ears. When the car broke a second time, hoping that he would save John any upset, Jay offered to water it. After, they stood either side of it, waiting in the sun.

'I didn't expect a full cure,' John said.

'No, no, of course not.'

'But I am better than I was.'

'Yes, definitely,' Jay said. 'Much better.'

'It's weird, isn't it?'

Jay looked at him, and at the knowledge of his unhappiness felt a shadow inside. 'Yes,' he said.

'I have a long way still to go. I have more churches and more holy men.' He held out both his hands and watched them for shakes, but they were still. 'It's what I promised,' he said.

The main road had a diversion without explanation and then took instead the left fork toward Buna and though Wajir before it led back around the Woyamdero Plain to Habeswein. As they came through country unfamiliar to both, Jay said the place-names to make them real to him. He used John's wrinkled map and traced the route over the many creases and tears that made of East Africa a jigsaw.

I am in Kenya.

If he was going back to Ireland he was going in the wrong direction, he had no money for a flight, nor did he know a single soul in that country. Nonetheless, he had decided this was the way. He could not have returned to the hospital and burdened them further by asking for money. He chose instead to believe the road took him now, and, by doing so, gave God and Man equal chance and travelled onward with the peculiar faith, parts zeal, innocence and desperation, of those in the place of last hope. The encounter with the Abaye Alem remained with him, and though he did not risk saying it even to himself, he felt he travelled now accompanied by spirit.

At nightfall they pulled in to the side of the road, bumping a little over the coarse dry ground and watching birds take flight into the pink twilight. Soon the vast canopy of African stars overhung them. Three-quarter moon made silver the grass. In the pale light Jay was prompted to take out his copybook, to try and put the place onto the page, to describe it so exactly and without emotion that it would simply be there for when he was elsewhere.

The windless grass of the plain.

The silver stillness.

The air like cloth; when it moves slightly a thousand insects fly.

'You are a writer,' John said, releasing the catch to let back the car seat.

'Not really.'

He placed his glasses carefully on the dashboard.

'I thought I would be a doctor,' John said. 'A surgeon.' Then, as the unsaid threatened the mood, he tapped with the flat of his palm on his ample forehead. 'I thought I would have a full head of hair, mind. Years looking in the mirror, taking care of the thin horrible hair I had. Never seeing all the time I had such a magnificent forehead.'

He laughed, and for the first time in a long time Jay laughed too, and the heat of the laughter clouded out the stars.

When they came at last into the sprawl of Nairobi, John asked, 'Where are you actually going?'

'Anywhere is good.'

'Anywhere?' He peered with huge eyes through his glasses. 'It is a big city.'

'Yes. No. Anywhere. Really.'

'You know somebody?'

'If you just pick a place that'll be fine.'

'You can stay with me, I don't mind.'

John kept his eyes on the road, the slow fumy traffic of truck and bus. His shoulder jumped. 'Sorry,' he said instinctively.

'I would like to stay with you, but I can't,' Jay said. 'I have to get out. It's hard to explain. It's chance. I have to . . . that's all.'

'Right.'

251

They drove on a little further, neither of them wanting the bond they had made to end. Then John pulled over, 'Here?'

'Yes, here's fine.' Jay took his bag and offered his hand. 'Thank you. Thank you for everything.'

John shook his hand. 'I am better, you know,' he said.

'You are. Yes. You are. You will be fine,' Jay told him.

'And you will be okay?'

'Yes.'

'Which way will you go?'

'I'll go . . . I'll just probably head down this way,' Jay said, pointing down a side road.

John palmed the crown of his head quickly back and forth. It made no sense. 'Sure?'

'Yes. Sure. Thank you. Yes.' Jay got out, turned, stooped to the window. 'You'll be fine,' he said, and said it with a confidence he did not know he had.

In a moment John drove away. Shortly he would circle back to convince Jay to get back in the car, but he would not find him, and it would be a long time and in another country before they met again.

So now, what?

Where?

You are in Nairobi.

Right or left? Straight on or back?

How do you live a life by chance? By whichever way you are blown, like a butterfly, like a kite? Is that it?

I am still giving You this chance.

For no reason he could tell then, or perhaps because there was the slightest wind at his back, he crossed the road and went down that way.

What now?

*   *   *

There was a collared man.

He looked like the Master. He had the same tufted grey hair and kind eyes and he stood in the road with his suitcase fallen open and his clothes spilled.

'Oh dear.' He was English. He hitched up the knees of his trousers to kneel to the contents and he looked up at Jay approaching and said, 'I appear to have made myself an obstacle, I'm very sorry.'

His name was Reverend Holt. He accepted the help that was offered with many thanks and apologies. The suitcase was thin and inexpensive and overstuffed not only with clothes but with books.

'My weakness, you see,' Reverend Holt explained. 'The good Lord knows. And sometimes chastises me with such challenges as this. Holt, he says, why do you need all these books?' He smiled the full of his false teeth that had grown loose as he thinner. 'I give Him that rather direct English of Northumbria. Well, thank you. Thank you so much.'

'The suitcase is broken.'

'Well indeed, yes.'

'The clasp has come off.'

'I see. You're quite right. Well then, that's it then, isn't it.' The teeth smiled again. 'It's books or clothes. Can't carry both. Time of choice, as indeed in Life itself, good friend?'

'I can carry the books. Have you far to go?'

'Ah! Providence answers. The question then, you see, is did Our dear good Lord know that the choice would be averted so? Holt's books continue with Holt. As tangible evidence of Holt's weakness, mind.' With a white handkerchief he patted the sweat on his brow. The grey cardigan and grey trousers, the grey socks in the open-toed sandals, guaranteed his perspiration. His forehead glistened an instant after. 'I forget my manners, I do apologize. Reverend Arthur Holt.'

'I am Jay.'

'My honour and my pleasure, as my father used to say. Indeed, Jay. You're English.'

'I'm Irish.' He said it before he had thought.

'I see. Wonderful. I enjoy the Irish. We had an Irish girl at the mission, very lovely, very good. No longer with us. But the Irish are wonderful. Well now, dear Samaritan, do you really think you can bear those volumes for me? I realize it might be considered cheating the good dear Lord, but really I make the case that your arrival results in His intentions being unclear, you see? Well . . . I'm a little breathless actually, but yes, well?'

'I can carry them.'

'Wonderful. Right then, answer given, we shall surrender the suitcase to fortune and may it be the bounty of the Good, Lord, and we shall persevere onward. Shall we?'

They went like figures in a story, strangers met in the plot, mismatched and unacquainted with anything of each other's history or purposes, the Reverend clutching a selection of fawn and grey clothing, and Jay the hardcover editions of various classics and books of philosophy. And this in a street in Nairobi.

'Which way are you actually going yourself?' the Reverend asked, patting his handkerchief onto his forehead again.

'This way.'

'Excellent. Further to my plea then.' He raised his upper lip and offered a crescent of teeth. 'Perfectly providential.'

They went a little way past stone buildings, but it was quickly clear the Reverend suffered pain in his stomach and he was forced to stop. He buckled as it pierced him and some of the clothes slipped from his hands. 'Sorry now. Just a . . .' he managed, and grimaced and leaned against the wall.

'Are you all right?' Jay put the books on the street and took the clothes from him.

254

The Reverend raised a hand to tell him to wait as the pain transfixed him. Two small boys appeared on the path and watched. Then, the piercing easing, he smiled.

'Ah,' he said, 'latest bulletin.'

The two boys were staring at him and he made a small wave to them and said something in Swahili and they giggled.

'Apologies, Master Jay. Trial of life, suffering. Nothing to be done.'

'Will I get help?'

'No no. It passes. The Good Lord is merciful after all. Just a brief rest. Apologies for delaying you once again. Do you mind terribly if I sit on my friends?' He indicated the books, and Jay brought the twin stacks of them and on these Reverend Holt rested. He told the boys then about the suitcase and they raced each other back along the street for it.

'Are you all right?'

'Oh yes. Dear me. Just a few moments now.'

He sat, they waited.

'Was that Swahili? Have you been in Africa a long time?'

'Oh yes. Since I was . . .' He patted his brow. 'Well, a young man like yourself. Hard to believe the old were young when you're young; hard to believe when you're old too.'

'Can you go on?'

'I think not.'

'I'll get help.'

'No no. You mistake me. Holt's Cryptic. You're not to blame. We will continue momentarily.' He suffered some further discomfort and bent forward and groaned.

Jay looked for anyone but the street was empty. Reverend Holt recovered once more, then again made the business of taking out his handkerchief and patting his brow.

'Terribly hot like this,' he said. 'Dressed for England you see.'

'You're going to England.'

255

'No no. Clearly not. Past tense. Was intended but not now advised.' He pointed to the sky. 'The bulletin.' He top-lip smiled. 'Holt's Cryptic again. Apologies. I had thought to die in Devon, but now otherwise. I remain, Yours truly, etc.'

Jay considered the puzzle of him.

'Now shall we?' Reverend Holt stood and blinked at the sun and the lightness of his head then.

Jay gathered the books.

'Where did you say again that you were going?' the pastor asked.

'I'm going home.'

Clarity came to Reverend Arthur Holt then, and he gave his Good Lord a smile of both sets, upper and lower molars, incisors, and he said, 'Of course you are.'

THIRTY-FOUR

Mick Daly was an impatient patient. The cast over his ankle was bloody awkward and uncomfortable and he couldn't wear a Wellington or drive the tractor and he had no liking for sitting still. His wife had cut a sleeve from a blue jumper and stitched the cuff together and this he wore over the plaster as he hobbled into the yard. He had waved away the crutches when the nurse had offered them, and used a black-thorn for the little support it offered. He came across the slab concrete that was sun-dried muck and dung and crisped sops of silage and long torn tangles of black plastic. He gave no time to adapting to the cast and his gait was a short intemperate shuffle, stabbing with the stick, dragging the sleeve-sock. He had told his wife he needed air; he had told her the doctors told him walk as soon as possible and she was too gentle a woman to confront the lie.

Rain, he thought, paused in mid-yard, taking in the day, considering the valley fields below, the quickened wind. He watched a scattering of blackbirds rise above the lately mown meadow, one then a few then all, following the wind then wheeling on it and landing again in another corner of the same field. He watched them for foreknowledge of rain, for pattern or purpose, and he saw none and spat gristle of rasher then hobbled crookedly across to the cabins. *Well you give us some rain for God's sake?* His ankle ached. *Bloody thing.* He tried to put no pressure at all on it, leaning forward on the blackthorn, making the briefest step on the sleeve-sock as he shuffled, but each time it sent him a sharp reminder of the break.

To get up into the cab was hardest. He had to use his good foot for the step and that meant his entire weight weighing briefly on the broken ankle until he could pull himself up. Then, it was the wrong foot, his left, and he would be wrong-way round and have to roll over to get himself in. He knew this before he left the kitchen. He had had time enough in the quiet of his breakfast to consider the difficulties and likely pain, but he measured this against his impatience and need and decided that he was going to do it. He reached with his left hand and took the side bar and stepped up with his good foot. Pain shot through the break in his ankle, staggering him with its ferocity. He moaned aloud and almost didn't pull himself up. He was backwards in the cab but he was up and he pushed himself in onto the seat and knocked the old cushion with the knitted cover and the ass-pressed yellowed copies of the *Clare Champion* and he grabbed the steering wheel and righted himself. He started the engine and she kicked first time and he used the stratagem he had planned to cross over and drive left-footed only. His action on the accelerator was rough and the tractor roared and drove with jagged jumpy motion out of the yard and past the astonished O of his wife's mouth at the front door.

He could manage it. Left-footed was better than the other possibility of using the blackthorn as a foot. He found a set angle for the speed and would be fine unless he needed to brake. The country road was narrow and curved with the orange spikes of montbretia thickly blooming and the black-berries early fruiting. Mick Daly was at home in the tractor. He rode above the hedgerows and looked into the fields he passed. The steady rocking of the seat, its consistent pulsing, was his own mother, and the ease of the world he felt there he felt nowhere else. Master of the town-land, surveyor of pasture and meadow, of beast bird and insect, of streams and springs, hills and dunes, familiar of fox and badger, pheasant and pine marten, he was a figure already becoming antique in that countryside. He knew that landscape with an intimacy he did not need to consider or measure; a second nature inseparably a part of his first.

So he drove the tractor down the narrow road and forwent the pain in his ankle. Where the road came to a cross he chanced his luck and drove right out into it, believing a broken ankle protected him from calamity for a while. Fifty metres from the gate where he wanted to stop he took his foot off the accelerator and let the tractor slow, bumping it in along the side of the dune-grass ditch.

He switched off the engine and considered how he would climb down. He managed with discomfort and effort, then, taking the blackthorn with him, opened the gate into the sea-field. The rain began softly. He paid it no mind. He could see the main herd and he stood, leaning, and let his gaze hold them for a time, the strange tranquillity there was in watching them graze. Then he saw her. Eunice was in by the shelter of the ragged gorse that was grown one-sided by the Atlantic wind. Her calf was beside her.

With slow, lopsided gait, the sleeve-sock beginning to unravel, Mick went some way into the field. Eunice watched him side-eyed. She did not turn her head, she did not move away.

When he came close, she breathed a little more loudly. Her calf, whether unused to man or too deeply secure in a mother's company, took no notice of Mick Daly until he was near enough to see what and how it was. Then the calf alarmed, and sprang away five steps and stopped.

Fine bull calf you had.

Mick scratched the wildness of his sideburn.

Even if you broke my ankle.

He went no closer. He stayed watching until cow and calf realized he was no danger and Eunice returned to slow languid grazing of sweet wet grass. A small smile Mick Daly allowed himself. He frowned raindrops from the furrows of his brow, blinked them.

He leaned on the blackthorn and did not move away for a long time though the rain thickened with purpose.

Later, he returned to the tractor and drove on, arriving soon at the high hedges when he saw the parked rental car. He pulled over, leaving the engine running. The rain was streaming into the afternoon. He listened then, leaning on the stick, he swung the blue-sleeve sock over and got himself down out of the cab and went in the gate to see who it was. Through the towers of weed he saw the woman up at the window of the old house.

'He's not there,' he called gruffly.

'Oh hello. I'm sorry. Yes, I know,' Bridget said.

'There's no one living there now.' He didn't mean to be brusque, but was.

'No.'

Bridget came away from the window and down the slippery overgrown path towards him. Her hair was drenched, the shoulders of her jacket saddled with wet. Then she saw his ankle cast and she said, 'Oh, I'm sorry for your broken foot. That must be painful.'

'Not really,' Mick Daly told her, 'more the bloody awkwardness of it than anything.'

'I see. Of course, yes, it would be.' She stood briefly in the rain and she remembered her father on the farm and sometimes uneasy conversations, and she decided pleasantness was the answer and she said, 'It's remarkable you're able to drive the tractor.'

'A challenge all right,' Mick crinkled a smile. 'First time anyhow. But you couldn't be sitting still all day.'

'Oh no, I'm sure. Still, some would.' Bridget held her hand flat like a minor roof over her eyebrows.

Flattered by her acknowledgement of his own nature, Mick tapped the cast with his stick. The bush of his wild hair was million-starred with raindrops. 'No you couldn't be sitting still,' he said.

There was a further moment, rain like a curtain moving; then Bridget stepped past. 'Well, speedy recovery, God bless,' she said and opened the gate.

Mick Daly did not believe anyone should know anyone else's business. He was not going to wonder why she was there, nor would he ask her. But the old Master had done him a favour and saved Eunice, and because he wanted to tell someone that story, he said, 'We thought him odd, you know? Well you would. Anyone would. Because of the way it happened. Funeral planned and all. And people can't turn their feelings around that quickly. Can't be sorrowful one day and then joyful the next. So we thought him odd after, and kept away. But he did me a good turn, you know? I have to say that now. I do. A good turn.' He grinned at the memory and then worked away an itch in his sideburn. 'I had a cow, Eunice I call her, and he sort of saved her I'd say.'

'I'm sorry?' Bridget put her hand up again, as if to shield the rain or begin to bless herself.

'The old man, I'm talking about. Him, used to live there. They call him the Master,' Mick said.

'Yes?' Bridget took her hand away and the revelation rained down on her.

'But he doesn't live here any more now.'

'Oh?'

'No.'

'I see.'

'He lives over at Dack's.'

THIRTY-FIVE

In the week that followed, on the pastor's insistence, Jay lived in the upstairs office of St Augustine's Mission in the Cibera district of Nairobi where the Reverend Arthur Holt had worked for his lifetime before being told he had advanced cancer of the pancreas that was now spread throughout. The diagnosis he took like a handed-in notice that there was nothing more he could contribute in Africa, and, without telling anyone, he had purchased a flight from Nairobi to London. It was cowardly, he told Jay later. 'But the Good Lord knows us well and in His wisdom decided cowardice is not a sin, dear friend. Indeed no.' He had thought to slip away because he could not bear to become an invalid in the place where he had laboured so long for others. Then his pains had worsened and come with greater frequency. When he was trying to escape them, his suitcase had fallen open in the road.

'The rest is where my history meets yours,' he said.

'You can still go to England,' Jay had told him. They were in a small room where a great old map of Africa that Reverend Holt had first brought with him still hung on the wall. Countries had changed since, frontiers and names, but he had not taken it down; he liked the old world right there behind the computer on his desk.

'Oh no. That's quite clear. I'm not for Devon again.' He folded his hands one over the other. 'I'm settled to that. Would you mind,' he indicated the books, and Jay returned them to the shelf where they had been for thirty years. 'Many thanks. They are probably best pleased to be back in their own dust again.' He saw Jay look at the titles. '*Our Mutual Friend*, my favourite Dickens.'

'I haven't read it.'

'Oh do. If you've time.'

'Time?'

'Before you go home.'

'Yes. All right.'

Reverend Holt looked down at the table, as though a jigsaw was there. 'As long as you stay here, in the mission, do please read. I don't think the book would do well elsewhere. Can you possibly stay a little time?'

'Yes.'

'Providential then. Wonderful.' Arthur Holt considered him with the wisdom of suffering and he smiled. 'I wonder if I could request one more favour? Would it be terribly improper of me to ask you not to tell Joseph I was running away?'

'Joseph?'

'He's my right hand. He's one of the wonderful souls you can come across in your life.'

'Of course I won't.'

'Only that he might be upset, you see, and that wouldn't be right.'

'No, yes. I understand.'

'Our pact deepens then. Thank you, Jay. Your second name I don't seem to remember.'

'I took my mother's name. It's Carpenter.'

'I see. Well then. So it is.'

Joseph was a Kenyan of firm manner who had worked with Reverend Holt for ten years. He knew the elderly man was ailing and he attended to him diligently. In all there were a dozen men and women who worked in St Augustine's, and Jay was struck by the similarities to the hospital in Addis, and the sense he had of such places in all the countries of Africa, and this gave him hope. One afternoon he told Reverend Holt about the House of Angels, and then asked if he could borrow the money for a stamp to send a card to say he was well.

'Money for a stamp? I see. Well, certainly.'

'Because I left in a hurry.'

'Yes, I see,' said the Reverend, although he didn't quite.

Then, because the need to speak of her was great, because the sorrow and love were in his mouth all the time, Jay said, 'There was a girl there called Desta.'

'Oh yes?' the Reverend invited.

Then Jay told him her story. He told it as all tellers do, first for himself, in the hope that the telling would lessen the suffering, that the story might find a shape and in the shape meaning, that loss and grief would have a place and be not the end. Then too he told it so that the love he had felt would live still. He told it because when he said the words out loud he felt he argued against the world that might think this a youthful passion of no consequence, another in the crammed back catalogue of: he loved her, she didn't love him, and she died. He told it because he wanted to believe it had mattered in some way. He described her face, her way of standing, her expression each night she came out into the corridor where Pellier was sitting. His eyes grew bright and his speech quick.

'Well, certainly you loved her,' Reverend Holt said.

'But she died.'

'Sadly yes.'

'So?'

'Well of course we all die.'

'But she wasn't even twenty.'

'No. No no, I don't mean to diminish the tragedy at all. Not at all. I mean only to say, still you loved her and she knew this. And that . . .' He paused and patted twice the tuft of silver hair on his crown. 'Now, there was something I said when I did sermons years ago, Holt's Epistles Volumes One to Seven sort of thing, youthful zeal and so forth. Something about the love you give being equal to, something and something and that, well I had it all in some manner of divine higher mathematics if you can imagine. I can't quite recall now. Was there a song about that? Doesn't come to me, the point. The point yes is that all love matters, no matter how brief, or how judged by the outside world. Of course yes. It matters. Yes, I think that was it. I dare say I probably came up with it in the suffering of some passion myself, but Holt's Law is that Holt will forget even Holt's Lessons so my apologies for less than exactitude, dear friend. But please carry on, tell me. Tell me your remarkable young life.'

And Jay did. He told it backwards from John to the House of Angels in Addis and Doctor Pellier and then to Bridget and Nuno in Portugal and all the way back to the studio in Germany in the summer of the bombings, and before there to London looking to find his father and thinking he was Ahmed Sharif.

'Who did you say?'

'Ahmed Sharif.'

'Isn't he . . . why do I know that name? Was he in the papers? Sharif?'

'He died in Frankfurt three years ago.'

'Really?'

'Yes.'

266

'Ah then. Holt's Mind,' the Reverend tapped his temple, 'Apologies. Omar Sharif, *Lawrence of Arabia,* my favourite film, yes. That and of course *Doctor Zhivago.* Sorry. I keep thinking everything is part of something else.' He considered the young man in front of him in all his singularity and he said, 'I'm sorry you lost your father.'

Then, thinking of the story he had just told for the first time, and rerunning it quickly back to the moment he was in, sitting before this man who looked like the Master, Jay said, 'I seem to have found many more.'

Reverend Holt nodded at the continuing surprises of the world. 'Well,' he said at last, 'Be sure to read some of *Our Mutual Friend.* It will take your mind for a little. I must say I do love the plot. Some of it improbable as Our Lord,' and he smiled both sets of teeth at the joy of epiphanies coming quickly now as the cancer spread. 'But so many voices in it, and the *suspense.* These are the keys. Yes, certainly. A book of death and renewal. You know, Dickens used the phrase quite a bit actually, "our mutual friend"; used it for several different characters and in different books. I do like it. Sort of a bridge between strangers. Mutual friend. Indeed, yes. Quite a Christian thing. I think I must be very nineteenth century myself.' His mouth made a wet clack as his teeth slipped and were sucked back. 'If you don't get much of it read, the last line is one of my favourites. "*Mortimer sees Twemlow home, shakes hands with him cordially at parting, and fares to the Temple, gaily.*" Isn't that just marvellous? That last "gaily" – so so wonderful. Fares to the Temple, gaily. Oh dear oh dear me. Well, we'll talk more tomorrow. Will we say noon?'

At noon then, the Reverend Holt told Jay, 'Dear Good Samaritan, I want to say goodbye.'

267

'Goodbye?'

'Yes. I'm afraid we have reached the turning of our ways. I do love that phrase. Elegance of expression. Apologies. Holt's Cryptic to be kept at bay. No, dear friend. Time for parting.' He spoke quickly, as though a pause might break his resolve and he might misplay his part. He offered his hand. 'Shakes hands cordially at parting, you see? Dear friend, it has been a very great pleasure.'

Puzzled Jay took his handshake. 'You're all right though,' he said, 'you're not . . .'

'No no. Not me, you. I'm afraid I still have further adventures in store here,' he said. And then, in what would become for Jay an act of further confirmation, of charity, of trust, of hope and of humanity itself, the Reverend smiled and added, 'You, dear friend, you. I have changed my ticket into your name. I wasn't sure you had yours booked. Detail of stamp-money, you see. Perceptions still part functioning in Holt's Mind. But time, you see. I do hope you don't mind. You're flying to London this evening.'

THIRTY-SIX

Because saints recognize each other, Ben Dack would say, Josie knew Bridget was important the moment she knocked at the door. She knew when she opened it and saw her standing with such trepidation and hope in her face and Mick Daly in his ankle-cast halfway down the garden behind her. She didn't need to ask, but already she knew this woman was here for the Master, and when Bridget asked for him Josie knew it was not news of death but life the woman brought. She invited her in, and offered the same to Mick Daly who hung back and said, 'No thank you all the same I won't.' As was customary, Josie asked him again, and Mick said, 'He did me a favour, the Master, and I'm grateful,' and made a slight gesture of ushering Bridget forward. It was as though he apologized for having been so wary of the man who had come back from the dead, but did so without saying.

'You'll come in,' Josie tried a third time.

'I won't. I must be going now or that wife of mine will be out hunting me,' he said, and scratched at his smile bashfully, grinning at the thought of her fierce love. 'I just wanted to make sure she got the right place. Tell the Master now,' he said, and then he was gone.

Josie sat Bridget down in the same room where Whatarangi had seen the photograph, and though she did not take it out or otherwise want to prompt what seemed to happen of its own nature, she had the sense of things opening and of revelation. She called the Master from the bottom of the stairs, and she waited there for him while Bridget sat and looked at the room and saw the puzzle of the sky that was nearly made and the books and she tried to breathe.

The Master too came down it seemed with foreknowledge, as if he knew it was the way things happened, three years nothing, and then in a single week a sudden confluence that swept the separated together.

'This is Sister Bridget,' Josie said, 'she is home from Africa.'

Bridget stood and she saw the old man and she saw in him the boy too and she brought her hands to her mouth because her feelings were too large for telling.

Quickly now everything happens, as though suddenly He remembers us, the Master thought. He had gone into the bathroom to put water on his face. *Jay thinks I'm dead and he's been in Africa all this time.*

He's been in Africa all this time, Mary.

He was on the verge of weeping but kept himself from it. He held onto the sink with both hands and his chin trembled and he raised his head and stood sorrowful and aged but undefeated. He kept his lips tightly closed and the old man in the mirror that looked at him was defiant of all outrageous loss and suffering and determined to endure. He stood until the sea inside him settled. He splashed water on his face again then he dried it and went back out to the sitting room where Bridget was about to phone Addis Ababa.

'Take this cup of tea, Joe,' Josie said.

'Yes, I will thank you.'

'All right then, I'll call.' Bridget picked up the receiver and dialled the hospital. She could not look up at the Master.

The call did not go through. She dialled again.

'It's ringing.'

That world away, Doctor Pellier answered. When she had explained where she was and that Jay's grandfather was beside her Bridget asked, 'Can you put him on?'

'*Mais non,* I cannot, Bridget. He is gone.'

She nearly said 'gone?' but she caught herself and said only, 'I see.' Then the doctor told her about Desta and her disappearance and Jay going after her. 'But he will return. *C'est certain,*' Pellier added, and she said again 'I see', though she had none of his faith, and thanked him and told him to tell Sister Eucharia she was well and had the Award and the cheque and that she would call again soon.

'Well?' the Master asked.

'He's not there. He's away for a couple of days doing this . . . this special job that . . . well, he'll be back in a couple of days.'

'Well then you'll stay with us, Sister,' Josie said.

'Oh no, I'll . . .'

'You will or Ben Dack would not be worth living with. Isn't that right Joe? You'll have the downstairs bedroom there and we'll be delighted to have you, Sister, and when Ben Dack gets home and you tell him that boy was with you in Africa all this time you'll see what I mean, you'll see him spin like a top, honest to God, won't she Joe?' She shook her head at the thought of her husband and then noticed the Master's disappointment and she put her hand on his shoulder and said, 'Joe, just a few days. He'll be back. Just a few days more.'

They sat then in the aftermath of the call with strange unease and sipped tea with a large company of wonder and fear. The things that were said mattered not at all. They were said for the smallness of their part in keeping at bay anxiety of what might yet come between Jay and home, what might be until what was untied was bound. Tea was drunk and more tea made and Bridget spoke of Jay and how he was in the hospital in Addis and the comfort he had brought to ones there. The Master listened the way he imagined the spirit of his wife listened too from the next life and he said very little. When Bridget had told all she could for a while, he rose and said, 'I will be thanking you for the rest of my life.'

'Oh no. Not at all. No, it was . . .'

'I will,' he said, and his manner was such that Bridget didn't say more.

'I need a little quiet now.'

'Yes, Joe. Of course you do, Joe. Go on up now,' Josie told him. 'I'll tell Ben when he gets in.'

'Yes.'

He went up the stairs to his room. He stood beneath the skylight some time, and then, not because he felt obliged or indebted but because it seemed a natural response to grace, he knelt.

Guide him home was his prayer.

Guide him home.

And afterwards, he sat again at the computer, and he waited for the screen to come where he could write his message. The cursor like a heartbeat pulsed. His hands trembled.

He had to dare to write: *he is alive. He is alive. He is alive.*

THIRTY-SEVEN

The flight left Nairobi at ten twenty-five in the evening. Jay was in the window seat that the Reverend Holt had booked for himself so that morning would show him the Alps then France and then Dover. The plane was nearly full, the passengers a mix of African and European businessmen, briefcased, pressed white shirts and elegant ties, then the pink and freckled returning Safarians, khaki families, excited children, and here and there stray single men and women, leaving home and with mixed emotion considering the mystery and promise of London. Jay had stood in the queue for check-in wearing the shoes the Reverend Holt had given him. He had his small backpack and the copy of *Our Mutual Friend*, which the pastor had insisted was another gift.

When the plane took off he felt both sorrow and relief and could not have separated one from the other. He was certain **he would** come back to Africa but certain too that it was right **he left** now. He had to return to the village. He had to see the Master's grave and sit by it and this would be the closure of that part of his life he had run away from and left open.

In the air over Africa, some hours after taking off, he thought: *I am beginning to believe in You.*

Not because You found me my father, You didn't. But because You found me many.

In Book the Second, Chapter Seven, he found the envelope in which the Reverend Arthur Holt had put four hundred pounds sterling and added a penned exclamation mark at the end of the chapter heading 'In which a Friendly Move is Originated'. And the lights in the cabin were turned off for sleep and he lay awake and said a prayer that the Reverend suffer no pain but one night die in his sleep *because You owe him that.* And in the state of illumination and grace that was not unlike that experienced by those returning from the altar rails, he believed himself less alone in the world now. He had the sense of something being repaired, but he could not have said what or why. He turned to the window and watched the lights of the villages and towns below, and felt he was over-watching the world itself and all those that the wings passed over, and he remembered long ago hearing suddenly the Master's voice say *it will be all right.* And he wished he could say this then to Africa itself and believe it might be so, but he knew what suffering and hardship there was and as the plane moved through clear skies over desert and mountain he thought only, *I will come back. I will come back to you again.*

He rose sometime over the Sahara and went down the passageway in the Reverend's oversized black shoes. The light was set low for sleeping and the passengers were mostly sitting in blankets and eye-masks or headphoned into films. It was strange to think of them all, this cargo for London, so many plots hanging there in the night sky. He went down to the galley and stood alongside two Africans, anxiously stepping around in the eight feet of space. They were brothers, and wore what seemed brand-new clothes. Jay knew they had never left Africa. They took turns, one leaning over to look out at the villages like candles below, then the other

274

tapping impatiently to see. One of them offered Jay a turn, but he shook his head: he had already left. They hadn't; nor would they for a long time yet, he thought. The engines droned on.

In an aeroplane like this you are neither one place nor the other. I can't believe yet that I will be there. I can't believe it's the same world and you can move from one part of it to another so easily. Can you?

Of course you can, in one sense.

Now I need to think myself there. I need to prepare. What will I do?

Bridget is in Ireland still.

I'll find her. I'll tell her she was right.

She'll like that.

Jay tried to concentrate on exactly what he must do when he landed, on practicalities, were there flights from Heathrow to Shannon, and from which terminal and how much one would cost. But across his mind kept coming the image of the house itself as he had left it. He had thought of it often in the three years since, but each time it had become a little more unreal. Now, he was going to be there in less than a day. He was going to go in the front gate and up the garden and look for the spare key under the kettle flowerpot by the front door. With the clarity of dreams he saw himself bend down to pick it up. He put the key in the door, but then tried not to see any further because he knew pain was there.

The plane flew into the dawn. Jay sat with his head against the window as the sleeping woke and the anticipation of arrival made a steady wavelike murmuring through the cabin.

London.

The last time I was here was the bombing.

He watched the first roofs appear, the plane passing over them with slow consideration.

How do you fit back into things?

275

You just do.

The wheels hit and bounced and the brakes screeched and the terminal buildings flew backwards as if spun.

'Welcome to London. The local time is nine forty-five.'

He stood in the line and showed the passport he had showed in England and France and Germany and Italy and Spain and Portugal and Egypt and Sudan and Ethiopia and Kenya. The photograph was no longer himself. He was become someone else since and the immigration officer studied his face until he found traces of the boy. Then he stamped a faded page and said, 'You'll need to change that soon. It's out of date Christmas.'

'I will. Thank you.'

'Next.'

He went forward, the black shoes and his shorts and T-shirt and light knapsack lending him an air of transience, so that when he came through customs without further baggage he was stopped and questioned. His bag was opened and the copy of *Our Mutual Friend* examined.

'Is London your final destination, sir?'

'I am going to Ireland.'

'I see, sir. Would you mind showing me your ticket?'

'I don't have a ticket yet. I'm hoping to get one just out in the terminal.'

'I see. And you've just come from Kenya?'

'Yes.'

'With no baggage but this book?'

'No.'

'I see.'

The officer re-examined the bag, its lining, the novel and the notebook where in the House of Angels Jay had written a description of the village in Ireland. He read it as if for clues.

'What's this then?'

276

Jay shrugged. 'It's writing.'

'You're a writer?'

And a moment after the customs officer raised the question with his eyebrows, Jay heard himself say, 'Yes, maybe.'

'I see.' The officer was accustomed to judging stories, and he put *Our Mutual Friend* back in the bag with the notebook and said, 'Write something nice about a customs officer sometime eh?' and he let him go on and beckoned forward the two anxious brothers. Jay looked briefly back at them: *it will be all right.*

There was no flight from Heathrow to Shannon and he bought a ticket instead to Dublin, and arrived at the gate early and sat reading the Dickens novel while around him gathered the faces and voices of Ireland. He tried to keep his mind in the story, in John Harmon presumed drowned, in the kind dustman Mr Boffin, and the enchanting Bella Wilfer. He tried not to think of arrival or ending, but only that the story in his hands would go on, that there were hundreds of pages and the comfort was in knowing there was more to come.

When his country had assembled around him and the flight was called, he boarded and took a window seat and folded his arms over the uncertain company of his feelings. He wanted to be there. He wanted the flight to last an instant and his journey to the West less. He wanted to be at the graveyard at the end of the village and find the grave and he could have no peace until he had. The closer he got – the flight taking off, the hostesses offering food, drinks, then perfumes, the flight landing – the more restless he became. It ate at him now. Now everything else was an obstacle to his urgency and he did not buy the newspaper offered nor see in it the article about Ahmed Sharif speaking out about the injustice of imprisonment without charge. He saw the eastern coast of Ireland an impossible green as the plane descended through cloud. He had forgotten such greenness.

At customs he held up his passport and was waved forward into the country without a word.

He felt he should stop and do something. He felt he should acknowledge that he was back, but the crowds were enormous and the space small and he was outside in the morning soon and looking up into grey drizzle both customary and strange.

He took a bus to the city, and in the streets of Dublin saw the old familiars, the pale-skinned, the long-faced, the rain-shouldered and the hunched-up of his countrymen, alongside and amongst another population of all nationalities, and in these many with African faces. On Dorset Street the bus passed Carey's Café, whose window had a poster advertising Fairtrade coffee from Ethiopia, and he felt a little dart of pride or hope and thought *maybe Africa is less of another world now.*

The bus to the west didn't leave for an hour. He sat in the cold spiritless terminal. He opened the novel again so that his feelings might be contained.

The Master did the same.

He opened *The Old Man and the Sea* and he read the part near the end where it says a man is not made for defeat, and he thought of his father long ago bringing him fishing and he thought of the boy too and the times they went fishing. He read on because he was waiting for God, because he was waiting for the part of the world that was still his to heal. He read on to the passage where it said: '*He was asleep when the boy looked in the door in the morning.*'

Then he stopped because the feeling was so strong, and he put down the book and cupped one hand in the other and held on.

Sometime later that morning, Jerzy Maski came to see him. He said that his brother and Whatarangi had gone back on the car ferry but that he had decided not to.

'I am staying for another time,' he said.

'For another while.'

'Yes, sorry, for another while.' Jerzy shrugged at his stumble in language and rubbed a hand across his mouth. He found some feeling had strayed to the back of his neck and he lowered his head a little and scratched there. The things he was not saying flickered about in his face. He did not say that something had happened. He did not say the undrowned girl whose name was Gabrielle had come to the door of the house in the evening and Uncle Laslo had pushed flat both sides of his moustache before asking her to come in. He did not say she had shyly refused and that Laslo had roared for him to come out then and he had, finding all his English knotted together in the base of his throat. She had come to thank him, and in those awkward moments he had found the map of the world changing, but he did not say this to the Master. What he said was, 'I will need more classes in English.'

THIRTY-EIGHT

I am here.

Jay walked from the station at Ennis and took the road to the west. He thought he might walk the twenty miles, but the Reverend Holt's black shoes were a size overlarge and he wore no socks and blisters came quickly. Five miles out, on the hill by Darragh, he stopped and faced the traffic and after a few minutes was picked up by two housepainters from Latvia who had thought he was not Irish but an immigrant like them. They had driven their car from Riga and the back seat contained their entire belongings as well as food, beer, paintbrushes, scrapers, overalls and a bag of rags. They were on their way to the new golf course and houses by the sea where in a café in Riga they had been told there was work and good pay. They spoke in their language and laughed and left Jay to himself in the back seat watching the countryside come back to him, the hedgerows, the brightly coloured houses, the ordinary marvellous in a drizzling rain.

At the turn-off for the village, they let him out. They were smiling men of little more than twenty in the adventure that for them was Ireland. Jay thanked them and one of them

281

said 'thanku', and the other laughed at his only word tried out in English and they drove away.

He stood by the signpost for the village some moments, remembering. He remembered the night he had left and how he had come out here onto the main road and run along the middle of it in the dark and fallen over the man. He remembered as he went now. He did not turn to the few cars that came up behind him and passed. There was a mile of road. He walked in the strange familiarity of everything, and it felt both as if he had been away a lifetime, and also in some ways that he had never left. He both belonged and didn't, and was coming now to realize that this was the nature of his place in the world. *It is all right. It will be all right.*

He went past Coughlan's and Considine's and Duggan's and in Ryan's he saw Mrs Ryan carrying in a basket of wet laundry from the line and she looked out at him passing by the front wall and called out, 'They're soaked through.' She went inside. He didn't know if she had recognized him or not, but he was surprised nonetheless, as if there was a key in his hand he didn't remember picking up. He walked on into the village and past where the hedgerows ended and there were houses on either side and in some of the gardens children playing in the soft rain, some of them the ages of Bekele and Dembe. He passed Fitzpatrick's petrol station and Michael Fitzpatrick, filling at the pumps, noted him and thought he knew him but just couldn't think of the name and Jay did not stop. He came up to the old graveyard and he found the thud of his heart had grown loud and he had to work to swallow back the feeling that rose in him now.

Between the pillars the old gate was pushed open permanently and grass grew over the bottom bar. There was a gravelled entranceway that led in by the oldest graves whose tombstones had surrendered their names to a century of rain. It fell softly as he went among them. He knew the names of

282

the parish. Some he remembered dying when he was a schoolboy and the Master brought him to the funerals in that time when entire communities went and by that were bound together. He went along the grave grid as though it was a street whose houses were black or white marble and sometimes flagstone.

Then he came to his mother's.

He wanted to keep from weeping, but he wept. His face buckled, and he knelt on the cold wet stones and bowed his head and could not say a prayer.

He wanted to lay his head upon her. He wanted to feel the peace and surrender of that, and tell her he was finding his way. He wanted to tell her about it all; about the night he had left because of her letter, because he wanted to find the man who had loved her. He wanted to tell her about the boat to England and the bombing and on and on through the entire journeying to Ethiopia and Desta and even to John and the Abaye Alem and the Reverend Holt. He wanted to tell her he had survived, and that in surviving he had found a kind of trust, and in that discovered that he was not lost. He wanted her to know and then he thought *she knows already* and he realized that what he longed for was to be held.

His face was wet and his mouth dry. Stones had printed his knees when he stood up and went over to the place where the Master was to be buried beside his wife. He knew they were to be side by side, the plot was double like a bed and the single headstone was to have his name carved below hers.

But it was not there.

At first Jay thought *no one has done it. Maybe no one paid for it and so it hasn't been carved.* And the neglect angered him, and then he looked at the small black glassy gravel that had been used for his grandmother and he tried to figure out if it should look different. *It's three years since the crash.*

He looked around him, but the graveyard was empty in the rain.

Only then did he notice that the flowers by the headstone had not been there long.

You're not here.

He's not here, Nanna, where is he?

He stood. The rain thickened. He walked out of the graveyard and went up the street through the far end of the village. He passed the post office where P.J. Crowley who had the entire parish in his head was loading the post van and did not see him. He went past the church and then stopped, turned back and went inside. He knelt in the back pew and he blessed himself and he said the 'Our Father' and nothing more. He blessed himself again and left. He went out of the end of the village where the kindly face of Frank Saunders watched from the front window of Saunders' shop and gave him a small wave salute, and he nodded back, unsure if he was known or not.

The road home went west for a mile through the rain. Saturate with memory and emotion, he tried to concentrate only on getting there. He looked at the road beneath his feet and for a time counted his steps, as though the exact measure of his journey was proscribed long ago and in three years and four months his feet would now step out the last number of paces. He counted six hundred and stopped, and the rain fell heavier and he blinked it from his eyes and tasted it on his lips where it was like the rain of always in Ireland, and he was glad of it. He passed fields where the after-grass was deeply green and cattle grazed intently and did not stop nor turn to consider him. No birds flew. The stillness of the country-side in the grey weather was dreamlike, and gave to that landscape a quality timeless and serene, as though it itself was a salve and could soothe anxiety.

Jay was nearly home. He was trying not to think. He was

284

trying just to have his feet get him there because he did not know which among the crowd of feelings in him he should feel. To keep him from thinking he ran his hand along a high fuchsia hedge and took some of the wet red blossoms that he remembered the Master teaching them in Irish were called *Teori de,* the tears of God. In the misting rain-wash the sky blended with the earth.

He was not a hundred yards from the house when the lorry came up behind him. He heard it approach but he did not turn around, and kept in closer to the hedgerow, mud coming up on Reverend Holt's shoes. Then the lorry stopped just behind him, and leaving the engine running, Ben Dack swung open the door and jumped down.

'By jingo. By jingo,' he said. His smile was enormous, his eyes wide above the high round curves of his cheeks. He looked at Jay and because he didn't know what to say he clapped. He clapped in the pouring rain, as if a master conjurer had performed. 'By jingo it's you! Down in Fitz's I'm filling and Michael says there was a young lad going over the road, and I asked him what kind. Because Ben Dack's not swift in the language department, not who but what kind, you see? He says a young lad, tanned. Tanned? I twigged that. I did. Fair play and credit due. Absolute. Tanned. So Ben Dack puts two and two for twenty-two as the fellow says and he'll be heading to the house because he won't know, he won't know. He won't, that part of the jigsaw is still turned over in the box maybe, you get me, so I'm away up the village then and I'm thinking it's him, it's him, and here, by jingo, it's you.'

Jay knew him at once, but not the reason for his wild happiness.

'Let me shake your hand,' Ben Dack said. 'Let me shake your hand and say welcome back.'

He did. Jay gave his hand but looked at the puzzle of this

285

short round-bellied man and told him, 'I have to go on. I am going home.'

'Of course you are. No question. One hundred per cent. But!' Ben prodded a plump finger at the underbelly of the air. 'There's no one there.'

'I know. I want to go anyway.'

'Yes. Correct answer as the fellow says. Next question. But!' Again a prod. 'Can you trust me? Or, cancel that, rewind, again, can I ask you to delay? Reason to follow. Forgive mystery et cetera et cetera. Can Ben Dack ask you to come with him a short distance by this lorry and thereby guarantee a smile on Josie Dack because she won't believe I won't have told.'

'Told what?'

'Precise mind. Wonderful. Absolute. Come on, same lorry same seat. My guest. Promise given return later.' He opened the passenger door, and after his hesitation melted on the man's geniality, Jay climbed in.

Ben drove them past the turn for the cottage and on along the narrow roads while all the time interspersing the journey by lifting his hands from the wheel and giving a series of quick short claps to which he added only 'by Jingo' and 'yes, yes, yes.' At one stage he glanced over at Jay and said 'You remember our little trip?'

'Yes, yes I do. Thank you for taking me.'

Ben chuckled. 'By cripes. By cripes. You've been some places since, I'd say.'

'Yes.'

'By cripes yes, says he. But!' the plump finger rose, 'hold your whist awhile till Josie.' And he chuckled again and smacked a hand on his thigh.

When the lorry came in the yard, Ben pressed hard on the horn three times and said, 'Here we go now! Here we go.' And he got out quickly and came around to make sure there was no slip now and that Jay was safely delivered. Josie was already out the door and came with floury hands wiping in her apron and she saw them and she said 'Oh heavens' and crossed and struggled to find words and then managed 'You're very welcome' and 'I'm sorry my hands are so . . .'

And Jay said thank you and took her hand, and Ben Dack had to get his arm around Josie because he knew she could fall down or float up then.

'Come on,' he said, 'come on.' He led the way across the front of the house along the narrow path. They passed the windows, but Jay did not look in.

Then at the front door, Ben stood back and extended his arm for the guest to go first.

Jay entered the little hallway and turned into the room off it.

He saw Bridget first.

He saw her sitting in an armchair before a small fire, her two hands together holding his map of the world on her lap.

'Bridget!'

In the instant it took her to realize he was real, for her hands to fly to her face and call out his name, in that instant he knew everything was changing. He did not know the exactness yet, but he *knew*, and it was as though a sea high and forceful swept in the door with him and foamed and carried in it a new life. What he felt was convergence and renewal, a surge of insight, as if the plot carried him ahead of himself and he was not sure yet of exactly what would happen but knew only that there was a plot, with something or someone, a Dickens, behind it. *It will be all right.*

Jay stood inside the doorway and Bridget came to him and he held onto her, and Ben Dack and Josie sidled in behind by the jigsaw table where the sky was nearly done. In a moment Ben saw the door up the stairs open and heard the first footsteps.

287

The Master descended slowly, his hand following the banister. It was as though he thought the thing so long dreamed could be a dream; he might wake yet on a loud sound or a slip of his foot. The possibility gave him pause and he moved with such slow deliberation in the stairs that he might have been travelling a great distance, he the one crossing continents and bearing the last frail stuff of his faith in the irrational, in mystery and chance. His heart hurt with hope. He dared not turn his head to see before he landed, dared not press against his prayers. Instead he studied the steps, one at a time, and brought himself at last into the absolute silence of that small room.

Jay opened his mouth to speak, but couldn't speak. The man he was looking at was greatly changed. Death and resurrection had paled him, had lent him a near translucence, so though he wore the same tweed jacket and blue shirt as always, he was somehow small inside them; his chin and cheeks prominent and the skin of his face a gentle gleam. He was white where he had once been grey. His hair, eyebrows, even his hands seemed whiter, the whole of him at first nearly a vision, as if there was a condition whereby men became light. In this, his eyes were unchanged. They were the eyes of suffering become wisdom.

The Master held open his arms, and Jay crossed the room and put his hands out and touched the face he loved and kissed it and cried out then with the pain of joy.

THIRTY-NINE

Postscript, in lieu of Preface

Our Mutual Friend

The old man and the younger man went up the hill to fly kites.

It was some weeks now since Jay's return and, though they would be recounted frequently as more details were recalled, the main stories were told. There had been a flurry of scenes: Bridget's departure back to Africa, her lower lip bitten away as she kept trying to tell Jay and not tell him that he had scored one for God, her leaving him a card he opened later to see it said, 'Congratulations on Your Confirmation'; a dinner at Dack's where Jay met Jerzy Maski and saw Gus in him at once and heard that the brothers spoke by text now and that Whatarangi wanted another book to read; the evening the Master opened a group email that began 'I am Joseph' and went on to say that H-47 had passed away peacefully in his sleep; the morning two days later when he saw inside the Reverend Arthur Holt's oversized black shoes the stamp H-47; it was a season of revelation, and of things being bound that had been untied.

The grandfather and grandson moved back into the cottage, though Josie insisted on supplying them with various stews, roasts, sauces and loaves of brown bread she had Ben drop off in the mornings. Jay and the Master were glad of the quiet then. Together the two of them worked to clear the cottage of cobwebs and fallen soot, to cut back the hedge and make passable the path. Often in the course of a day's working, one or the other would stop and consider if the entire story were a dream, but soon then carry on because if so the story-dream had reached a place where the dreamer was contented. They had each felt it, the strange satisfaction in the pattern, in how things had come together, in their supposed deaths and then returns, in the circularity of the journey, in Ben Dack, their mutual friend. They were like figures of a less fractured time, or ones who lived only in the pages of a book of the nineteenth century, Joe Carpenter, the old schoolmaster and his grandson. But in those weeks when they were back in the cottage they didn't care if they might have seemed out of time or unreal to any because each felt returned to some elemental truth, to love. They worked in the house or garden side by side in the tremendous quiet of the countryside, where soft showers of rain came and went as the year stepped further into autumn.

In the evenings Jay had read the Reverend Holt's copy of the Dickens novel as though it too were part of a mystery. When he reached the last sentence he remembered the old pastor's delight in it, *'Mortimer sees Twemlow home, shakes hands with him cordially at parting, and fares to the Temple, gaily.'* He had read it aloud for the Master who asked him then: 'Besides "the Inimitable", you know what Dickens liked to call himself?'

'No.'

'I read about it one time. A Resurrectionist.'

'Really?'

'Oh yes.'

And they had each considered the strangeness of that a little while, and that evening when he lay in his bed, Jay had taken out the copybook he had carried with him. In it were written various scraps of description, and he had read them all and then drawn a line under them before beginning to try and bring alive in words the Reverend Arthur Holt.

Then, some weeks after moving back to the cottage, a morning when the west wind took down the leaves, they were sitting in the kitchen with the radio on. There was a talk show they were not listening to. Jay would remember that he was standing at the sink rubbing a circle of soap water onto a plate. Then, as though the volume increased or their hearing sharpened, they had each heard the host say 'Good morning and welcome, Mr Sharif.'

Neither of them had spoken. Jay moved the sponge in slow circles on the plate and stared out of the window, listening then to the man called Ahmed Sharif tell of his years of imprisonment without trial, and how he had survived. He was calm and clear and firm. He was neither fanatical nor disjointed, but told what it was to have lived so long in absolute isolation. When his fifteen minutes was up, the host had thanked him in a bright voice and played some music.

Joe Carpenter looked at Jay at the sink but did not say anything. Jay finished the plate and took another, circling with the sponge again, looking out at the leaves flying cross-ways into the garden. Then the music had ended and the host came back and said, 'I should have mentioned, of course, Mr Ahmed Sharif is the guest speaker tonight of Amnesty International. That's in Trinity College here in Dublin, at, let's see, yes, eight o' clock. Okay now, let's move on.'

The grandfather had stood up then and switched off the radio. 'Come on, let's go up the hill.'

So, now they went, bringing the kites. When they reached

291

the hilltop they stood a little apart and each caught the wind quickly and the two kites climbed. It is silent sport, its only sound the wind. For a time then they were there on the hilltop, flying their thoughts in a grey-white sky that threatened rain. Then at last the old man moved a little closer. He kept his eyes fixed on the kite above, and he said, 'We should both go, shouldn't we?'

They took the yellow car. They took it as an act of faith that no accident would befall them now, but the old man secured extra insurance by driving very slowly across the country, making the four-hour journey in six. 'You never know,' he said, 'God has his moments.'

They arrived in Dublin and parked and walked to Trinity College with the wind whirling, their unbuttoned coats winging out as though they were themselves being flown. The audience was larger than they had imagined. When they were seated the grandfather leaned over and said, 'We're cynical and negative and fat with money, but still this country . . . look, it's packed. Young people.' Then, knowing the anxiety was more intense each moment, he asked, 'Do you want me to get you anything? Do you want some water?'

'No, I'm all right.'

'Good man. Whatever you want, all right? We listen, we get up, we go away, whatever you think.'

'Yes. All right.'

Jay looked down. Because it was Dublin, because he wanted to look older and more serious, he was wearing a jacket of the Master's and the black shoes of the Reverend Holt.

A woman came out on the stage and the crowd quietened to hear her introduction of a journalist she described as believing in the power of the written word to change the world. Ahmed Sharif, she said, was that rare thing today, an innocent, and – even more rare for someone with his history – a believer in good.

He came out on the applause. He was a thin man with black hair and brown eyes and a manner humble and grateful. The clapping was prolonged and he was moved by it and clasped his two hands together and made a slight bow.

The moment he saw him, the Master knew. He knew this was the man from all those years before, one he had never met and whom for a long time he had hated. He knew this was the beginning of all that hurt, and resentment and sorrow glutted on his heart and he put his two hands down and held onto the sides of the plastic chair. He pulled air in through his nostrils. He turned his eyes up to study hard the high cornice of the ceiling and then he reached across and pressed firmly on Jay's arm. Neither of them spoke. Like a wave the applause subsided and the man came to the microphone. He did not speak at once. He let the realization of where he was and what had brought him there settle in the hush of anticipation. Then he began by saying, 'Some years ago, I wrote only about a time of hatred and what I called the beginning of the end. I had forgotten there was also love.'

Ahmed Sharif spoke for an hour. He spoke in the quiet voice of a witness, and sometimes his anger and hurt made shiver his words and the hall was stilled as though each one held their breath. And as he spoke the Master found his daughter again. He found her in the quality of this man, in his conviction and passion, and he knew why she had loved him. The more the man spoke, the more she was present; the more she was present, the more the pain dissolved.

'I was a prisoner,' Ahmed Sharif said, 'of judgement, of hatred, of resentment, and of my own of each of these. With each I took away from myself some of the world. But it was given back to me.' He raised his shoulders, put out his palms. 'Who can say why?'

293

He spoke on. He told in detail the day he was released and it was to see the ordinary things of the world again. When he finished the applause was again long and the audience stood.

Ahmed Sharif did not leave the podium. He thanked everyone, he asked that those who hadn't already please consider joining Amnesty, then the woman who had introduced him came over and they continued speaking together while the audience began to file noisily away.

'Come with me, ' Jay said.

He went against the flow of people, the Master behind him. He came to the stage and was looking along it for where there might be steps when Ahmed Sharif noticed him.

There was a table and Jay climbed onto it and onto the stage, and when he turned back the Master said, 'Don't worry about me, go on, go ahead. I'll go round.' And already Ahmed Sharif had told the woman, 'It's all right. No no, it is fine,' and he had stepped away from her to meet the young man he thought was asking about Amnesty.

Jay stood before him then and he took a moment because all of him was beating like a bird held from flight and what lay before him was vast and dizzying and he said, 'My mother was called Marie. She was a nurse.' He swallowed hard. He wanted to be very clear. He wanted to be telling facts, each one hard and precise and fitting piece by piece into a whole. He feared his own intensity and he did not realize yet that Ahmed Sharif had recognized himself.

'She was a nurse,' Jay said again, and again swallowed. 'She went to England, to Birmingham. She fell in love with . . .'

There was a slight pause.

'. . . with me,' said Ahmed Sharif.

Jay looked at his father. 'Yes.'

Ahmed Sharif put his left hand on his chest as if he had

294

been struck. Understanding was swift and fierce. He shook his head very slowly. 'I did not know,' he said.

'She died. My mother died.'

The Master came out onto the stage, and there was a strange awkwardness such as is when people meet pieces of their history.

'What is your name?' Ahmed asked at last, his voice nearly a whisper.

'I am called Jay, but she gave me the name Joshua,' he said.

'God rescues.'

'What?'

'It is what it means. Joshua, God rescues,' he told him.

Jay could not speak. He stood on the stage and when Ahmed Sharif held out his hand he took it. And Jay did not know if this was an ending or beginning, or whether there were such things or if the whole was not some continuous circle, each piece joined, marked by suffering or joy. He did not know what he thought, only what he felt, and this had been his compass for so long he could not have chosen differently. He did not know the plot ahead nor care then nor consider any possibility other than at that moment it seemed as if something had been defeated and the victory although quiet was certain.

His father squeezed his hand. He could not speak.

THE END

What's next?

Tell us the name of an author you love

Niall Williams   Go ▶

and we'll find your next great book.